Also by Dor

The Cameo Clue

A Shadow On The Snow

Secret For A Satyr

Snowhedge

Dorothy Bodoin

HILLIARD HARRIS

HILLIARD HARRIS

P.O. Box 275
Boonsboro, Maryland 21713-0275

First Edition-September 2008
ISBN 1-59133-274-5
978-1-59133-274-9

Book Design: S. A. Reilly
Cover Illustration © S. A. Reilly
Manufactured/Printed in the United States of America
2008

To my niece, goddaughter, and dear friend, Emilie Bodoin.

Acknowledgements:

I wish to thank my good friends and remarkable critique partners, Marja McGraw, Susan Shaw, and Shirley Schenkel, who have supported me in more ways than I can count. Also thanks to Stephanie Reilly and Shawn Reilly for their faith in my work.

Chapter 1

An autumn sun burned down on Greengrove Farm, flooding the charred skeleton of the kennel with harsh morning light. The fire had swept through the structure with the fury of an avenger on a mission. In the end, only the main house escaped with minor damage to the veranda. It hadn't been the arsonist's target.

I stood on layers of crushed leaves and scorched vegetation, allowing myself one last look at a dream in ashes.

The home of Larkspur Collies was as dead as the dried stalks at my feet, as dead as the point of this sad, sentimental stop on my way out of town. Impatiently I blinked away the tears and walked back to my car, eager to begin the long drive north to Maple Creek before anything else happened.

I had a plan: All of my possessions packed and a road map of Michigan in the glove compartment. A place to go, my black collie, Romy, in the back seat of the Taurus, the puppies in a safe home.

It felt like running away, but that wasn't accurate. Call it a strategic retreat or moving on or, simply, a temporary job in another county. Burning bridges? That too. However I chose to describe my leave-taking, I knew I'd never return to Greengrove again.

I pulled the keys out of my jacket pocket and opened the driver's side door.

Now, hurry. Out of here.

A familiar old Chevy turned off the main road and rattled up the drive. Romy woofed and stuck her head out the window as Marsha Vernon, the farm's owner and my former landlady, brought the car to a stop. She stepped down carefully on the gravel drive, using her umbrella as a walking stick.

"Susanna! I wanted to see you before you took off." The sunlight sparkled on her coral earrings and the silver glints in her hair.

"I'm just saying goodbye," I said.

"I'll never understand it." Her voice broke as she looked away from the ruins. "Who would set fire to a kennel?"

"The same monster who torched those stables in Essex and killed six horses."

"That lowlife Tag Nolan. I hope he burns in hell."

"Or the judge throws him in jail for a couple of decades."

"I wish you'd change your mind and stay," she said. "It'll take a little time to rebuild, but by spring, you girls can be up and running again."

I kept the bitter edge from sharpening my tone. "That won't happen. Amy has a new partner, and I've already accepted a job upstate."

"Oh, too bad. You two worked so well together. You were my best tenants. I was hoping…" She peered into the back seat, stroking Romy's head, frowning. "Where are the puppies? Did you sell them?"

Frosty, Cherie, and Cindy. My two blue merles and my tri. I'd pulled them out of the flames while waiting for the pokey fire department to arrive, herded them to the house, and watched the blaze devour the kennel. In the end, the entire structure, even the sign cut in the shape of a collie, was gone.

But I was fortunate. My dogs were alive and Larkspur could rise again some day. Only not here and not with Amy Brackett. The tears were close again. Too close.

Susanna, don't you cry, I thought. *It's going to be okay. Better than okay. The Kentwoods and their dogs are survivors.*

"I dropped them off at a kennel yesterday," I said. "It's only fifteen minutes from where I'll be staying. My new employer doesn't mind if I bring one dog with me, but not four."

"Then I guess we'll see each other at the shows."

"In Lakeville at Fairoaks, the week after Thanksgiving. I'll be there."

"Well…" She hesitated for a moment, then hugged me. "Take care of yourself, Susanna. Have a safe trip to wherever you're heading."

I promised to do that and said goodbye. She turned away and walked slowly up to the silent house, stabbing at the gravel with her umbrella tip.

As I inserted the key in the ignition, a twinge of pain raced down my right arm and came to rest on my fingers. I stared at my hand, at the heirloom diamond ring I always wore, at nails glossy with shell pink polish.

Not again. Not today when I had miles and miles to drive.

The burns had healed; there was no medical reason for discomfort and only the slightest trace of redness on my skin. Still, sometimes my hand hurt. When it did, my imagination yanked me back to the night of the fire. Smoke poured into my lungs again, and flames licked at my clothing. Inside the barn, the trapped dogs screamed. Panic closed its fist tightly around my throat. I couldn't breathe through the acrid mist, couldn't call their names, could hardly make my feet move. But I had to.

I have to save them!

I gripped the wheel and waited for the images to dissolve and the pain to subside. Romy whined softly. I glanced toward the house. Marsha had gone inside, and the ruins of Larkspur lay still and black in the sun.

Quickly I turned the ignition key and drove out to the road. Coming back to the farm had been a mistake. In approximately twenty-five minutes, with light traffic, I should reach the I-75 entrance ramp. By late afternoon I'd be settled in a borrowed country house a hundred miles away from the memories, far from the faint smell of smoke that seemed to linger in the air.

The novelty of traveling to a new place on a perfect fall day soon cast its spell on my dark mood. I opened the window, breathed in fresh sweet air, and let the wind toss my hair into a tangle of waves. Happiness was suddenly possible again, if not imminent.

While I'd been packing suitcases and boxes in a rented gatehouse, the countryside had burst into brilliant color. When I left the freeway, I turned on a narrow byroad that meandered through endless miles of green and russet woodland. 'Horses on the Road' signs hinted at habitation. I didn't see any riders but once caught a fleeting glimpse of leaping deer in the distance.

This corner of Michigan was a mix of thick woodland and vast cultivated fields with an occasional dusty hamlet thrown in to break the monotony. Horses grazed behind white paddock fences, and lakes shimmered through leafy screens. As I drove past richly embellished new structures and weathered old farmhouses with classic lines, leaves drifted through the air. They touched the windshield lightly before flying away to layer the ground.

Goldengrove unleaving, I thought. *That's Michigan in October, this enchanted month.*

In a few more weeks the color show would be over, but the days were still fine with mild temperatures and sunshine. I intended to live in the present, seizing every opportunity that came my way.

Like this house sitting job. The newspapers had carried the story of the kennel fire and, later, of the arrest of prime suspect, Tag Nolan. That was how my mother's long-lost second cousin, Valerie Lansing, found me in the old gatehouse down the road from Greengrove.

Valerie had purchased an historic house in north Lapeer County as an investment and staged it for a quick sale, never doubting that a buyer who shared her vision would snap it up. In a depressed economy, that didn't happen. Now she was about to move to Florida for the winter and needed a trustworthy person to take care of the property in her absence. "An unattended house is an invitation to vandals," she had said at our reunion lunch last month.

Valerie was a statuesque woman with bright chestnut hair twisted into an elegant chignon. She wore vibrant summer colors, spoke softly, and had the face of a stranger.

"I thought after that terrible fire you might want a change of scenery," she added.

Romy lay in the doorway eyeing Valerie with an uncharacteristic wariness. The puppies were in their crates, quiet for once and out of sight.

3

Valerie's only acknowledgement of my collie was a terse question. "Does she chew woodwork or furniture?"

I assured her that Romy was well-mannered, and she nodded thoughtfully, smiling her approval of good canines.

"You'll both like country living, Susanna," she assured me. "But there's no fenced yard. Your puppies wouldn't be safe there."

"I could board them. For a while. Short term only."

"Please say you'll come," she said.

My duties would be simple: Keep the sparse furniture dusted and buy fresh bouquets for the front hall and dining room. A local handyman would handle leaf and snow removal.

"I'd like you to decorate the outside and maybe simmer potpourri on the stove," she said. "Meet the neighbors. Let everybody know you live there. The location is a bit remote, but you'll fall in love with the house, and I'll feel better hiring somebody I know."

"You don't know me," I said.

"I did—when you were a little girl. One Christmas I gave you a doll— Little Red Riding Hood. Don't you remember?"

"I'm afraid not."

I had vague memories of Valerie at rare lake outings, and I must have fading pictures of her in a photograph album. She was a name on a family tree. A scrawled signature on a holiday card. Not even that since my mother's death several years ago.

But I had no recollection of a storybook doll.

She said, "Over time, relatives drift apart. That's life. But your mother and I were close when we were young. You're an artist too, aren't you?"

"Sort of. I'm an art teacher without a job. My school dropped art and music from the curriculum this year and laid me off. I'd like to find another way to use my degree."

"Maple Creek has some breathtaking scenery, especially with the leaves changing. You'll find plenty of interesting places to paint."

Aside from being separated from my puppies, I didn't see a downside to Valerie's proposition. I agreed to watch over her house as if it were my own. She gave me a ring of keys, a checkbook with a balance to cover household expenses, and her Florida address, along with the name of her real estate agent. As soon as she left, I began to pack my possessions and made arrangements to board the puppies.

Afterwards, it occurred to me that Valerie's offer had come out of left field, rather like Valerie herself. No matter. The rent was free, the pay generous, and the work practically non-existent. As soon as the house sold, I could reclaim my pups and look for a permanent home for all of us.

The rural location was a bonus. Balsam Lane, twenty miles north of Maple Creek. I had never heard of either one. No one would know where I'd gone, not even Marsha Vernon, and certainly not Amy Brackett. Anonymity was important to me. At the time I wasn't quite sure why.

4

Now, as I navigated a dizzying chain of curves through the crimson and gold wonderland, I thought I knew. The fire had been the most devastating of the misfortunes that had plagued me these past months. Every now and then, in anxious moments, I wondered if something even worse was going to happen next.

Tag Nolan, Amy, acquaintances with friendly smiles and hostile intent, or even a stranger might strike again at any time. In simpler language, I feared that someone was out to get me.

That's because someone is. Move fast and far and your enemy won't find you until you're ready to face him.

I slowed down to avoid a deep rut, averting my eyes from the dark animal body that lay motionless in my path, probably a raccoon, although it was hard to tell.

When had I become so paranoid? When my best friend betrayed me? When my boyfriend stopped calling me? When a malicious stranger set fire to the kennel? Or the day I first became aware of Amy's vicious lies?

All of the above.

The enormity of my situation threatened to overwhelm me. To add to my discomfort, I was hungry. I steered the car to the side of the road and surveyed the remnants of my picnic basket: Two jelly doughnuts, a Hershey bar, an empty coffee mug, and a six pack of bottled water—not exactly what I wanted. When I reached the house on Balsam Lane, I'd make Romy comfortable and go out again to look for a restaurant.

Still hungry and growing more tired with every mile, I drove slowly down the main street of Maple Creek, admiring its Norman Rockwell charm. Maple trees lined the sidewalks, their foliage as red as crackling flames. Quaint stores blended smoothly with storybook Victorian houses, and American flags flapped in the wind. The only other sound was a rustle of leaves.

Where were all the people? In those picturesque houses on streets named Walnut and Beechnut and Willow, or inside the shops? How could any place, especially the main artery of a town, be so quiet, so dead?

I saw them then. A little girl with blonde Alice-in-Wonderland hair pulling a doll in a wagon. A brawny bearded man emerging from a barbershop with a black Belgian shepherd at his heel. A red-haired woman carrying an oversized bakery box. Ah, good! Maple Creek had a bakery.

A lone traffic light blinked red. I came to a stop at the intersection. As I scanned the storefronts, hoping to see a café or pizza parlor, I noticed a vintage brick building with letters in Old English script on the front: *The Blue Lion Inn. Prime Rib—Fish—Spirits.*

The Blue Lion would do for dinner tonight, and if I needed a nut or bolt, its neighbor was a feed and hardware store. If I required anything more elaborate, Maple Creek probably had it tucked away in one of these little shops.

5

So I wasn't really in the middle of nowhere.

Still, for the first time since I'd accepted Valerie's offer, I had a moment of doubt. Could I adjust to life in this small northern town where the winter would be colder and snowier than the same season downstate?

You're not going to live in town, I reminded myself. *The house is twenty miles north of it.*

Valerie's homemade map lay on the seat beside me. It consisted of wavy arrows and miniature landmark sketches, all of which led to a cloud shape labeled Marble Lake. This route would take me to Hunter and from there to 7 Balsam Lane. Printed instructions filled the bottom half of the page:

Main Street turns into Hunter. Stay on Hunter until you pass the lake. In five miles, you'll see a fork in the road. Turn on Balsam. You're going northeast now. The house is on your right. It has blue siding and a wraparound porch. There's a hedge and a pond in front.

When the light turned green, I drove through the intersection and promptly found myself heading out of town. Before long, I was traveling through deep country again. The land rose high on the left side and dropped down so low on the right that the treetops were level with the road. The woods were filled with pines, tall and imposing. They shadowed the way, diminished the afternoon light, and chipped away at my earlier exuberance.

Romy barked at something I couldn't see, possibly more deer.

Onward to nowhere, I thought, resisting an irrational impulse to turn the car around and drive back to Main Street. Contrasted with this forest of giant conifers, it seemed bright and friendly.

Marble Lake, however, was a luminous body of water fringed by hardwoods wearing autumn's vibrant colors. Beyond the lake, I saw the fork in the road and made the last turn on Balsam Lane.

Blue, porch, hedge, pond...I kept my eyes fixed on the right side of the road, sailing past hidden driveways, cookie cutter farmhouses, rustic mailboxes, and street numbers so far away they might as well be non-existent. At last, beyond a sharp curve, I saw a blue house.

Rather, a blue palace behind a high hedge with a pond nestled in an embrace of woods. Valerie had neglected to mention how large the house was.

"Well, we're here, Romy," I said. "Journey's end."

But I didn't get out of the car, and Romy only yawned and pressed her nose to the window.

Our destination was a grand Victorian at least a century old, a silvery-blue, three-storied extravaganza of gables and graceful arches and windows. Besides the wraparound porch, it had two high balconies at opposite ends of the house and a tiny one in the middle. Every inch of trim dripped with gingerbread that gave the exterior the frosty appearance of a massive ice sculpture.

This is a cold house, I thought. *A winter place.*

Fallen leaves rose in high waves up to the foundation, hiding the walkway and steps, and trees grew close to the sides, reaching out with long branch-arms as if to catch the house in a grip of wood and imprison it forever.

What a weird notion! I'd been driving too long without proper food.

But the encroaching branches and that wild overgrown hedge inspired gruesome fancies. Apparently Valerie didn't understand the value of curb appeal. She should have had the trees trimmed, the shrubs neatened or replaced, and, definitely, the hedge taken out. It seemed somehow sinister, a dark barrier between the house and the rest of the world.

The old Victorian itself was magnificent, however. Storybook beautiful. It needed a nineteenth-century family to fill the rooms with laughter and children to skate on the lonely pond when it froze in the winter. One woman and her dog would get lost rambling around in those dark halls.

But they wouldn't be dark when I moved in and turned on the lights, and, of course, this wasn't my home. I'd leave as soon as the right buyer came along, and surely that would be soon. Who would let this place languish unsold if he had the means to purchase it and a desire to live in the country?

Then...I imagined the house restored to its former old-century glory with light in every window to temper the ice-cold façade and a warm welcome inside for the weary traveler. Illogically, that was what I had been hoping to find at the end of my long trek north—an unknown somebody to say,

"Come inside and sit by the fireplace, Susanna. Burn your troubles with the pine logs, and when you leave, you'll be free and strong again."

Abruptly I forced myself back to reality. Nobody waited behind that massive ornamental door to greet me. I was the one hired to provide the welcome, and I would. Only...

My eyes swept the blue house in its wooded setting and bed of leaves, wondering what was missing. Then I knew.

There was no sign in the yard. How would anybody know that the place was for sale?

Chapter 2

Nothing communicates neglect as clearly as a house sinking in a sea of leaves. Either Valerie's handyman hadn't visited the property in days or the leaf fall had been sudden and excessive.

I freed Romy from the back seat and walked around the car to the trunk. The two suitcases contained everything I'd need tonight, including Romy's bowls and a portion of kibble. I could unload the boxes tomorrow.

It's too quiet here, I thought. *Almost spooky.*

Wood creaking in the wind and a crunching sound under my feet couldn't fill the deep country silence that wrapped around me. But quiet and isolation were good. It meant no nearby neighbors to complain about a noisy dog and, more importantly, no one to observe my comings and goings.

This remote location was exactly what I'd hoped to find. Valerie needed me to help sell her house, and I knew I could meet this new challenge.

Carrying a suitcase in each hand, I waded through ankle-deep leaves, forging my own walkway. Romy ran under the hedge's high arch, barking her joy at finding herself in a new yard. She sent waves of leaf dust high in the air and leaped up onto the porch, tail wagging, dark eyes bright.

Oh, for a modicum of her exuberance.

Setting the luggage down in front of the door, I looked to my right, entranced by the shine of the pond in its frame of trees. Beyond the water, the land rose sharply. Graceful balsam firs appeared to march up to the sky, their top branches brushing against low-lying clouds. On the western side, a slender stream threaded its way through yellow-leafed lindens. Across the lane, the woods grew thick and dark.

The spectacular view alone was worth the house's high asking price, but the exterior would hardly entice a prospective buyer. Drifted leaves gave the wraparound porch a sad, abandoned look. A large branch lay on the railing, and two dead chrysanthemums flanked the entrance, their rust-colored flowers shriveled and cheerless.

Snowhedge

Buy fresh plants and a harvest wreath for the door, I thought. *Track down that handyman. Decorate the outside with cornstalks and pumpkins. Orange and brown will contrast nicely with the blue.*

But first, the floor needed a thorough sweeping. If I could find a wicker chair this late in the season, I'd place it in front of the bay windows for an inviting homespun touch.

Now for the interior.

I turned the key in the lock and stepped into a vast frigid vestibule. Romy dashed ahead of me, circumventing a mahogany table topped with an empty vase. At the foot of the staircase, she came to a stop. Tail frozen, ears at high alert, she stared into the shadows above.

"One floor at a time," I said, resolving to explore the upstairs rooms in the morning light.

I slid the suitcases inside and stood still, letting first impressions wash over me. High ceilings, exquisite crown moldings, ivory walls. Closed doors on either side of a dark hall. Stairs with an ornate banister. Evocative and elegant, but nothing said 'Welcome.'

The inside was a little less quiet and much spookier. Romy's nails clicked on the hardwood floor as she padded down the hall. Wind-tossed branches scratched against glass. Somewhere a clock ticked. With two stories above me, it was easy to imagine ghostly footsteps pacing overhead or grotesquely-shaped shadows descending the staircase.

And it was so cold. Freezing. I found the thermostat and turned the temperature to seventy-two degrees. The furnace fan hummed on, but still I shivered, waiting for the heat. Valerie had mentioned a furnished bedroom with an electric fireplace. That was where I'd sleep, in a bed made with my own flannel sheets, under a heavy comforter.

"Keep moving," I said aloud. "You'll warm up."

An echo threw my voice back to me.

Returning to the vestibule, I opened the first door on my right and surveyed an airy expanse of burnished floor and lavender walls. The room had a white brick fireplace but no furniture. Frosty condensation had etched graceful patterns on the bay windows. The scallops and scrolls matched the design on the beige curtains.

According to Valerie's rough sketch, this was the parlor. A twenty-first century owner would most likely find another use for it. A library, perhaps, or a home office.

I took a deep breath, puzzled by a faint woodsy scent that hung in the air.

Romy padded past me and sniffed at the fireplace. Swept clean, with a bare mantel, it was practically invisible. A single decorative piece like a grapevine cornucopia would give it a dash of seasonal color.

My head teemed with ideas, but I couldn't stop shivering. It hadn't been this cold in the hall or outside either, come to think of it. I crossed to the windows, suspecting they hadn't been securely closed, but they didn't open. Still, a draft seeped in through the panes, along with the scent. What was it?

Something with pleasant associations. Incense? Cedar? No, balsam. I glanced at the firs on the hill. Definitely balsam, and it seemed stronger now, more potent. I might be standing in the middle of a Christmas tree lot, inhaling the aroma of freshly-cut firs.

Maybe I was smelling polish or cleanser. How could the fragrance of the hillside balsams travel all the way across the acres to this closed-up room?

It couldn't. No doubt I'd find Pine-Sol in Valerie's well-stocked broom closet. But that wasn't the answer. Why would anyone clean the parlor and leave dead flowers at the entrance? And who would that person be? *I* was the house sitter.

Calling Romy to heel, I closed the door. Whatever the scent was, it stayed behind. I made a hasty tour of the rest of the first floor, leaving doors open and turning on lights wherever I found them. That helped a little.

Helped what? Don't let a little scent spook you when so many other things are eager to do that.

The room with the electric fireplace had a nostalgic sleigh bed and night stand, an antique white armoire, and a roll-top desk—everything I'd need except a mirror. The walls were mint green, the exact shade of the glass parlor lamp and the pillows on the window seat.

On the other side of the hall, I found a spacious country kitchen painted sunny yellow. A set of dishes with a busy pink pattern gleamed in a glass-fronted cupboard, and a copper tea kettle brightened an aging stove. I froze at the sight of an orange pillar candle in the center of a drop-leaf maple table.

I'd find another centerpiece as soon as possible, one that wouldn't remind me of leaping flames and crying collies.

Rescued collies, I reminded myself. *Focus on the present. Forget the past.*

Romy needed to eat. So did I. Her dinner makings were in my suitcase, but, for me, that meant a trip back to Maple Creek. I should leave soon, before the Blue Lion closed for the day. As I would be coming home after dark, I'd better leave the lights on.

I moved quickly then, giving Romy a drink and her dinner, unpacking suitcases, and making the bed. After freshening up in the tiny bathroom, I changed into a long plaid skirt and warm black turtleneck sweater. As I brushed my dark brown hair, I recalled Valerie remarking on my resemblance to my mother.

I had inherited my mother's small stature and coloring, but I was tougher than she'd ever been, capable of taking care of myself in most situations. Even in an isolated country manor with only a dog for back-up.

Remember that, I thought. *In case the house on Balsam Lane isn't as remote as it seems.*

At six o'clock Maple Creek resembled a small metropolis. Cars cruised up and down the street, and pedestrians strolled past store fronts framed in twinkling lights. I found a parking space in front of the bakery and set off on a leisurely stroll to the Blue Lion.

In the window of the barber shop, posters advertised next Saturday's Apple Fair and the Lakeville Players' Halloween production of *Dark of the Moon*. Apparently small town life had its share of diversions.

I pushed open the restaurant's heavy door and waited for a moment while my eyes adjusted to the dimness. The place was crowded. Wait staff carrying trays and order pads glided deftly around the tables. Soft lighting set a mysterious, romantic mood, and the Medieval-themed border on the dark-paneled walls created a quaint old English ambience.

My idea of old English ambience, that is, with all the warmth and welcome that eluded Valerie's house. The Blue Lion provided comfort food, too, judging by the specials printed on a chalkboard at the entrance.

A short, rosy-cheeked hostess in black and white gave me a cheery smile. "Good evening, ma'am. How many in your party tonight?"

"One," I said.

"Right this way."

She ushered me to a booth near a fireplace. In the midst of subdued conversation and laughter, I felt suddenly alone, which made no sense. I *was* alone. How else should I feel?

But the couples and convivial groups seated around me provided an illusion of company. For now, that would have to do, and even an illusion would balance the silence waiting for me at the end of the evening.

I can eat out every night if I want to, I told myself. *Maybe I'll meet new people, and the next time I come to the Blue Lion, someone will sit across from me.*

Like the brawny, blond state trooper eating pie at the next booth. He had a clean-shaven face, handsome rugged features, and a grim take-no-prisoners expression. Was he a brilliant conversationalist or the strong silent type?

Well, you'll never find out, Susanna.

Smiling at my foolishness, I picked up the menu. The entrées ranged from pricey prime rib to plain fare like homemade beef pasties with mashed potatoes. I ordered a petite filet, considered adding a glass of wine, then remembered the drive back to Balsam Lane in the dark.

"Large ginger ale with extra ice please," I told the waitress.

This done, I settled back in my chair to watch my fellow diners. Before long, however, my attention strayed to the painted figures in the border: Knights in hunter's green, ladies resplendent in royal blue, lions and unicorns, and hounds with jeweled collars around their necks, all against a background of earth tones and red in various shades.

The detail and wealth of color dazzled me, and, speaking of color, the lions were caramel brown and the unicorns purple with silver horns and wings. Why call the restaurant the Blue Lion then? Why not the Brown Lion or the Purple Unicorn?

Making a mental note to ask someone, I studied the hounds with their proud heads and sleek, shining coats. They were so realistically depicted that they seemed about to leap off the wall onto the table.

My waitress brought me a tall frosted glass of ginger ale and murmured that she'd be right back. I took a tentative sip, then a longer drink, deciding that it tasted almost as good as wine.

Here's to the entire canine race, I thought. *To Romy, my best friend, and to the puppies.*

For me, dogs had always been a genuine passion in the blood. My child's dream of owning a dog like the heroic collies who ran through Albert Payson Terhune's novels or graced the pages of *Collie Vistas* had never died.

Feeling a sting of tears, I swirled the straw through crushed ice and took another sip of ginger ale. *And here's to the lost one.*

For a brief happy time, I had co-owned a gorgeous blue merle champion, a dog so magnificent that everyone who saw him wished to own him.

That's the fairy tale of my life, I thought. *A convoluted web of treachery and trial by fire with a still-to-be-determine ending.*

Damn Amy Brackett with her cold green eyes and counterfeit smile. Damn her for intruding on my thoughts yet once again. The memories stirred by the hounds pushed their way to the front of my mind, determined to carry me back to a time I wanted to forget.

Amy and I were dog show friends who had pooled our money to purchase a young show prospect out of a famous Connecticut kennel. True to his breeder's expectations, Larkspur Blue Frost grew into a breathtaking beauty, with the form, sweet temperament, and thick, lustrous coat for which his line was known. Before his first birthday, he had earned ten points toward his championship.

And he was such a good dog, so gentle and loyal. Like the Terhune collies, Frost had spirit and heart. Basking in his sterling reputation, we leased Greengrove Farm, hired a talented dog handler named Preston Anderson, and planned a stellar future for ourselves in the Fancy.

Then in an instant and without warning, my world fell apart.

The waitress set a basket of French bread in front of me and moved on to the trooper's table to refill his coffee cup. I helped myself to a slice and ate it quickly, concentrating on the crisp golden crust, the slightly sweet taste, and the fall of crumbs on the tablecloth. Anything to distract myself from the anger that still burned inside me as relentlessly as the Larkspur Kennel fire.

In one bold, brazen move, Amy stole my share of Blue Frost from me. Then she blithely ripped my reputation to shreds by starting a rumor that I had set the fire out of spite.

The accusation was ludicrous. Previously, we had both identified Tag Nolan as the vagrant who had been hanging around the kennel, trolling for odd jobs. Another witness had seen him trespassing on the property with a can of gasoline. Still another had implicated him in a chain of stable arsons.

So no one could have believed Amy's lie, but at the Middlebrook show, a few people I considered friends had been cool to me. Maybe, some of them *did* believe her. Even Preston, which hurt me deeply, as I thought he cared for me. Only Marsha Vernon appeared oblivious of the stories, but then she shied away from unpleasantness of any kind.

I didn't know why Amy turned on me. Because of an innate mean streak I had never suspected or an imagined grudge? Or because possession and prestige meant more to her than integrity? Or for some private reason I couldn't fathom?

I only knew that I would never forgive her.

Still, I realized that sustained anger has a painful rebound effect. It couldn't touch Amy. It could only harm me as it was doing right now, throwing a shadow on my first evening in Maple Creek.

Don't let it.

I made my way through salad and filet mignon, casting surreptitious glances at the handsome state trooper until he paid his bill and left the restaurant. Then I wove fictitious histories for the people seated closest to my table. Finally, while waiting for dessert I made out a long mental list of chores and errands for tomorrow.

My attempts at self-distraction succeeded. By the time I finished my chocolate cheesecake, I was able to push Amy back into the past where she belonged, at least temporarily.

She had taught me a valuable lesson, although that wasn't her intent. In the future, I vowed to form friendships more slowly, if at all, and to hold fast to what I had, no matter what happened.

Bands of pink streaked a mauve sky as I passed Marble Lake and turned onto Balsam Lane. By the time I reached the first of the curves, the pink was gone, the mauve had deepened to black, and stars and headlights replaced street lamps. Night driving made me nervous, but I knew how to navigate country roads.

Keep your eyes on the center line. Look out for leaping deer. Hope to sight another car so this lonely road wouldn't seem like the way to World's End.

If I did all that and ignored my rising anxiety, I should make it home safely. Not home, I reminded myself. The place where I was staying. Where I'd left Romy.

I kept glancing to the right, waiting for a well-lit blue house to materialize beyond the next curve. Several miles and thirty minutes later, I still didn't see it. When a quaint covered bridge loomed out of the darkness, I knew I'd gone too far north.

Making a U-turn, I slowed to twenty-five miles and headed south again, now looking on my left. I passed a gray stone cottage that reminded me of a mausoleum, tree-shadowed estates, and a scattering of old farmhouses, interspersed with stretches of woodland. Nothing looked familiar.

But the house had to be here. Somewhere.

I tried to swallow away the dryness in my throat and found that I couldn't do it. My heartbeat quickened, and I tightened my hand on the wheel, frowning as a familiar pain jabbed at my right hand.

Stay calm, I ordered myself. *Panic attacks and driving are incompatible. It's impossible to get lost between Marble Lake and 7 Balsam Lane.*

Was I even on Balsam Lane? Where were the road signs?

The hands on the dashboard clock seemed to spin around; the numbers on the odometer raced forward. How could I have let this happen on a simple drive to town for dinner?

On one of those dark curves, I might have inadvertently turned onto an unmarked byroad or taken the wrong fork back at the lake.

"You'll like country living," Valerie had assured me. At the moment I didn't, not one bit.

Lost in the woods. Lost in the night. Lost...

I drove on. To the edge of Nowhere. To World's End.

Calm. You have to stay calm and clear-headed.

I'd made a mistake, but it was fixable. If I'd chosen the wrong road, all I had to do was return to Marble Lake and take the right one. Start all over again. Maybe I was on Balsam Lane after all. Things always look different at night. I wasn't familiar with the area.

Wait! There...

I stepped on the brake as my headlights illuminated a towering blue house held fast on either side by encroaching trees. There was the sinister hedge. There was the shimmer of the pond and the hill where balsam firs grew up to the sky. Everything was as it should be, ice blue and magical under a starry sky.

With one exception. The place was steeped in darkness. Every light I'd left on had been extinguished.

Chapter 3

All the panic I'd felt earlier on Balsam Lane rushed back as I raced through the shadows up to the porch. *It's happening again...again....* The words thundered in my mind. *Someone broke in. Someone took Romy.*

My hand trembled as I unlocked the door and continued to shake as my dog padded out of the darkness and nudged my knee with her snout. I gave her a long, loving pat. She was safe. Thank God. But what happened to the lights?

I felt along the wall and pressed the switch. The hall flooded with dim illumination, showing itself to be empty—as far as I could see. The vase still topped the mahogany table. Doors remained closed, and stairs ascended into an even deeper blackness.

I listened carefully to the household sounds to make sure they were innocuous. The clock ticked in the living room, the refrigerator fan whirred, and the furnace hummed, sending blessed heat throughout the house. I didn't hear anything unusual, but an intruder could be hiding on the second or third floor, or even this one, waiting.

For what?

Impatient with my newly emerging jitteriness, I considered taking another quick tour, this time covering the upper stories. Not really wanting to do that tonight, I settled for a question, using a louder-than-usual tone. "Is everything all right, Romy girl?"

Her wagging tail and sparkling eyes assured me that it was.

I walked down the hall, turning on lights in the kitchen and bedroom, searching for an easy solution to the mystery. Valerie had warned me to expect brown outs and power failures in the country. But would the electricity come back on at the exact moment I touched the switch? It was possible but not likely.

Suppose the Realtor had noticed the house lit up and let herself in to investigate? This made sense, except Valerie had alerted her to my arrival. Once inside, she'd have seen Romy. No one with sense and compassion would leave a dog alone in the dark.

Another possibility, that a neighbor or friend of the previous owner had a key, alarmed me. If a stranger could let himself in at will, I'd better have the locks changed. I didn't like the idea of a real estate agent having access to my living quarters either.

Incidentally, why would Romy have allowed a stranger to enter the house?

"This job will be a piece of cake," Valerie had promised me. After only a few hours, I suspected that she didn't know the old Victorian any better than she knew me.

At my side, Romy whined, reminding me that she had to go out.

Like most collies, she was an extremely vocal dog, chatty and alert to anomalies in the environment. On the night of the fire, her frantic barking had awakened me out of a deep sleep, giving me a chance to save the puppies. I knew I could count on her now.

After a trip out to the yard, she scrunched the bedside rug into a cozy nest and closed her eyes while I changed into a nightgown. Still, sleep didn't come so easily to me. I lay under the quilt, tense and anxious, listening for an alien sound to infiltrate the familiar ones.

But no untoward noises disturbed the silence, only natural ones. The clock chimed eleven times, so loudly that it might have been just outside my door. The winds picked up, and branches scratched against the windows, creating a ghastly sound. Romy sighed in her sleep.

At last I let myself relax. Tomorrow was soon enough to deal with capricious lighting and assorted strangeness.

In the morning, emboldened by bright, wholesome sunlight, I embarked on my delayed tour of the house's upper stories. Romy padded along behind me. I kept up a running conversation with her in an attempt to inject a little normal noise into the silence.

We stopped at the landing where a lacy Norfolk pine languished in a corner, far from the closest sunbeam. Still, it looked healthy enough. I touched a branch and discovered that it was silk. It should be in a downstairs room surrounded by real plants. The house needed something green and growing.

As I made my way down the hall, my footsteps echoed in the lonely expanses. Romy dashed excitedly from door to door, eager to explore unseen wonders. Then, changing her focus, she darted up the stairs to the third floor.

The rooms on the second level were sparsely furnished and painted creamy white or soft gray. One contained twin beds covered with beige spreads in the classic wedding ring pattern. Another held a vintage Singer sewing machine. In a third, a maple rocker, oddly placed in the center of the floor, appeared to move for a fraction of a second. Somewhere above me, wood creaked—from four legs running, I hoped.

With its empty spaces and neutral colors, the house radiated cool spookiness—and something else that I couldn't quite identify. A sense of waiting? A growing impatience?

16

Don't be so dramatic, I scolded myself. *As soon as curtains and rugs and furniture leave a room, it looks and feels different. There's nothing unnatural about that.*

Spooky was a frame of mind, an illusion, and presented no real danger. No one had hidden up here, poised to wreak havoc on an unsuspecting house sitter. This was simply an aging Victorian minimally staged for sale, desperately in need of homespun touches to whisper in a buyer's ear, *"You must have me! No matter what the cost."*

The bathroom was ordinary enough with an old-fashioned white tub standing proudly on clawed feet. A set of snowy towels lay on the top tier of an iron stand, and to the left of the vanity, a jar of vanilla bubble bath kept company with heart-shaped soaps in an apothecary jar. The mirror had a dull surface and a small jagged scratch in the center.

Empty rooms, bland walls, motionless shadows, and echoes—the house offered predictability, which was good. I reached the end of the hall and backtracked, imagining dainty vintage wallpaper and authentic period furnishings. Color, even in small doses, would provide a lived-in feeling, as would lamps burning from sunset to late at night.

On the third floor I found a large, airy room with a magnificent view of the grounds. This space would be ideal for a person who wanted to sleep close to the birds and the sky. It deserved special treatment, a crowning touch to seal the deal. But what? The Norfolk pine strung with lights?

I walked over to window and stood for a moment looking down at the pond. From this height, it seemed smaller, like a piece of unevenly shaped glass set down in the grass to reflect the balsams on the hill. In the winter, with the water frozen and the trees steeped in snow, the scene would turn into a living Christmas card.

As breathtaking as the scenery was, I didn't care for these higher elevations. They were too far from the exits.

After a quick survey of the rest of the floor, I decided to end my exploration. The upper levels held no discernible secrets, and if I heard mysterious noises, it could only be the house settling, combined with imagination.

I called to Romy. She appeared immediately, standing as still as a shadow in the meager light that filtered through the stained glass oval at the hall's end.

Downstairs again, I drank a tall glass of water, then unpacked the car, dividing boxes between the kitchen and bedroom. As soon as I plugged in the coffeemaker, my new surroundings began to feel almost homey. While Romy crunched her morning biscuits and I ate a day-old jelly doughnut, I leafed through the papers in the folder that Valerie had given me. One contained a newspaper advertisement:

Maple Creek Victorian. Enchanting blend of charm and history. Three stories, formal dining room, parlor, country kitchen, eight bedrooms. Pond and stream on wooded acreage. All this in a village setting. Three Pines Realtors.

Atmospheric and a little sinister, I added. And did the village setting refer to Maple Creek?

Nonetheless, the property sounded wonderful on paper. I jotted down the address and phone number of the Realtor, Karenell Miller. We should meet soon, today, if she was available, to discuss the missing 'For Sale' sign and last night's lighting glitch. And the possible existence of an extra key. I mustn't forget that.

The clock chimed ten times, leaving ten echoes in its wake. I found my shoulder bag on the hall table where I'd left it last night.

First stop, grocery store. Second, florist—if you can find one. Third...

A scent of balsam slipped into the air. Fresh and spicy, the most aromatic and evocative fragrance in the world. I breathed it in deeply, as images of Christmas trees and wreaths and branches tucked on top of picture frames formed in my mind.

Check the parlor. That's where it's coming from.

Ignoring my accelerated heartbeat and the rush of chilled air, I opened the door to the same view I remembered from yesterday: A white brick fireplace that no one had used in years, bay windows rimed with condensation, curtains that appeared to move as if a breeze had stolen through solid glass and coaxed them into motion.

I blinked and came closer. The scroll-and-swirl pattern in the beige panels resembled waves breaking on a frothy surface, or snow blown eastward by the wind. Or a diamond edging of ice racing across the hem.

I was cold again, shivering in jeans and a warm red sweater. Why couldn't the heat reach this ground floor room when it traveled all the way up to the third story? And why, as I moved closer to the bay windows, did the balsam fragrance intensify?

These were good questions that must have answers. I just couldn't think of any yet. Maybe Karenell Miller could enlighten me.

As I turned to leave, the light ping of an object falling on hardwood broke the stillness. Expecting to see one of my buttons or a broken piece of earring, I looked down.

A little green paper star lay at my feet. It was the kind of sticker sold in any drug store or craft shop, used for...what? An envelope decoration? A child's party? I hadn't seen one in years.

Where could that have come from? Surely not the thin air.

I picked it up, squelching the prickle of fear as soon as it appeared. This might be a house of mysterious happenings, but a tiny, shiny star from Whereverland wasn't one of them.

It must have attached itself to my clothing or hair as I toured the house, maybe when I examined the old sewing machine. Then, just now, it fell to the floor. That was the only possible explanation, but, like the power failure, it wasn't very likely.

What was going on here? And how could a light object made of paper make any sound at all?

The star glittered on my palm as bright as a five-pointed emerald. I couldn't just toss it in the trash.

But why keep it? I could buy a whole package of stars in all colors for a few dollars.

Not like this one, I thought.

Setting it on the mantel for safekeeping, I left the parlor, closing the door tightly. Suddenly I wanted to do something—anything—outside the house on Balsam Lane.

By noon, I'd bought a week's worth of groceries, two red-gold chrysanthemum plants, and a handful of autumn bouquets. Later, on the way to the Realtor's office, I discovered a field filled with pumpkins, cornstalks, and lawn decorations. Here on a rolling half acre called Jones Farm was everything necessary to transform the old blue house into an autumn showplace. Except for the wreath.

I took my time to select the perfect decorations for the porch. A lanky young man in overhauls set my cornstalks carefully in the trunk and loaded a dozen pumpkins on the back seat.

"Do you know if Maple Creek has a florist?" I asked.

He ran a callused hand through his spiked red hair. "There's one on Main Street. It's called the Flower Cart."

"I wonder if they sell grapevine wreaths."

"Can't say. If you're in the market for a decoration, how about one of my sculptures?" He pointed to a row of life-sized wooden animals: Rabbits, raccoons, foxes, deer, and a brown bear standing upright with outstretched arms and massive paws. "Old Grizzly is my best seller. He's yours for a hundred bucks."

All of the creations had ferocious expressions, even the bunnies. "They're nice," I said. "But I'm looking for something to hang on the front door. Something pretty and bright, with fall decorations."

"Go to the Apple Fair next Saturday," he said. "They'll have all kinds of crafts for sale and lots of good stuff to eat."

"Thanks for the tip. I couldn't squeeze anything else in the car anyway."

"Come back after Thanksgiving for your Christmas tree," he added, with a wave.

I drove away from the farm, my mood brightening at the prospect of attending a country festival. I had no idea what to expect, but that didn't stop visions of doughnuts and cider and hand-woven baskets from dancing through my head. I could finish my shopping for the house and have fun at the same time.

Now for my last stop of the day, the realty office on Maple Road. The agency headquarters was a tiny white cottage with lavender shutters and a window box where shriveled ghosts of plants choked out their last breaths in dried dirt. The remains of a large pumpkin lay splattered on the winding stone walkway. Stepping over innards, seeds, and chewed chunks, I noticed a small 'Closed' sign propped in the window.

Not open on a weekday afternoon?

The general air of neglect about the place, specifically the pumpkin mess, raised a bright red flag. Unless Three Pines was a one-woman operation and Karenell Miller was out in the field showing a house, I might have a problem. Apprehension jabbed at me as I contemplated this latest development in a venture that showed every sign of going awry.

Apparently no one was actively marketing Valerie's house. The Realtor was away, her headquarters unattended, and where was I? Wandering in a Twilight Zone of strange and stranger happenings.

A girl comes to a mysterious blue house in the woods and finds herself trapped in a series of weird circumstances that lead to . . . Terror?

Only in a mystery story.

But something was wrong. What if I'd come to the wrong office, having made a mistake when copying Karenell Miller's address? Or, could I possibly have come to the wrong blue Victorian on Balsam Lane?

Impossible. The sign identified the place as Three Pines Realtors. The address and description in Valerie's folder matched the house. Most importantly, the key worked. The answer lay elsewhere. Once again I searched for an elusive explanation. I could only think of one.

Valerie might have left for Florida, not knowing that the Realtor had gone out of business. That would explain the missing sign—and, unfortunately, leave me and the house in a state of limbo. Only Valerie could straighten out the muddle by listing the house with another agency or, better still, coming home to Michigan to handle her own affairs.

If that happened, I might have to pack up and move on. And Romy...oh no! Romy! How could I have forgotten about my dog? She was in the house, alone again.

I hurried back to the car, propelled by a sense of urgency.

Hurry, hurry...before it's too late. Before something terrible happens.

I had to get in touch with Valerie immediately. My cell phone lay on the seat beside me, but her Florida number was in the folder she'd given me, back in the house.

Hurry.

But there's no reason to be afraid for Romy. She's all right. You have to stop overreacting.

I'd intended to stop at the Blue Lion Inn for a leisurely lunch before heading back to the house. Now I couldn't get home fast enough. I had sandwich makings in the trunk and the coffeemaker at home. But I couldn't think about food until I knew where I stood in this rapidly shifting scenario.

First, make sure that Romy is all right. Second, call Valerie. Third...

At present, I didn't know what to do after that. As I headed back to Balsam Lane with my load of harvest decorations, I had a sinking feeling that in accepting Valerie's job offer, I might have made my bad situation worse.

Chapter 4

The siren came out of nowhere, shattering my jumbled thoughts into tiny fragments. That couldn't be the police. Could it?

As I glanced in the rearview mirror, hoping to see an ambulance or fire engine, a fast moving vehicle with flashing lights on the roof rack materialized through a cloud of dust and grit. That meant a cop, and mine was the only other car on the road.

Where had he been hiding? More importantly, why didn't I see him? And most important of all, I couldn't spare the time to deal with a delay now. Did I have a choice?

The speedometer needle quivered at seventy-five. Automatically I pumped the brake. The Taurus shimmied, and the tires skidded on the gravel, taking me to a respectable forty miles per hour. Too late. But at least I wasn't speeding now.

I turned on my signal and steered to the side of the road, hoping the officer would be in warning mode or, better still, that he only wanted to pass me. Of course, with my run of dismal luck, I was his target, and he would soon give me a ticket.

As I waited, a fantasy of outrunning the law played in my mind. If I'd seen him sooner, I could have turned down one of those shadowy byroads and wished myself into a cornfield. If only it were possible. If only I dared.

But I wasn't living in a movie. I was guilty and had allowed myself to be caught, another unanticipated wrinkle in the fabric of my new life in Maple Creek.

The officer brought his cruiser to a stop and strolled over to my car with heavy, determined steps, while I pressed the window button and searched in my shoulder bag for my wallet.

He was a state trooper, tall and imposing, with attractive sun-weathered features and waving blond hair. He was also familiar. I had seen him last night at the Blue Lion Inn eating pie. This afternoon, he was a hundred percent business, with a stern, cool demeanor and no recognition of me. None of which mattered at this particular moment.

I squinted up into the bright sunlight, forcing myself to look directly into his eyes. They were blue-gray with ice glints in their depths. "Was I doing something wrong, officer?" I asked.

"Didn't you see me following you with the lights on, ma'am?" he demanded.

"Just now I did."

"Do you know how fast you were going?"

"Fifty?"

"Seventy-five."

"That fast? I didn't realize. Well, there aren't any other cars around, and..." I trailed off, not wanting to appear argumentative. He must have heard variations of this theme a million times. No words were going to alter the outcome.

"I'm sorry." I handed him my driver's license and registration. "I'm just trying to get home."

"The idea is to make it there in one piece." He began to write in his pad, an ominous sign.

"Yes."

He was right; I was wrong.

"That's speeding and reckless driving," he added.

I shifted in the seat, impatient to be on my way. "I just moved to Maple Creek yesterday. I'm not familiar with the area yet."

"It's forty-five on this stretch. You need to be able to stop if an animal runs out in front of you." He pointed to the silhouette of a leaping deer on a nearby warning sign and handed me the ticket. "It happens all the time. We had a bad crash here last week. Luckily no one died."

I signed my name quickly, letting the last letters drift off into an illegible line.

"Good afternoon," he said. "Keep that speed down."

Promising to drive carefully, I steered slowly back to the road, lamenting the lost money and what it could have bought: The puppies' boarding, entrance fees for the shows, days and days of lattes, if this godforsaken backwater had a coffee house, and new toys for Romy.

Country living had its hidden costly side. I vowed never again to tangle with the law, at least, not while exceeding the posted speed limit.

Still, the encounter had provided a dusting of sparkle in an otherwise humdrum day. The blond trooper possessed a certain appeal, if you liked the tall, fair-haired, and handsome type. What woman didn't?

But I'd never see him again, unless we happened to be in the Blue Lion Inn at the same time. Anyway, my stay in Maple Creek wouldn't be long. In fact, my job might be evaporating at this moment, which reminded me that, along with needed funds, I'd just lost precious time.

The officer was long gone, and I had the road to myself again. With a quick look in every direction, I increased my speed by ten miles per hour. Balsam Lane and Romy were still a half hour away.

As I turned into the driveway, I heard the distinctive roar of a leaf blower. A strong burning odor made its way through the opened window.

Fire! Where?

My heart began to beat more rapidly. Quelling the rising panic, I parked behind an unfamiliar black truck and surveyed the grounds.

A coil of smoke snaked high above the trees on the left, well away from the dwelling. There was no need for alarm. Someone was burning leaves or wood. Or junk. No doubt the handyman.

The front lawn had been transformed into a neat, rolling expanse of dull green and brown with a 'For Sale' sign in its center. Beyond the hedge, the old Victorian glowed in the afternoon sunshine, the porch swept—or rather blown—clean, the gables rising high against a deep azure sky.

All of my misgivings vanished. The fallout from my multiple ordeals had made me overly imaginative and prone to find problems where none existed. Valerie had said she'd hired a man to take care of the grounds, and here he was, out of sight at present but obviously hard at work. The place was definitely on the market. As for Karenell Miller, she was simply too busy making sales to keep her own cottage tidy.

In other words, all was well.

Please let it stay that way, I prayed. Because even with manicured grounds and a newly trimmed hedge, the house maintained its cold blue countenance. Appearing to lean on the trees for support, it communicated desolation, along with another quality that I still couldn't identify.

That façade needed every bit of color I could give it and a healthy dose of seasonal good cheer.

I followed the noise to the back where a man in a red flannel shirt and hunter's cap herded leaves into a burning stack. I stared at the blaze, transfixed by its power to destroy.

Flames leaped high. Dried leaves sizzled like little living things trapped on a grill. The heat reached out to me with desperate fingers, grabbing hungrily at my hand. I slipped my keys into my jacket pocket and tried to rub the sudden stabs of pain away.

It's only a bonfire, I told myself. *There's no need to overreact. None at all.*

But smoke choked the country freshness out of the air. I struggled to breathe and was surprised to find that I could.

From inside the house, I heard Romy barking angrily. She hated unusual sounds and noise-making machines. She'd continue to fuss until the monster died. That should be soon. It looked as if the clean-up was winding down.

I stepped back, away from the smoke and crushing waves of heat. Onto safe ground.

My right hand throbbed. Tears stung my eyes—from the smoke. I wiped them away, wincing at the tenderness in my fingers. Would I ever be well and whole again?

The handyman began a slow saunter back to the house, sending leaves flying in his wake. He had an elderly man's lined face and a young man's physique. I waved, and he turned off the blower.

In the fall of silence, I said, "I'm Susanna Kentwood..."

He nodded slightly, running his hand over his gray handlebar moustache. "You're Ms. Lansing's gal?"

"Her house sitter."

"Virgil Jones here." He tipped his cap.

"Did Ms. Lansing give you a key?" I asked.

"There's no need for that. I work outside."

His voice had a gruff edge; his clipped words made me feel like an intruder.

I added, "Did you bring the 'For Sale' sign with you?"

"It was here all along. Just buried." He gestured toward the trees, still heavy with vibrant color. "I'll be coming by every week till they're all down."

Leaves continued to fall even as we stood in the yard, locked in uneasy conversation. They floated down in a scarlet shower to spoil the clean-swept perfection of the lawn. He brushed one off his sleeve with an impatient swipe.

"I'll let you get back to work," I said. "Be sure the fire's out before you go."

"I know about safety, miss." His sigh held reproach and perhaps a hint of resentment. 'You're not the boss here,' he might have said. 'You're hired help, just like me.'

He pushed a switch, and the blower roared back to life. Without a further word, he headed toward the pond.

Romy's face appeared in the dining room window. Her barking turned into a high-pitched keening that tore at my frazzled nerves.

I need it to be quiet, I thought. *Just for a little while.*

Quickly I unloaded the car, leaving cornstalks, pumpkins, and chrysanthemums on the porch, bringing groceries in the house and holding them away from Romy who forgot her agitation as she sniffed the brown bags for one of her treats.

In the vestibule I paused to look at the mahogany table with its empty vase, the stairs leading up to the darkness above, and the hall that ended in a gathering of shadows. Nothing had changed since I'd been away, but for the first time, I felt as if the blue Victorian was welcoming me home.

After Virgil Jones finished clearing the grounds and drove away, after lunch and a brief quiet spell, I arranged the pumpkins at cozy intervals along the front of the wraparound porch. With cornstalks and bright chrysanthemums flanking the entrance, the house looked almost cheerful. Only the door begged for a decoration of its own.

This Saturday at the Apple Fair, I hoped to find the perfect wreath, one adorned with autumn flowers or red winterberries.

What else could I do to whip the place in shape? A colorful rag rug? Gourds? Outside furniture? The maple rocker that had seemed to move of its own volition would be a perfect addition to my Halloween-themed décor.

By the time I'd carried it down from the second floor and set it in front of the bay windows, the sun had vanished behind swollen gray clouds. A cool wind blew, chilling the temperature and blanketing Virgil's immaculate lawn with a fresh leaf cover. The bonfire had shrunk to an ashen blob on the landscape, every spark dead, its smoke still hanging on the air.

I was about to go inside through the back door, when a tinny voice from the front called out, "Hello...hello. Is anybody there?"

Romy bolted toward the sound, barking excitedly. I called her to heel and followed more slowly.

Our visitor stood on the porch, patting her silvery blonde hair in place. She was a petite woman dressed in a long denim jumper with sprays of daisies embroidered across the bodice. She carried a basket filled to the top with dried purple flowers.

"I'm Flora Brine from next door," she said with a wide smile. "I should say, from down the road. In the white farmhouse."

"Hello. I'm Susanna Kentwood. This is Romy."

I told Romy to sit, and she did, tilting her head. One ear pricked and promptly fell back in place as she offered the newcomer her paw.

"Should I?" she asked. "Is she friendly?"

"She's a lamb."

Flora shook hands with Romy. To me she said, "I came over to see your pretty decorations up close and welcome you to Snowhedge."

"Snowhedge?"

"That's the house's name. Because in the winter, the hedge looks like it's made out of snow."

Like an austere country manor in a nineteenth century book, the old Victorian had a name and a poetic one, at that. A neighbor had stopped by to compliment my decorations. I felt a burst of pride in my vision, in my accomplishments. Pride of possession?

You're hired help, Susanna. A paid tenant doing her job.

"The owner didn't tell me that," I said.

"Oh..." Flora's smile faded. "You didn't buy the house?"

"I'm just watching over it and trying to fix it up a little," I said.

"You won't be staying then?"

"For a little while. Until the place sells."

"That may take forever. It's been on the market for two and a half years."

"I'm going to do everything I can to get buyers to notice it."

"They will, Susanna," she said. "I did. You're not staying here alone, are you?"

"It's just Romy and me."

"Lila Rose lived alone too," Flora said. "You hardly ever saw her outside. Never, toward the end. 'My house is my life,' she always said. 'Why should I go anywhere else?' They say that once people settle down at Snowhedge, they never leave."

"The Realtor should use that line," I said. "Who was Lila Rose?"

"The last lady who used to live in the house. In the end, she didn't have to leave. She died here."

"I didn't know that," I said.

"Don't let it bother you. People die all over the place every day. This is exactly where Lila Rose would have wanted to be when it happened."

"I suppose so, if she loved her home."

"Well..." Flora rested her hand on the porch post, looking toward the stream. "That's all I wanted—to say hello. It was nice meeting you."

I wasn't being the slightest bit hospitable. She'd think I was unfriendly.

"Would you like to come in and have a cup of tea or a soft drink with me?" I asked.

"Oh, no. Thank you, but I...I have to take my lavender home, and I can see that you're busy. So, goodbye."

"Come again," I said, but Flora was already walking briskly away. She crossed a small decorative bridge that spanned the stream and stopped to gather more flowers on the other side of the property line. I called to Romy and went inside, closing the door.

Alone at last. Alone . . .

But, darn. I'd missed an opportunity to learn more about the neighborhood and possibly the history of the house.

I still had to finish unpacking groceries and call Karenell Miller who should have returned to her office by now. Then...I frowned. Then, what? The rest of the afternoon and an entire evening lay ahead of me. Endless hours to fill. Ghostly halls to wander through. Spooky rooms in an old Victorian where a woman had drawn her last breath. Too much space and not enough to do. Too much time to think.

What I wanted was to engage in some lighthearted, mindless activity where lights were bright, people laughed, and I didn't have two unoccupied floors above my head.

Then do it. Go out for dinner again tonight.

If I could lose myself in some happy place like the Blue Lion Inn, a lonely country life would be mildly tolerable.

This job isn't a good fit for you, Susanna, I told myself. *Call Valerie, tell her you can't stay here, and move on."*

Where? And do what?

Besides, I didn't want to resign. Valerie was depending on me. So, oddly enough, was Snowhedge. Going out for dinner and coming home with a new perspective would be easier.

Having decided on my evening plans, I arranged the flowers from the grocery store in vases. They were spicy sweet carnations in autumn reds, oranges, and yellows with plenty of baby's breath. One bouquet would stay

26

in the kitchen, replacing the centerpiece candle. I'd put the others on the vestibule table, in the dining room, and on the mantel in the parlor.

I wished that Flora hadn't told me about Lila Rose dying in the house.

And she probably wasn't the only one. Snowhedge is over a century old. People die all over the place every day. Words of wisdom from Flora Brine.

I'd rather have heard about Lila Rose's life and why she was alone as her life drew to a close.

Presumably because she had loved her home above all. I couldn't imagine anyone being so attached to a wooden structure that they would be reluctant to leave it.

I set the large vase on the mahogany table and headed toward the parlor with the other one. Bracing for an onslaught of frigid air and balsam fragrance, I opened the door.

There was the cold and the scent, right on schedule—and there, in the middle of the glossy hardwood floor, was a dark red stain.

Chapter 5

The stain looked like blood, but that couldn't be. No drops led to or away from it, and it appeared to have the consistency of clay. Holding the vase in a tight grip, I ran my fingers over the surface.

It wasn't clay but warm candle wax, pooled and hardened, stuck fast to the wood.

Warm? Impossible.

I scraped a piece of the substance with my fingernail and smelled it. The scent wasn't the room's signature balsam. Heavier and sweeter, it conjured visions of cookies and coffeecakes. *Cinnamon?*

The last time I'd looked in the parlor, the floor didn't have a single disfiguring mark on it, not a scratch, not a scuff. Had the red glob fallen from thin air like the green star?

You're missing the significance.

Someone had carried a lighted candle into this strange room and stood in the exact center, letting it drip hot wax. This must have happened within the past few hours, which meant that I wasn't alone in the house—or hadn't been. The thought of an intruder holding a dangerous fire-maker terrified me.

I realized that I was shaking, that I couldn't stop. Without a doubt, this was the chilliest room in the house, possibly fifty degrees. The frosty condensation on the windows had climbed higher, forming unrecognizable shapes in glistening white. Why? It wasn't that cold outside.

I set the vase of carnations on the mantle next to the star, aware that the combination of red, orange, and yellow looked like flames. Was everything in this house designed to torment me?

But I'd bought the flowers and chosen the colors myself, never noticing their resemblance to fire.

Quickly I backed into the hall. I'd have to scrape the rest of the wax away and try to remove the stain, if possible, but I'd deal with clean up later, when I felt a little braver and had warmer clothes on. Now I only wanted to get out of this icy room.

I closed the door and almost stumbled over Romy who lay beside the table, quietly watching me.

"Come," I said and started up the stairway, turning on lights as I went along. She grabbed her stuffed duck with her mouth and bounded along after me, tail wagging.

Second floor, third floor...everything in place, all quiet.

I walked slowly, over territory I'd covered yesterday, carrying on a lively conversation with Romy, even peering into empty closets and behind furniture. I half expecting a figure to leap out of the shadows and pounce on me, but the sounds of footsteps and breathing were my own.

Every room was exactly as it had been, except for the one from which I'd taken the rocker. No mysterious stains splattered the floors or walls and, if an intruder had walked through the house, he left no tell-tale sign of his presence behind.

I was definitely and undeniably alone. Now. But maybe Virgil Jones had entered the house earlier and spilled wax on the parlor floor to frighten me. Or Flora Brine. Perhaps she was the neighbor to whom Lila Rose had given a key to use in case of emergencies. For some unfathomable reason, one of them wanted me gone.

Neither explanation seemed likely. But how could I explain this latest anomaly? Most telling of all, nowhere on my travels did I find a red cinnamon-scented candle.

The intruder took it with him?

I didn't know; I had no idea. Once again the house had flung a mystery at me. I couldn't live in a place where I was often baffled and constantly afraid.

Don't be, I told myself. *Every puzzle has a solution. Finding it is only a matter of time and ingenuity.*

The clock chimed seven, reminding me that I'd missed lunch, but my desire for a nice dinner at the Blue Lion was gone. Besides, Romy shouldn't have to stay alone unless it was necessary.

Turning on the lamp in the living room, I said, "Come. We're going out."

With my dog riding in the back seat, I drove away from the house, down Balsam Lane, through Maple Creek, and onto unfamiliar country roads. When I noticed a drive-in restaurant outlined in blinking lights, I stopped. Here was a safe, unpretentious, normal place where I could regain my equilibrium.

After a quick meal, a cheeseburger for me and one for Romy, I felt that I could return to Snowhedge and make that call to Karenell Miller. If I had someone to confide in, I'd be able to cope with this excess of strangeness, and who better to serve as confidante than Valerie's real estate agent?

All the way back, I worried that the light would be out when I reached the house, but that didn't happen. The lamp glowed softly in the living room window, not quite welcoming me tonight, but...what was the word I wanted? Oh, yes. Beckoning.

As I walked up to the porch, a frightening thought assailed me. Could I have imagined the red wax? Out of my deeply ingrained fear of fire, did I create a dangerous burning candle that I'd never allow in my living quarters? In a few minutes, I could be gazing at a smooth expanse of hardwood floor without an unsightly spill on its surface.

Perhaps, but that would bring its own terror.

As soon as I unlocked the door, I steeled myself to check the parlor, by now convinced that the wax would have vanished.

It was still there.

Two days passed. It seemed as if the clock was always chiming, but the unending hours grew progressively longer. My calls to Karenell Miller went straight to her voicemail. She didn't return them. Virgil Jones made another taciturn appearance and once again swept the grounds clear of leaves. The wind blew in from the north and promptly brought more of them down.

Inside the house, I dusted, mopped, washed windows, and changed the water in the vases. With a thin bladed spatula, I scraped away the wax and applied several coats of polish to the parlor floor. A faint red impression remained, a mere ghost of itself, with a disturbing shine in the sunlight. I needed to find a rug large enough to hide it, but the only suitable one proved too heavy for me to move.

Nothing else unusual happened. Too soon the dust came back, the carnations began to droop, and the condensation on the parlor windows reformed. Keeping house, I discovered, was a never-ending, thankless chore. No one stopped by to inquire about the property.

On Saturday, more than ready for a little diversion, I leashed Romy and headed to the Apple Fair. The day was perfect for an outdoor activity with warm weather, a slightly overcast sky, and a light wind sloughing through the trees. I found a parking place two blocks from Main Street and walked back to the center of town in a shower of leaves, trying to keep an exuberant collie from pulling me off my feet.

I knew how she felt. Freedom is infinitely sweeter to one who has just escaped from prison.

At the corner of Walnut and Main, I merged smoothly into the crowd, holding tightly to Romy's leash, both of us aware of the admiring glances coming her way.

At least three or four hundred people strolled up and down the street and roamed through the shady municipal park. Flags flapped from store fronts and picturesque Victorian houses, and red balloons moved languidly in the breeze as "Yankee Doodle" played softly over a medley of chatter and laughter.

I relaxed and surrendered to the spell of the festival, to the promise of fun, good food, and the illusion of company. This lively rural celebration was my real welcome to town.

Booths set up on either side of the park offered apples of all varieties in every conceivable form—heaped high in bushels, coated with candy and

30

caramel, baked into pies, and woven through wreaths and swags—while the Maple Creek Cider Mill sold doughnuts and cider in paper cups and gallon jugs.

Long live the Apple. Long live the Fair.

I paused for a moment at a table crowded with rosy-cheeked harvest dolls. They were cleverly fashioned little creations whose baskets overflowed with fall fruits and vegetables. Some of these Thumbelina-sized maids seemed to have wicked, knowing eyes. That was a ridiculous notion. Still, they cast a fleeting chill on the festive mood.

Move on, then...move on...there's nothing evil about harvest figures and plenty more to see and buy.

The booth closest to the park held an impressive selection of colorful baskets and wreaths, many of them adorned with maple leaves that were reminiscent of the mess around the blue Victorian. Interspersed among the decorations were candles of all kinds from Halloween and Thanksgiving novelties to chunky pillars: Orange scented with pumpkin, green with peppermint, and red with cinnamon.

The sight of cinnamon candles transported me back to the blue Victorian and the stain in the parlor. I told myself that scented candles were as readily available as apples, especially at this time of year, and forced the matter out of my mind. Just for this afternoon I didn't want to relive a nightmare moment.

I'd come to the fair to buy a wreath, cider and doughnuts, and maybe.... Mentally I added an apple pie, fudge, and a pound of chocolates shaped like miniature gourds as a welcome for prospective buyers.

Instead of wandering from booth to booth, I needed a plan. I'd buy the essential items first, stash them in the car, then return for lunch and more browsing. Possibly I'd allow myself an impulse purchase or two. I had to be careful how I spent my money, and only the wreath and chocolates could be charged to Valerie's account.

Romy sniffed the air and turned in a new direction, quickening her pace.

What *was* that delicious smell?

A tantalizing aroma of franks grilling wafted on the wind. Romy lunged forward, forging her own path through the crowd, our roles reversed as she led me toward the hot dog stand where she stood, casting imploring glances in my direction and whining, her desire clear.

I pulled her back. She tugged on the leash and gave a series of short imperious barks.

We had an audience. Two little tow-headed boys watched the battle line being drawn. Between bites of hot dogs, they discussed the possible winner in loud amused tones.

"Later, Romy. We'll eat later!" I said, dismayed to hear hearty male laughter behind me.

Feeling like a mother whose child is throwing a tantrum at the candy counter, I ordered her to stop. She put on her brakes and sat down, staring straight ahead at her chosen destination. In the end, I fairly dragged her away from the stand, deeper into the park.

"Now someone will report me for animal cruelty," I told her. "You are a bad dog."

But I was the one who felt bad for not giving in to her.

A young girl in a red gown with a crown of apple blossoms in her long black hair and a basket in her hand emerged from the crowd. She was handing out caramel apples at random to whoever reached for one. As Romy licked her chops, a voice said, "Jess makes a pretty Apple Queen, doesn't she?"

"She looks like Snow White," said another.

"Hey, Jessie, over here!"

Romy yelped, attracting the Queen's attention.

"What a beautiful dog," she said. "Hello, baby." She gave me a caramel apple in a cupcake paper.

"Thank you," I said, as she walked on, smiling, and bestowing apples to her subjects as if they were favors.

Maple Creek might be a small town but it knew how to host a fantastic fair, and this was a pretty little park, tucked away amidst the shops and houses that lined Main Street.

I found a stone bench near a bubbling fountain and sank into it, giving Romy a guilty pat and telling her to lie down. While she watched me, dark eyes begging for her share of the bounty, I bit into the apple. Lord, that tasted good. Sweet, crunchy, and sweet again. I added caramel apples to my list. The Queen knew what she was doing by giving away free samples.

"What kind of dog is that?"

The tow-headed boys who had witnessed Romy's initial rebellion stood close to us, two pairs of blue eyes fixed on my dog. They were dressed alike in crisp Levi's and Apple Fair shirts, and their features were so similar they might have been twins, but the one who had asked the question was an inch shorter than the other. He had a mustard stain on his shirt and a wide gauze bandage around his left wrist.

"She's a collie," I said, and Romy let her ears fall smooth against her head and wagged her tail.

"Isn't she supposed to be brown like Lassie?" he asked.

"Dogs come in different colors. Romy is a tricolor; that means black, tan, and white, but mostly black."

"That's her name, huh? I'm Danny...this here's my brother, Davey. You ought to give that poor dog something to eat."

"She can't have caramel."

"Why?"

"It isn't good for her. I feed Romy kibble mixed with meat."

"You could give her a hot dog then."

"I guess I could."

Danny reached out to pet Romy just as a brawny man materialized at his side and grabbed his arm in a rough grip. I recognized the blond state trooper but didn't think I'd see him again so soon and in another confrontational situation. Today he wore Levi's and an Apple Fair shirt, like the boys. He looked as austere as he had on the road.

"What did I tell you about getting close to strange dogs, Danny?" he demanded.

Danny had no answer. The trooper still held his arm, eyeing Romy as if she'd changed into an attack dog with blood dripping from her mouth.

"I wish we had a collie like that," Davey said.

"Romy loves children. I guarantee she won't bite. But..." I turned to Danny. "It's a good idea to offer her your hand to sniff before you touch her. Then she won't feel the least bit threatened."

I demonstrated by showing Romy my palm. Her long pink tongue swept over it. In her own way, she'd gotten a taste of caramel for herself. Even the grim-faced trooper smiled.

"I remember you," he said.

"I hope so. You gave me a ticket yesterday. I was driving a little too fast, you said."

"I'm glad to see you're slowing down. Your name is...?"

"Susanna Kentwood."

"That's a nice old-fashioned name," he said. "Does anybody call you Sue?"

"They wouldn't dare."

"I'm Mike Slater. Captain Slater when I'm on duty." He laid a heavy hand on each boy's shoulder. "Let's let the lady eat her apple in peace."

As Mike led the boys through the gate, I heard the first words of a lecture about safe behavior around strange canines.

I hoped Danny wouldn't grow up to be afraid of dogs. As for Davey, he couldn't keep the wistfulness out of his voice when he'd wished for a collie like Romy.

Some day, if the Fates smiled on us, we'd all get our heart's desire.

I still had to make those essential purchases that had brought me to the Apple Fair, and the smell of hot dogs grew more enticing by the minute. I was hungry, and, if a snoopy do-gooder was watching from behind some tree, I didn't want him to report me for starving my collie.

But that wouldn't happen. Only three people knew where I lived. Two of them weren't here, as far as I could tell, and Captain Slater would never remember my ad

In the late afternoon, the sky darkened, and the winds picked up. Flags flapped more energetically and the balloons resembled red apples making their break for freedom. Vendors scanned the clouds anxiously.

I'd bought everything on my list except for the fudge. Stopping at a small booth set up near the fountain, I decided on large squares of maple walnut and vanilla fudge for myself and chocolate gourds for the vestibule table, a nice touch to go along with the potpourri I planned to simmer.

I turned around, candy in one hand, leash in the other, and froze.

Preston Anderson stood in line at the hot dog stand, not three yards away from me, a glittering golden man in a cowboy hat. A single glimpse was enough to make me remember how much I'd once cared for him.

I clutched the candy bag tightly. In seconds, we'd be facing each other. He couldn't fail to see me. So—should I go over and say hello to him or walk in the opposite direction?

He must have heard Amy's lies.

But he knows me, or should know me. Say something. Give it a casual spin. *Talk about a small world! What have you been doing?*

Preston didn't have my current address. He might have been too busy to call. From his perspective, I'd disappeared without a trace. Didn't Preston deserve the benefit of a doubt? Didn't I?

He turned. I took a few steps forward, tugging gently on Romy's leash. The sun broke through the cloud cover, casting him in a spotlight. Surely that was a favorable omen.

Then I saw Amy, small, slender, and fair with that delicate air she assumed by using only the most natural makeup. She strolled up to meet him, smiling and taking one of the hot dogs out of his hand. With a closeness that told of a long and intimate association, they walked out of the park.

Disjointed thoughts ran through my mind. *I should have suspected. I wished I hadn't seen them. Thank heavens he didn't notice me. And Amy...I never want to see that lying, thieving tramp again, not even in her coffin.*

How had they found their way to my new town? Was this a weird coincidence, or were they about to initiate Phase Two of their plan to destroy my life? And why did I still care about Preston?

I gave them a reasonable head start, then walked slowly down Main Street, to Walnut. The wind blew harder now, sending candy wrappers and paper napkins scurrying down the street, along with the leaves. An apple colored balloon had flown into a tree and gotten caught on a high branch, too far up to reach.

As I neared the car, warm raindrops splattered down on my face and fell like tears.

"We stayed too long at the fair, Romy," I said

Chapter 6

The newsprint screamed at me. Dogs Die in Kennel Fire. Susanna Kentwood burned to death at Greengrove Farm last night in a failed attempt to rescue three young collies.

No! That didn't happen.

I turned on the bed and faced the dream flames. They leaped skyward, greedily devouring fresh wood. Their long red tongues licked at my nightgown.

Dear God. My puppies were trapped in that inferno. Their screams filled the smoke-thickened air, drowning out the deadly crackling.

Somewhere behind me I heard Romy's frenzied barking. Farther still, a siren wailed.

Taking deep gulps of air, I cried, "I'm coming!"

A post toppled forward and sizzled on the ground. I spied a narrow passageway not yet touched by the fire. I could go that way. The pups should be on the southern side of the kennel, about a yard from the door. Only three feet away. With luck I could reach them in time.

I forced myself to walk into hell. Impressions flashed on and off in my mind. Canine screams on the right. Heat. A crash. The siren. Shouting.

Another post fell. The fire spread its hideous wings, igniting the roof. I tread on red-hot ground, trying desperately to evade the flames' grasp.

There they were!

Frosty and Cherie huddled together against a fallen wall. I grabbed them by the scruff of the neck and called Cindy's name.

With a terrified yelp, she dashed out of the smoke and raked desperately at my leg. I flung Cherie and Frosty out into the night, picked up my little tri, and ran.

Sheets of flame followed us. Tears blinded me as I stumbled out of the burning kennel into the blessed, cool air. The vile smells of singed fur and burnt flesh came with us.

I wasn't alone. People stood by like grim motionless death figures, their shadowy faces illuminated by firelight. I didn't know them. Voices reached me from a great distance.

Susanna! Thank God! I thought you were a goner.

Look at your hand!

Here, let me have her.

35

A woman standing close to me took Cindy from my arms and whispered soft words of comfort to her. Panicked screams subsided to whimpering as Romy danced around the two pups, licking them. A massive fire engine braked in the yard, and men jumped to the ground.

Two pups?

"Where's Cindy?" My voice was a broken croak. I began to cough; I couldn't stop.

"Yeah, nothing but cinders left," a male voice shouted.

Where was the woman who had just taken Cindy? Valerie? No. I didn't know Valerie then. Marsha?

"You saved those two little dogs," the man said. "That was a damn fool risk you took. Let me look at that hand."

He was wrong. I'd saved three.

Or did I?

Cindy was still in the burning kennel!

Flames swept down the passageway and swallowed the door. I felt a strong hand on my shoulder.

"You can't go back in there. Everybody—move! Now!" That was a fireman, taking charge of my situation. "Get her out of here. Keep those dogs back."

A faraway voice said, "Nothing could live in that."

"No!" I wiped the tears out of my eyes, newly aware of a burning on my arm and a sharp pain in my hand. I'd held Cindy too tightly.

But not close enough. Somehow, between the kennel and the vast grassy area that bordered it, I'd lost her. An unknown man held me back, but restraint wasn't necessary. I couldn't get through the passage again.

I awoke, shaking under the comforter, as cold as death, even with the electric fireplace throwing its heat across the room. My right hand throbbed.

I lay in bed, rubbing the pain away and sorting the distorted dream version of the rescue from reality. I'd tossed two pups over the flames to safety and carried the third out, and I didn't die.

But to save Cindy, only to lose her in some inexplicable way? How had my sleeping mind created that unthinkable scenario?

I didn't know, but it was irrelevant. All three of the puppies were safe in their temporary new home, only a fifteen minute drive away. I could visit them any time I liked. A dream had no power over me. The next time I woke, it would be a tangle of slowly dissipating memories. Like all the others.

Amy and Preston together was the real nightmare, and it wouldn't dissolve with the morning light.

Something was different about the view from the porch this morning.

I paused in the doorway, wreath in hand, studying the grounds through a rain of falling leaves. The wild hedge seemed to grow higher every day, but that wasn't it. I looked again, noting every section of the landscape separately.

Woods cast long skinny shadows on the lane, the pond shimmered in the sunlight, and balsams marched up the hill to the low-lying clouds. Everything was in its place and familiar. Then I realized what bothered me. The 'For Sale' sign had disappeared again.

If Karenell Miller was serious about marketing the blue Victorian, she should take care of these details or at least return her calls.

Maybe the house doesn't want to be sold. It's happy with the status quo. You're bringing it back to life.

I smiled at the odd fancy as I hung the circlet of winterberries and willow stems. I'd made the blue Victorian sparkle with a few seasonal decorations, but from the beginning, this whole affair had been cloaked in strangeness. An out-of-nowhere offer, an absent Realtor, and a vanishing sign, combined with a scent of balsam and mysterious candle wax.

I looked longingly at the lane. How easy it would be to load the car and drive away, to find a new town and a different position.

Run away again? No. Snowhedge wouldn't like it.

The next time I went into Maple Creek, I intended to tape a note to Karenell Miller's door. If she still didn't respond, my only recourse was to tell Valerie that the Realtor wasn't giving her full attention to the property and ask for further directions.

I'd assumed that the house sitting job would be temporary, but if the blue Victorian languished on the market indefinitely, I'd be trapped here for months, dusting, mopping, arranging bouquets and simmering potpourri for buyers who never materialized.

Or I could leave.

After seeing Amy and Preston together yesterday I felt like starting over again in another place, even though they couldn't possibly find me at 7 Balsam Lane. Only Valerie and the elusive Karenell Miller knew where I was living. Oh, and Captain Slater.

Preston hadn't seen me at the fair. Had he?

I didn't think so, and in a way it was fortunate that I'd learned about his new alliance. When I encountered Amy and Preston at the next dog show, I wouldn't be surprised. I'd have had time to get used to the idea of them as a couple.

So all was well. But when I searched the area where the 'For Sale' sign had been, I couldn't find it. Exasperated, I swept the leaves aside with a large branch. I couldn't even detect an impression in the ground where the stake had been.

It's official, Susanna, I thought. *The house wants to keep you here.*

Once the thought of finding a job in a new town entered my mind, it refused to leave. Long hours dragged their way toward another Saturday. Every morning, I wandered through the house with a feather duster and mop. Wearing a heavy cardigan to ward off the parlor's cold air, I tried to remove the stain on the floor, sanding, polishing, and sanding it again. No matter what I did, a faint impression of the red mark remained, taunting me whenever I stepped into the room.

The window panes kept frosting over, and the spicy balsam scent seemed to grow stronger every day. Or perhaps, trapped by the walls of Snowhedge, my imagination was running amok.

To break the monotony, I shopped for groceries and fresh flowers and took Romy for long walks up and down the lane. Karenell didn't respond to the note I'd left on the Realtor cottage's door, and my calls to Valerie took me to her voicemail.

"It's a conspiracy, Romy," I said. "What do you think? Should we pick up the puppies and move on?"

She pushed my hand up with her nose as if to say 'Whatever you decide. You're the leader of the pack.'

In spite of my frustration and unrelenting boredom, I wasn't ready to do that. Not yet. When a generous check arrived in the post office box Valerie had set up for me in Maple Creek, I decided to treat myself to a Saturday night dinner at a restaurant in the hope that an hour or two of diversion would help me endure one more week.

And if you run into Preston and Amy having a romantic dinner there?

I wouldn't. The location was too remote.

But if you do?

Then I'd know that their appearance at the Apple Fair wasn't a coincidence.

Captain Mike Slater lounged in the doorway of Hunters Roadhouse, scanning the room with a cool, appraising look that landed on me. He walked slowly toward the table where I sat alone, sipping a club soda.

Why did that man turn up everywhere I went?

Because you're lucky, Susanna. Because Maple Creek is a one-horse town with zero nightlife. There are only a half dozen places people can visit after dark.

He wasn't in uniform this evening. I wasn't speeding down a country road, and my collie lay snoozing by the electric fireplace in the blue Victorian. The Captain and I should be able to exchange a few bland pleasantries. Besides, having someone in Maple Creek recognize me was a pleasure, even if he was a law enforcer who had snatched a hefty sum out of my savings.

"Susanna—mind if I join you?" he asked with a hint of a smile that softened his austere expression just a bit.

It sounded more like a statement than a question. As I said, "Not at all, Captain Slater," he pulled out a chair and sat down.

Tall, fair, handsome in a roughhewn, high-cheekboned way. Why would I object? Now if he would make that ticket disappear, this would be a fortuitous encounter.

"Remember, it's Mike," he said. "Did you have fun at the Apple Fair?"

"Pretty much. And you?"

"The same. The boys enjoyed themselves. Davey hasn't stopped talking about your black collie."

"Romy attracts attention wherever we go. I call her my show stopper."

He laughed and reached across the table for the dessert menu. His hand was rough and weathered with long, sturdy fingers and neatly clipped nails. He wasn't wearing a wedding ring.

So he was a single dad, divorced or widowed. Or a man who simply didn't care for jewelry? He could have a wife at home as blonde and attractive as he was. He probably did, but could that be a faint spark of interest in his eyes? I hoped not—unless he was free.

Even then, I didn't need another complication in my life. Men and trouble were synonymous.

Suddenly ill at ease, I looked around—at the bar with its rows of shining bottles and glassware, at the deserted pool table, at an old-fashioned juke box that probably played yesteryear's music. These plain uninspiring surroundings held more appeal than a lonely old house with a spooky parlor, but if Captain Slater was a married man, if he was hoping to get to know me better... *Be warned.*

A state trooper has a lady in every northern hamlet from Maple Creek to Harrisville. Someone had made that cynical observation once, probably a trooper's girlfriend.

I searched his face, looking for clues. There were none. Only a sparkle that lurked in his eyes; only that inscrutable not-quite-finished smile. He *was* a handsome devil, and his hair and eyes seemed darker in the dim lighting.

Don't anticipate trouble, I told myself.

Captain Slater showed no sign of leaving soon, and I couldn't make a quick but graceful exit when I'd ordered a burger and fries. I didn't want to do that anyway.

Keep talking about dogs.

I said, "Romy is three points away from wining her championship. I expect to finish her by next spring."

"Anyone can tell she's a superior specimen."

The awkwardly worded praise went straight to my heart. "She is a beauty. She's also my best friend."

"Do you know where I can buy a puppy like her?" he asked. "Black, with the same markings, but a male?"

Ah. Here was the reason for his friendly overtures.

Silly Susanna. Not every tall, blond, handsome man is trying to hit on you.

"Davey has a birthday coming up," he added. "I'd like to surprise him with one."

"I had the impression you didn't like dogs," I said.

"You're wrong. We all like them, but Danny got bitten last week. I'm trying to teach him how to act around strange dogs."

I was on familiar ground now. "Michigan has some top rated collie kennels. Depending on whether you want a pet or a show quality pup, you'll pay from about $200 all the way up to $2000 or more."

"You seem to know a lot about collies," he said.

"I do."

It was true. With my store of textbook lore and hands-on experience, I could tell him anything he might want to know, from the history of the breed to the qualities to look for when choosing a show pup.

But in spite of my background, I hadn't been able to hold on to my prize champion or keep my kennel safe from fire; and I couldn't call myself a breeder any more. I was a woman who owned one exceptional collie, three promising puppies, and a dream that wouldn't die.

"You might try contacting Georgia Leigh at Silverleigh Kennels," I said. "They're not too far from here. Georgia guarantees her puppies' health, and she breeds for quality. That's important."

A petite red-haired waitress in a trim white apron came up to the table. She had a flirtatious smile for Captain Slater and a neutral one for me. "Beer tonight, Captain?" she asked.

"Pabst, please." He glanced at my almost empty glass. "Can I buy you a drink, Susanna?"

"I'm waiting for dinner. Maybe later."

"That reminds me. Would you mind unpacking my take-out order, Lin? I'll eat here with Ms. Kentwood." He turned to me. "If that's all right with you?"

"It's fine."

He leaned back in the chair, appearing more at ease, almost in date mode. "I'll give this kennel a call," he said. "Tell me, did you move out to the country to have more room for your dog?"

"Not exactly. I'm watching over a relative's place while she spends the winter in Florida."

"Then you're not staying in the area permanently?"

"I'll be here until the house sells. After that, I don't know."

He gave me a full smile this time. "There's always something going on in Maple Creek. We have a haunted house tour on Halloween and the Snow Blast at Christmas. You'll be happy, if you like the quiet rural life."

"I thought I did."

"Now you're not sure?"

How much could I say? Certainly not the cause of my growing disillusionment. Perhaps a tiny slice of the truth?

"I feel like I'm in the middle of the woods," I said. "The house has three stories. It's a little overwhelming, not what I'm used to."

"You're not living there alone, are you?"

"Yes, with Romy. Why?"

Instead of answering, he said, "Where is this place located?"

"At 7 Balsam Lane. It's a fancy blue Victorian with tons of atmosphere."

"With a hedge in front and a pond. I know it," he said slowly. "I'd be surprised if anyone bought that place."

"Why do you say that?"

The waitress set his beer on the table. He took a long swig and set the bottle down with an emphatic bang.

"The real estate market is bad these days, and the economy is worse. Unloading a house is an uphill battle, especially one with three stories to heat and a hefty asking price, probably in the high three hundreds. "

Everything he said was true, but I had a disturbing feeling, based on nothing tangible, that he knew more about the blue Victorian than he'd revealed, something beyond plummeting housing sales.

But when was reading people my forte?

"It's over a century old," I said, remembering the ad in Valerie's folder. "That makes it an historic house, and the view is spectacular. It would make a charming bed and breakfast."

"That it would. Your buyer will have to be rich to renovate it."

"It doesn't need much fixing up. A new heating system. Maybe replacement windows and updated landscaping."

"You're still talking about major money and work."

"You're right, but I hope the buyers will come along. Soon."

"They will, eventually," he said with a sly smile. "Then you may decide to stay on in our town."

"I *will* need a place to live."

His eyes met mine. The spark had vanished. He seemed to be looking at something beyond me, and his gaze was wary. "In the meantime, I hope you'll be careful."

I'd given myself variations of the same order, but coming from an outside observer, this one had sharper edges. Again, I sensed an undercurrent in his words, along with a subtle contradiction. He would be surprised if the house sold. He thought it would. Or was he simply making casual conversation?

"Why?" I asked.

"Like you say, you're living in a forest. Most girls like lights and people around."

"Romy is a good watchdog, and this girl likes variety. For a while anyway. I might want something different than the deep woods in the future."

We fell silent as the waitress delivered our orders. They were identical. Thick cheeseburgers with steaming golden French fries and sides of slaw. She took my empty glass away and set a fresh drink in its place.

As she left, Mike handed me the bottle of ketchup. It made a dark red glob on my plate. Like something unpleasant, but my mind didn't catch it.

"What exactly are you warning me about, Captain Slater?" I asked.

"Vandalism, break-in's, arsonists, escaped prisoners, serial killers—you name it. We're not immune from big city problems up north."

Arsonists, I thought. *Not here, not again.*

"Are all the police alarmists?" I asked.

"It's part of the job," he said. "We like to keep people safe. On the lighter side, Halloween is just around the corner. Our local devils can get pretty feisty."

"Well," I said, "so can I," and took my first bite of cheeseburger.

Chapter 7

An icy draft seeped out from under the closed parlor door. Shivering in the arctic air of the hallway, I dropped my handbag and keys on the vestibule table. If I didn't insist on keeping that troublesome room closed up, warmth from the furnace could reach it.

Or its frigid temperature would freeze the rest of the house.

What a strange thought. The cold in the parlor couldn't travel down the hall and up the stairs.

No, but the atmosphere could.

I turned the knob and opened the door to a dazzle of color and light. Frozen in place, I stared at a startling transformation. The room was filled with furniture: A sofa and chairs arranged to create a cozy seating area around the fireplace; an octagonal coffee table holding a basket of pine cones; and close to the entrance, a round table covered with a bright red cloth and crowded with picture frames.

A painting hung over the mantel, shadowing a row of fancy plates; and in the bay windows, a balsam fir stood firmly in an iron stand, its top grazing the ceiling. Spicy fragrance scented the air.

Impossible. But impossible to deny. How could this have happened? By what strange alchemy does a bland empty space change into an elegant, furnished parlor?

I had to be dreaming again or hallucinating. That was it. The handsome captain had drugged my drink.

For what purpose?

The oldest one in the world. Seduction. He'd dropped a date rape pill into my club soda. Possibly he'd followed me home. He could be outside right now, waiting outside the window.

To have his way with me? Don't be foolish. I'm alone. This is real. Even though it can't be.

All I had to do was take three steps forward and I'd enter somebody else's world.

Everything is ready. The room is waiting.

With a tremendous effort, I wrenched myself away from these ghostly thoughts. The Oriental carpet had a design of pink cabbage roses and green vines on a rich black background. The chairs were plush gold, the sofa a muted shade that my grandmother had called old rose. A package wrapped in shiny green paper lay on the coffee table.

I might have stumbled into a parlor in a giant's dollhouse, assembled in a heartbeat, looking as if every item had been in place for years. I moved nearer to the round table, absorbing every minute detail.

The painting depicted a winter garden scene with snow drifted high on a bird bath and icicles dripping from a trellis. On the round table, light from a ruby shaded lamp shone on small ornate picture frames set amidst red candles, all of which appeared to be new. The fireplace was alive with flames that burned soundlessly, casting an eerie glow on the seating group but not an iota of heat.

That was the strangest and most frightening aspect of the phenomenon. And it was cold. So cold.

Clutching the sides of my suede jacket closer together, I touched the tablecloth. The material was satin-soft and cool, and the metal frames were as cold as popsicles just taken from the freezer. Hastily I withdrew my hand.

Oh, this was real. Solid. Tangible. I was awake and couldn't have been drugged because I felt fine. My vision was clear, my thoughts sharp and focused. But how could I explain this unholy transmutation? This terrifying piece of devil's work?

Let's see...maybe the answer was simple. This might be part of the house's staging, quietly engineered by the unknown Karenell Miller. Tonight, while I had shared a roadhouse dinner with Captain Slater, she'd had furniture moved into the parlor, choosing each piece to evoke Christmas nostalgia in a prospective buyer. She had gone so far as to set up a tree and place a present on the coffee table.

Who wouldn't be inspired to buy an old country house after viewing the Christmas room? Of course. Yes.

Christmas is coming. The goose is getting fat.

With its festive red hues, the parlor exuded a certain magical pull, issuing a silent invitation to sit in front of the fireplace and entertain a visitor.

Everything is ready. The room is waiting.

I noticed a silver tea service on the coffee table.

Just lift the lid and see if there's anything inside.

I didn't move any farther. Staging couldn't explain the great cold and the unnatural fire. Besides, what Realtor works in the dark of night without the house sitter's knowledge?

What was going on at Snowhedge then? Or, more accurately, with me?

A thought yanked me back to my senses. *Where's Romy?*

I slammed the parlor door shut and called her name. The house flung my voice back at me, a higher, desperate version of it that I hardly recognized.

Snowhedge

You forgot her again. Your best friend. Your loved one.

"Romy?" I cried. "Where are you?"

The bedroom? The kitchen? I began walking, calling her name, hearing my panic mirrored in every echo.

With a jingle of tag on chain, she padded out of the kitchen and stretched lazily. Wagging her tail, she lifted her head to my hand for a reunion pat. My beautiful, sweet, good dog. This, at least, was the way it should be.

I buried my hand in her fur, trying to coax warmth and feeling back into my fingers, attempting to ignore the familiar stabs of pain.

Dear God, what was happening to me? Had the trauma of the fire burned away my grasp on reality?

I longed to run into the bedroom, to lock the door and climb into bed. To sleep and wake to another day. But first...

"Come with me, Romy-girl," I said and went back through the hall toward the parlor, walking again into a rush of ice-air.

Nothing had changed. Only now the objects were more clearly defined, their colors more vivid. The vintage frames held photographs of men and women, some sepia toned, others tinted in pastel shades. The candle holders were a mixture of brass, silver, and crystal; and the tree was as fresh and green as if it had just been chopped down. Tiny particles of snow and ice balls glistened on its branches.

The thick scent of balsam surrounded me. I felt as if I were going to be ill.

I was. The entire cheeseburger seemed to be lodged high in my throat. No matter how many times I swallowed, I couldn't get past it.

"Oh, Romy," I whispered. "This can't be happening."

'Get out of bed. Go back to the parlor.'

It wasn't a voice but a command from my mind, a faint hope that a new day would restore the normalcy I'd previously known at Snowhedge.

Normalcy? You can't be serious. When was this mysterious blue house ever normal?

Last night before drifting off to sleep, I'd thought of another explanation for the eerie phenomenon. It was out in left field, but I grasped at anything that left my sanity intact.

Suppose the house had twin parlors, side by side, one empty, the other furnished? Last night I'd gone through the wrong door.

Into a hidden room I hadn't discovered on my previous wanderings?

I had lain in bed, recreating the floor plan in my mind. In the end, my theory fell apart. Beyond the fireplace wall, trees grew close to the house. There was no place for a secret space to exist. However impossible the idea, it still comforted me. I didn't let it go.

This morning, after breakfast, I intended to make another extensive search of the first floor, looking for the phantom room. Then I'd try again to contact Karenell and Valerie. In the meantime, maybe I could come up with another explanation.

Stop thinking. Get up and check the parlor! It may be too late.

I swung out of bed and stepped over Romy who lay stretched out in the doorway in a deep slumber. Down the hall, past the kitchen where the first daylight poured through the windows, past the vestibule table with its spent country bouquet I hurried, not fully comprehending the need for haste.

The closer I came to the room, the more keenly I sensed a subtle shift in the house's temperature and a barely discernible alteration in the atmosphere. A deadly chill enveloped me. My heart pounded. Still I moved forward.

As soon as I verified what I'd seen last night, I...would do what?

Never stop until I understood it.

In order to stay at Snowhedge, I needed answers from someone. Living in a house with a room that transformed itself was too stressful.

I opened the door but kept my hand firmly on the knob, ready for anything.

The parlor was empty. There was no furniture, no rose-patterned carpet, no painting on the wall, not even a hole where a nail would have been. No balsam fir in the bay window dripping snow melt on the floor. Nothing on the mantel but the flame-colored carnations that I'd placed there myself. The white brick fireplace, swept clean and cold, couldn't have seen a fire in decades.

Everything was as it had been ever since I'd first come to the blue Victorian except for that ten or fifteen minutes of time-out-of-time when the parlor had changed into an actual, usable room. The faint impression of a red stain seemed to glare at me from the middle of the hardwood floor.

I crossed to the bay windows and looked out over swirls of frosty condensation to the balsams on the hill. At least the view was familiar.

Yesterday I'd been sure of what I was seeing. This morning, doubts assailed me. Karenell Miller couldn't possibly have returned with her shadowy band of movers to clear out the parlor while I slept, and there was no hidden room, no unaccounted for space.

Back in the kitchen I found Romy wagging her tail, eager to begin a new day with her morning Milk-bone biscuit breakfast. Transmuting parlors didn't faze her. Nor, it seemed, did the anxiety I couldn't control.

I poured water in the teakettle and opened the bakery box. A lone maple-iced doughnut remained. Combined with a cup of steaming tea, it would give me needed energy to face the task ahead, which was to explore the blue Victorian yet once again.

I felt as if I were going through the same motions over and over, walking on an endless treadmill, heading nowhere.

That was a fairly accurate description of my life these days.

After searching the first floor thoroughly, I climbed the stairs to the second story. It occurred to me that perhaps the parlor wasn't the only room in the house capable of changing itself into a model for a *House Beautiful* spread. What a terrifying prospect! But I had to know what—or who—I was dealing with.

As I paused on the landing, I reviewed my choices. Track down Karenell Miller and see if she could shed any light on the mystery room. Call Valerie with the same request. Follow my instincts and leave Maple Creek, which was what I really wanted to do.

And take the problem with you?

If I had created a parlor filled with furniture out of my wounded mind, how could I know what I'd imagine next? Besides, I didn't want to run away again. If I could only muster the courage and tenacity to unravel the house's eccentricities, I'd emerge a stronger person.

If not, the next unexpected blow could destroy me.

So, what's going on in this house? What can I do to find out?

Flora Brine! She had known the previous owner, Lila Rose. Maybe the strangeness didn't originate with me. Could Flora tell me anything relevant about the blue Victorian's history? Would she? Perhaps, if I framed my questions diplomatically.

I added her to my list: Karenell Miller, Valerie, Flora.

The answers I sought might be within my reach. Meanwhile, a morning sun was shining on what appeared to be a perfect autumn day. Reeling from an unfamiliar burst of optimism, I ascended the last flight of stairs to the third floor.

Here the air was thin and cool. Light streamed through the windows at the hall's end, setting dust motes into mad motion. The off-white walls and light-stained hardwood flooring made me feel as if I were walking through clouds—or in some otherworldly place.

I stopped first at the large room at the front of the house where I'd considered placing a plant strung with lights, something to draw the observer's attention upward. The Gable Room, I thought now, although its gable was only one of many.

The blue Victorian had been built for a large family. I could almost see a gaggle of children dressed in vintage clothing. They would love playing and sleeping away from the rest of the family and close to the sky. The oldest child would have this room with the view of the woods across the lane.

She would feel like a princess in her royal chamber. When she grew older, she'd set up an easel in the window where the light was strong and paint scenes inspired by the countryside, twisting them with a touch of fantasy—a centaur trotting out of the woods, a fairy girl skating across the pond, a tree with reaching arms and a seductive smile.

If she was adventurous, she could climb through the window and step carefully on the slanted shingles. Down, up, and down again, crossing the gables, she'd made her way to a thick and sturdy branch and climb down to the ground below.

I could do it too! But taking the stairs was less risky.

Amused at the mock history I'd created, I walked across the room to a door, recalling that I never opened all the closets on this floor. I turned the knob and pulled it forward. It didn't open.

Impatiently I tried again, then noticed the dull brass lock. This wasn't an ordinary bedroom door like others in the house. It could lead someplace. Where?

I imagined a flight of steps descending in cold darkness to the first floor and the outside. A secret exit!

Didn't many old houses have hidden features known only to their owners? Fireplaces that swung forward at the touch of a brick? A tunnel to another location? A panic room?

Maybe this door led to something wonderful—or dangerous. Maybe to something deadly. No matter. This was the most exciting discovery I'd made at Snowhedge. It might even be my clue. If only it weren't locked.

Eager to prove my theory, I rushed down the stairs and flung open the front door. Romy, waiting in the vestibule for her morning outing, dashed out, running ahead of me.

Outside I stood under the Gable Room, looking for another entrance. It didn't exist. All I saw was the smooth exterior of the house, an unbroken expanse of blue-sided wood.

Where my hypothetical door should be, a pair of windows offered a desolate view of a living room with a lone chair taken from the dining room set and a wrought iron floor lamp. Any secret entrance would have been boarded over with the coal and milk chutes when the siding was installed. I couldn't take the house apart looking for it.

Reining in my disappointment, I returned to the Gable Room and tried the door again—and again. Three times is a charm, but it wouldn't budge. Aside from hacking it down with an ax, which was unthinkable, I wouldn't be able to access the area beyond unless I found the key.

I now had two more questions for Karenell Miller. Did she have a key and why lock a door in a house that you hope to sell? Certainly any savvy buyer would want to see every square inch of his prospective home—from basement to attic.

Attic! Ah, that was it. The stairs behind the door must lead to the attic rather than down to the ground floor. To test my theory, I covered the rest of the floor, opening doors, searching for steps or a primitive board opening in the ceiling. I didn't find it. The closets were simply closets, small, empty, smelling faintly of lavender.

Everything is ready for the new owner's wardrobe. Bring your own hangers.

The attic entrance could only be in the Gable Room. Unfortunately, Susanna Kentwood, girl detective, had run out of ideas and now had another puzzle to solve. What secret lay hidden behind the locked door?

Chapter 8

Could there possibly be anything of interest in the attic? Most people take all their possessions with them when they leave a house. But not always. My mind fastened on the exceptions. What if I could unravel the secret of the parlor simply by opening a door?

You might find a cardboard box, a fragment of wrapping paper, or string. Or a clue.

Although I had no idea what I hoped to discover, the idea of stumbling over some forgotten item took root and grew. After searching for a key without success, I drove past Karenell Miller's cottage and discovered that the note I'd taped to her door had disappeared. That was progress. Still, she didn't return my call. As for Valerie, she might have vanished into thin air; and Flora Brine was never home during the day.

Find out how to pick a lock, I thought. *Buy an ax and break down the door. You can always have it replaced. Just end this incessant speculation.*

I did neither. Reminding myself that I was the house sitter, I swept leaves off the porch, watered the chrysanthemums, and bought fresh bouquets every fourth day. I kept the furniture relatively dust free but stopped simmering potpourri on the stove. A neighbor's child selling chocolate bars for her school's band was my only visitor.

Several times a day I checked the parlor. I couldn't seem to stay away. Always I found it cold and empty with the sinister stain on the floor and white condensation on the windows. If I lingered in the doorway, I thought I could see a definite pattern on the glass. Giant, silvery flowers that appeared to sway in a non-existent wind. And if I didn't move on to another part of the house quickly, the red mark began to look like blood.

Romy avoided the room, although she often stood on the threshold, tail still and ears in alert mode as she sniffed the air. The fir tree might be gone, but its scent remained.

And that should tell you something.

Yes, but I wasn't ready to hear it.

One morning the 'For Sale' sign reappeared, standing slightly askew on a mound of leaves. Karenell Miller must be back at work, although I couldn't understand why she hadn't knocked on the door and introduced herself. I placed another call to her and again found myself listening to a recorded message.

Nothing about this affair made sense; and suddenly the week ended. How easy it is to lose track of time when your only contact with humanity is a grocery store clerk.

In the afternoon I took Romy for a run up Balsam Lane, then changed into a black dress and silver hoop earrings that could take me from the post office and assorted errands to an early dinner at a proper restaurant, my one night out on the town. Such as it was.

Before leaving, I walked across the porch to the bay windows and peered inside. The parlor was a plain, empty room with a white brick fireplace, its only decorative touch a vase of bright Gerber daisies.

Stay that way, I thought.

I took the new issue of *Collie Vistas* from my post office box and stared at the classic winsome face of Champion Larkspur Blue Frost. It filled the cover. His colors were exquisite: Misty gray mottled with ink black, snow white, dashes of golden sable. A black diamond mark under his left ear. Dark, grave eyes that could look straight into my soul.

My stolen collie.

I turned to the Index, then to page three where color pictures alternated with graceful Gothic script. *Frost welcomes his first litter. Out of Brookspring Blue Sprite.* A row of fluffy collie infants gathered in front of a picket fence. *Four tris, five blues. Show homes only.* A side view of Frost running into the wind, his fur blown back. One of Amy holding a blue merle puppy. Another of co-owners Preston Anderson and Amy Brackett standing together, beaming their pride in their acquisition.

Co-owners?

This was the July issue, as usual three months late to arrive. Amy and Preston had been together for a long time. Since last summer. Since the month of the fire. I'd never guessed.

What had Amy desired more—my boyfriend or my share of our champion? And how had Preston become co-owner of Frost?

I want him back.

The dog or the man?

Fighting tears, I left the post office, reminding myself that I still had Romy and my three pups. Almost as important, I was officially free of Amy and Preston. Now and forever.

Still the old anger surfaced, mixed with a familiar hunger to compete. I hadn't looked at my collie calendar in days, not since moving to Snowhedge. There was the show in Lakeville the week after Thanksgiving and another smaller one in Spearmint Lake in December. The best way to prove that Amy's treachery couldn't hurt me was to enter Romy and beat whatever dog Amy was showing.

It never occurred to me that Romy wouldn't at least win a ribbon, and the puppies would shine even though I'd neglected their conformation training in recent weeks. They were little hams, demanding more than their fair share of attention, and no matter the competition, Larkspur Romany Revel, my Romy, had no equal.

Let the games begin! Susanna Kentwood and her collies needed to make a comeback in the Fancy.

For the first time all week I was thinking of something besides the old blue house on Balsam Lane and its devil's parlor. That was another kind of progress.

If three times is a charm, then what is a fourth encounter? The Fates conspiring to make a match? Hastily I withdrew the thought. Captain Mike Slater was an unknown entity. Last week, for one frantic moment, I'd suspected him of dropping a date rape drug into my drink. I still wasn't sure if he was free of romantic entanglements or marital bonds.

But he looked so bright and handsome walking up the path to the roadhouse that I couldn't help being a little enthusiastic over another meeting, mainly because I hadn't talked to a single person all week except for the clerk at the Flower Nook. Or so I told myself.

Seeing me, he paused on the walkway and smiled. His hair caught the last of the day's light, and fine lines crinkled around his eyes and mouth. He was wearing a dark brown jacket and a blue shirt open at the neck. Translation. He was off duty.

"Good evening, Captain," I said. "Are you back for another burger?"

"Or something. It's Mike. How about you, Susanna?"

"Something." I had a brief, unpleasant memory of a cheeseburger lodged in my throat as I stood in the doorway of the parlor. "Something lighter, like a sandwich," I added.

"That makes two of us."

He held the door open and followed me inside, into dim lighting, past pockets of activity. The song on the jukebox had a quaint folksy melody. I didn't know the selection and didn't recognize any of the people in my view, but I felt at home, or at least not like an outsider. I was, after all, entering the establishment with a native of Maple Creek who happened to be one of its law enforcement officers.

"Did you buy your puppy yet?" I asked as I scanned the room looking for a place to sit.

"On my first shopping trip. I found a pint-sized version of Romy at Silverleigh Kennels. His name is Jack. That's short for Blackjack. He's a real live wire."

I was pleased that he remembered Romy's name and happy that he'd taken my advice. "Was Davey surprised?" I asked.

"He will be. His birthday is next Wednesday. Till then, the pup is staying with me."

Mike didn't live with Danny and Davey then. That suggested that he was a single dad and quite possibly unattached. Breathing more easily, I said, "I'll bet he's chewing your house to pieces."

Mike laughed. "He'd like to. I bought him a supply of rawhide toys. Tonight, he's confined to his crate."

"That can be a life saver," I said. "Let me know how the first meeting between boy and dog goes."

I took a step away from him toward a vacant booth near the pool table.

"If you're not meeting anyone, would you like some company?" he asked.

"I'm not, and I would. Yes."

"How about that table by the window?" He laid his hand on my shoulder. "What do you think?"

"Let's take it."

I settled myself on the hard chair and slipped out of my jacket. This casual meeting felt comfortable and right, and an hour of good company in a lively place would make up for a string of solitary days.

The roadhouse had a certain roughhewn charm. It seemed like a holdover from another century with a personality as quirky as the life-sized papier-maché witch sitting on a barstool. Someone's macabre idea of a seasonal decoration, she cast a dark shadow on the floor. A dessert menu written in black Magic Marker rested against a chunky orange candle in a hurricane jar. I shivered, noticing a slight draft.

The candle isn't lit. It can't harm me.

But every table had a similar centerpiece, and many of the candles were burning. If somebody got careless or a little tipsy...if he knocked a jar over...how far was it to the exit? Glancing at the door, I estimated the distance to be thirty footsteps.

"Is something the matter, Susanna?" Mike asked.

He was watching me, frowning, concern in his eyes.

"No—nothing. It's a little chilly." To cover my confusion, I arranged my jacket over my shoulders.

"Hunters is famous for their soup," he said. "On Saturday it's chicken noodle."

"I'm still thinking of a sandwich."

"They have apple pie tonight." Mike flipped the menu over. "I enrolled Davey and Jack in obedience training. It's part of his present."

"That should be fun for both Davey and the puppy. Your son is a lucky boy."

"He's expecting a video game." Mike's blue-gray eyes twinkled. "Davey is my nephew, but the boys are like sons to me."

"Oh..."

"My brother was killed last year in the line of duty. I give my sister-in-law a helping hand with them whenever I can."

"I'm sorry," I said.

He nodded. "Dan was a good man. I can see a lot of him in his children."

I remembered the boys at the Apple Fair and Mike striving to give them a normal day, complete with hot dogs and canine safety lectures. I suspected that he was a good man too.

"I drove by your house yesterday," he said. "That fancy porch display should attract buyers. Have you had any prospects?"

"Unfortunately, none at all," I said. "The 'For Sale' sign disappeared, but it came back."

"Some enterprising kids might have moved it to their school yard as a Halloween prank."

"I never thought of that."

"What did you think?"

I couldn't tell him that I considered the vanishing sign a part of the general strangeness that plagued the house on Balsam Lane. It would be better to stay with seasonal trickery. "I assumed there was some kind of mischief afoot."

"Aside from stolen signs, how are you managing?" he asked.

"Fairly well. I don't have much to do. After a week of country solitude, I'm more than ready for a little noise and life."

"You came to the right place."

"Would you like to see the take-out menu tonight, Captain?" The waitress, Lin, stopped by the table, order pad in hand, avid curiosity in her eyes.

"Thanks, but we're eating here. I'll have a Pabst. Susanna?"

"Ginger ale, please."

"Back in a few," she said, dropping our menus on the table

"Has anything unusual happened lately?" Mike asked. "Besides your missing sign?"

"Like a visit from an escaped convict or murderer?"

"Nothing so drastic. Just something out of the ordinary?"

For a lawman, Mike wasn't particularly subtle. Why would he think something unusual might have happened? I suspected that he had some private knowledge of the blue Victorian that he didn't want to reveal. Not yet.

"Do you know something about the house that I don't?" I asked.

He met my gaze squarely. "Only that 7 Balsam Lane is reputed to be a hard sell. It's one of those places with a past."

Ah. Finally. "A checkered past?"

"I wouldn't go that far."

"Tell me more," I said.

"The last owner died there."

"I heard that from the woman who lives next door."

"There were rumors of suicide, but Miss Rose was elderly—in her eighties—and reclusive. No one knows what really happened."

Dorothy Bodoin

"I understand that she lived there for years," I said. "That she loved her home."

"So they said. Then there was another tragedy there years ago. A murder or a suspicious accident. I don't know the details. It was covered up. Now it's lost in time."

"How fascinating! Is this public knowledge?"

"I heard it here at Hunters when I first came to town."

"So you think the house is haunted by past tragedies?"

"Not haunted. Maybe shadowed."

"That sounds like the same thing. I haven't seen any ghosts floating through the halls."

Only a room that had slipped seamlessly into the past, and I still hadn't found an explanation for that impossible incident except for my wild date rape theory. I felt myself blushing. Yes, wild. How could I think for even a minute that this kind man would be guilty of such a heinous act?

Lin set our drinks on the table. I unwrapped the straw, took a sip of ginger ale, and resisted the urge to keep my hand over the glass. I wished I hadn't remembered that. I didn't want to be afraid of food and drink—or men.

With little effort, I brought myself back to the present. Here was my chance to learn more about the blue Victorian and keep our conversation in motion.

"One possible suicide, one old tragedy. That seems about right for a century-old house," I said.

"Most people don't want to move into a gloomy old mansion with a troubled background," he added.

"That isn't true of everybody. Snowhedge would be a perfect winter retreat for an author. Think of someone like Stephen King. All those partially furnished rooms in the blue house remind me of the hotel in *The Shining*."

"Funny that you mention Stephen King. One of the previous owners was an author."

"Did he write horror novels?" I asked.

"The author was a woman, Eve or Eva Something, and she was pretty obscure, but she had some stories published. I don't know what they were about. We're going back several years now, maybe decades. When you find out her name, you can look her up on the Net if you're interested."

"I am. If I could find her books, I'd scatter them throughout the downstairs rooms. They'd make a good selling point, and I could tell people about her—all those buyers I'm expecting to show up any day now."

"My guess is that her work is out of print. There's a small antique shop on Main Street. You could check there."

"Good idea. What else do you know about the house?"

"Not much." He picked up the menu. "Only that it's been on the market for over two years now. Going on three. When you see that"

54

nobody's snapped up an attractive property in all that time, you think something's wrong with it."

I glanced at the sandwich section, trying to decide between a turkey club and ham and Swiss on rye but I was really mulling over Mike's words. The blue Victorian was a country lover's dream come true, dressed for autumn in a surround of woods and water. Most likely the average house hunter had never heard vague tales of past and possible tragedies.

Why didn't it sell?

I came back to the depressed housing market and Valerie's high price tag. Those were facts. Mike's observations were subjective, but his words kept playing in my mind: "Something's wrong with it."

With the house, I thought. *Not with me.*

Chapter 9

I thought that time in a lively place would balance the long hours at Snowhedge, but that didn't happen. The next day, the blue Victorian seemed quieter than ever and strangely colder, even in front of the electric fireplace.

Sunday's weather turned gloomy with a fine drizzle, reinforcing the air of isolation that hovered over Snowhedge. As I neatened the house for the coming week, my thoughts drifted back to the roadhouse and Mike's revelations about Lila Rose and an obscure female writer named Eve or Eva. Mike believed that Snowhedge remained unsold because something was wrong with it. I still suspected that he knew more about the house than he'd revealed. Of course, I hadn't told him about the Christmas room.

What if I wasn't the only person who had seen the furnishings and the fir tree in the window? How could I ever know the answer to that question?

Look behind the locked door.

If I managed to open that door, would I find a dusty old attic with a rose sofa, gold chairs, tables, and a winter painting stored under white sheets? And if I did, where would that leave me?

Setting the vase of carnations with its fresh water on the vestibule table, I glanced toward the parlor.

Go ahead and check it out, I told myself. *This will only be the sixth time since breakfast.*

I opened the door slowly, bracing for a blast of frigid air. The room was empty. All was well. At this moment.

Maybe it had always been a vast, cold expanse of polished floor and pale lavender walls. Maybe it always smelled of balsam. Maybe the stain only seemed redder today and the frosty condensation just appeared to cover more of the windowpanes.

No. I closed the door and wandered into the dining room. Something was wrong with the house. Mike said so, and, being an objective, no-nonsense state trooper, he wouldn't be inclined to wild imaginings.

We were going to see each other again next week. Last night, as we lingered over pie and coffee, he had asked me out on a date. That was something to anticipate, a step above accidental encounters at a roadhouse.

Also he'd promised to try to open the locked door, which I'd described as a minor inconvenience.

Still, time seemed to move backwards at Snowhedge. Surely the clock had chimed eleven an hour ago.

The roar of a leaf blower cut into my thoughts. Through the window, I glimpsed Virgil Jones plowing a wide path to the back of the yard. He usually appeared in a burst of noise, cleared the grounds efficiently, and refused any conversation beyond a grudging 'Morning, ma'am' or 'Afternoon.'

Today I stayed inside the house watching leaves fly through the air to their appointed mounds. With the frequent autumn winds, the trees of Snowhedge would soon be bare, reaching long gaunt arms out in a futile attempt to trap the house in their grasp.

I shuddered at the image I'd created. As long as a single leaf clung to a branch, I could hold on to fall.

Christmas is coming. The goose is getting fat.

That line from the old Christmas song slipped into my mind, raising a faint alarm. I wasn't looking forward to the holidays, and I wanted to be gone from this place before the first carol aired, taking my entire collie family with me.

In order for me to do that, the house would have to attract a buyer.

By noon Virgil was gone, the grounds were immaculate, and the rest of the weekend stretched out in front of me, a parade of dull interminable hours. Sundays are for rest, I decided—and afternoon drives.

Preparing a thermos of hot chocolate to ward off the day's chill, I called Romy and attached her leash to her chain. This was a perfect day to visit the puppies. I only had to call Tara Saywin to tell her I was on my way.

Tara rented a farm in nearby Foxglove Corners where she bred horses and aspired to establish a collie kennel. She had a tri-factored sable named Honey and a twelve-week old litter. She had agreed to board my puppies until I could make a home for them. I'd paid her through the end of October, which was a week away.

A damp gray mist hung over the long unpaved driveway and the white farmhouse at its end. No one had raked leaves at the Saywin homestead. They lay in soggy heaps, squishing under my boots as I led a wildly excited Romy up to the wide front porch.

She had spied three brown horses grazing beyond a paddock fence. In her view, high adventure lay ahead.

My puppies would be inside the snug, freshly painted barn to the right. Not, I hoped, outside playing in the gravel-lined runs. I didn't see them and couldn't hear them. Still I frowned at the thought of my beautiful babies streaked with mud. How could they keep clean in such dreary wet weather? No one took care of my dogs the way I could.

They shouldn't be here. Why had I sent them away?

I wiped my feet on the doormat. *Because of Valerie*, I thought. She didn't want puppies at Snowhedge.

Romy whimpered as excited barking drifted out of the house. Tara flung open the door, telling Honey to sit and be quiet. Tara was a thin, dark-haired young woman in jeans and a light blue shirt rolled up to her elbows, an ideal outfit for working around animals.

"Hi, Susanna—and Romy," she said. "Come on in. Don't worry about the mess."

"We just came to see the puppies."

I stepped inside the warm country kitchen. It smelled of fresh coffee and wet dog, smelled like home, the way Snowhedge never did.

"I thought you'd stop by before this," Tara said.

"Is everything all right?" I asked quickly.

"Right as rain, but your little ones miss you. They think you've abandoned them."

Her words deepened the guilt I already felt. "Is it okay to go out to the barn?"

"Sure. I'll come too. Just let me grab a jacket."

As she disappeared into the hall, Honey ambled over to Romy and sniffed her. I noticed an empty cup on the table, alongside the July issue of *Collie Vistas*, the one with Blue Frost's face on the cover and that telling photograph of Amy and Preston inside.

"I'm trying to find homes for my litter," Tara said, buttoning her brown suede jacket. "But people end up wanting your puppies instead. You could have sold all three of them last week."

"They're not for sale," I reminded her.

"One woman who came by insisted that I give her your cell number. Naturally I didn't."

In the overly warm kitchen, I felt a chill. It seemed as if some unknown enemy had been trying to find me. Someone new.

As we walked to the barn, toward a chorus of yips and yaps and assorted noise, I asked, "What woman?

"Janice Rivier from Flint."

"What did she look like?"

"She was tall and a little on the chunky side. About fifty maybe. She had red hair and wore a big diamond ring. Usually I don't notice jewelry, but this stone was spectacular. Almost too heavy for her finger."

"I don't know any plump redheads," I said.

"Then she came back a few days later."

Tara opened the barn door. A horse whinnied, and the pups threw themselves at me. Fluffy little missiles, warm and eager, with wet tongues and sparkling eyes. They weren't streaked with mud. Their coats were as clean and bright as if Tara had just finished brushing them.

"Oh, my little girls..." I swallowed a lump in my throat. "They've grown."

Snowhedge

Tara chuckled. "That's what puppies do the best.

"I'm missing so much of their lives," I said. "It isn't fair."

Cindy pawed at my leg while Cherie and Frosty began to chase each other around Romy in a dizzying blur of blue and gray and blue...and gray. Stepping to one side, I almost lost my balance on the uneven floor. I grabbed the post for support, felt the solid wood.

"Susanna! Are you okay?" Tara's voice had an anxious edge.

"It's these heels." I'd left the house in such a hurry that I hadn't thought to change into sensible footgear or even don a pair of jeans. "They're not meant for walking in barns."

"Let's take the puppies up to the house," she said. "Come on, little gals."

They followed us like wind-up toys, loping through the muddy grass, leaping over leaves, turning around to nudge me with their snouts, yipping frantically.

"When this Janice Rivier came back, did you make it clear to her that my puppies weren't for sale?" I asked.

"I did. She was looking for show prospects sired by Blue Frost."

"He isn't their sire," I said. "That's Caroland's Blue Revenant."

"So I told her. She said she wanted to look at my litter again, but I don't think that was the truth. She didn't pay any attention to them. Anyway, she hasn't been around since."

"It doesn't make sense to me," I said. "Who buys three litter sisters?"

"That's what I thought. Unless you want an instant kennel." She opened the door, shepherding the canines into the kitchen. "Make yourself comfortable in the dining room. I'll get us something hot to drink."

Inside the house, Cherie discovered Honey's stuffed dragon and began a friendly game of tug of war with Frosty. While Honey tried half-heartedly to retrieve her toy. Cindy lay down near the table next to Romy and crossed her front paws, watching me gravely.

Never, never trust anyone with your precious dogs. I should have learned that lesson last summer.

On the surface, there was nothing threatening about an unknown woman wanting to own my gorgeous pups, but past experiences had made me wary of strangers and friends alike.

Tara had a tall, muscular husband, one of the sheriff's deputies, who was away during the day. Most of the time, though, she was as isolated as I was at Snowhedge. Honey was no watch dog, and the barn was several yards away from the house.

I made another mistake, I thought.

Tara appeared with two mugs of steaming coffee. "This should warm you up."

I sipped slowly and did some quick calculations. If I had a large crate, I could keep the puppies confined during the night. I'd spray the woodwork with Bitter Apple to save the Snowhedge woodwork from their sharp teeth.

59

I'd have to watch them carefully, but they'd tend to congregate around Romy and we'd all have Romy to look after us. It would work out.

"I changed my mind about boarding the puppies," I said. "There's no reason I can't have them with me."

"Did your employer change her mind too?" Tara asked.

"No, but she's in Florida, and we're not in contact with each other. The chances are good that she'll never know. I want to put them through their paces for Lakeville."

"You're going to enter! Oh, Susanna, you should. Show everyone what little gems you have. I'll be there too."

Tara must have heard Amy's lies, but she'd never mentioned them to me. I didn't let myself think about that now. The show was to be my comeback, my star-spangled, winner-takes-all weekend.

"I'll write you a refund check for the boarding," Tara said.

"No, don't. Just keep them for a few more days while I get the house ready. Call me right away if anyone shows interest in them."

"Do you think that woman had ulterior motives?" she asked.

"Probably not. I'm just being extra cautious because of the fire. You understand."

"I do," she said.

"And you'll make sure they stay safe," I said.

Tara laid her hand on Honey's head. "I have Ted's shotgun, and Honey looks like a big ol' marshmallow, but she lets me know if anyone comes skulking around the house."

"That's good. I'm just anticipating the worst, I guess."

"I know what you mean. Whenever I think of one of my pups ending up in a bad situation...well, I try not to think about it, or I'd never breed another litter."

On the way back to Snowhedge, the drizzle turned to a sloppy rain-snow mix. I drove cautiously over mashed leaves, keeping the windshield wipers moving at a steady speed and watching for deer crossing the road. A strange, unsettling foreboding rode with me. Something was going to happen soon, and it wouldn't be good. The very wind seemed to wail a warning.

Keep my puppies safe, I prayed.

I tried to remember if I'd ever seen a red-haired woman wearing a diamond so large that you'd notice it immediately. I couldn't recall a single redhead—not at college or my school or any of the shows; not in any place since I'd moved to Maple Creek.

Titian, auburn, chestnut, copper...hair could be dyed. Some women wear wigs.

I should have taken the pups with me.

I almost made a U-turn on the narrow road and headed back to Foxglove Corners. But I kept driving, telling myself that I was overreacting once again. Tara knew my concerns, and she'd be extra vigilant. In a few more days, we'd all be together.

It was only the weather, so depressing and anxiety-inducing that it made me feel like crying. This was a good afternoon to sit in front of the fireplace wrapped in a warm throw, and let the rest of the day burn itself out while I read a good book.

It was a dark and stormy night…

Or something lighter. Thank heavens for Valerie's spooky house with its sturdy walls and strong roof. The wind shook the car, tried to drive it to the edge of the road. Thunder rumbled in the distance.

I passed a series of upward sloping curves and drove into sudden folds of white fog. Slowing my speed, I let the Taurus creep the last quarter mile to the Snowhedge driveway.

The porch lamp shone through the mist, casting an eerie glow on the orange pumpkins and tall cornstalks. I parked and freed Romy who dashed up to the steps, wagging her tail. Pulling my hood up over my head, I followed her, holding my own against wind gusts, treading on leaves that had been attached to trees earlier this afternoon. Going home.

This isn't our home, I thought. *It's our shelter from the storm.*

Inside the vestibule, I turned off the porch lamp and switched on the dim hall light. Shadows leaped into place and lay still on the floor, waiting. The silence overwhelmed me, and the air was cool, about ten degrees below my comfort level; but I expected that. At least it was dry.

And I was wet and cold. As I dropped my purse and keys on the vestibule table, I noted the sorry state of the carnations. They had lost their vibrancy, which was odd. The bouquet was only two days old and had been fine earlier when I'd changed the water.

A whispered command came from some far place. *Look in the parlor!*

I opened the door, recoiling from the icy rush of air that I knew would be there.

Everything was back in place: Furniture, vintage photographs, painting, fir tree in the bay window. Impressions battered me like drops of assaulting rain. Color and light and substance. Red, green, silver, gold. Lamplight and firelight and candlelight. Solid objects. Shadows. An unspoken invitation.

All you have to do is step inside and you'll enter somebody else's world.

Chapter 10

Come in. Come in.

Sometimes an unspoken invitation can be loud enough to hear.

Leaving the door open, I stepped inside. The parlor seemed to hold out its arms in welcome. Lamplight shone on the round table, illuminating vintage photographs and candles. The fireplace flames leaped high. In the bay window, the balsam fir had undergone an astounding transformation. No longer dripping snow from bare branches, it glittered with multi-colored lights, ornaments, and strands of shiny tinsel.

No room on earth was more alluring. I could almost overlook the pulsating waves of arctic air that washed over me.

Since the last materialization, someone had scattered presents under the tree and added festive touches to the décor. Fresh greens sparkled between the plates on the mantel, and a red velvet ribbon framed the winter garden painting. A two-tier silver server claimed the place of honor on the coffee table. Its trays held Christmas cookies and chocolate squares topped with miniature holly berries.

Where was the tea service?

I crossed to the round table where the picture frames and candles had been pushed close together to make room for a brass angel-and-candle decoration that revolved lazily on its stand like a toy merry-go-round. They were Swedish angel chimes, designed to ring when heat from the candles turned the angels. Although they moved, they were silent.

Fire that doesn't generate heat can't burn. Holding my hand over a flame, I dared myself to test it. At the last minute, giving in to my fear, I pulled it back.

You can't be afraid of ghost fire, I told myself.

But I was—and of soundless chimes and of the room itself. My apprehension warred with pure fascination.

Although I wanted to stay in the parlor, I wished I were in another place, one I could understand. I felt like an intruder wandering around in someone else's house, while she stood by, helpless to intervene.

There's the door. Still open. Go back and close it behind you. Maybe it'll all go away.

I didn't. The mystery of that unknown Someone Else's identity cried to be solved. Who had brought the tree in from outside and hung the ornaments? This person had wrapped presents, lit the angel chime candles, set out candy and cookies, and decorated the room for a holiday celebration that might have taken place years ago.

Or years in the future?

The alternate was like a hard, unexpected slap in the face. Was this a vision of the parlor in a Christmas season-yet-to-be?

Susanna, stop! I thought. *You're not living in a Dickens novel. If you have to move in time, move backwards.*

Because the furnishings had a dated look. Swedish angel chimes were antiques. I wouldn't know what they were if I hadn't seen them advertised in the Vermont Country Store Catalogue. Most modern indoor tree lights had tiny flower petal shapes. I touched one of the photographs, a sepia image of a young boy with a grave smile and an outdated hairstyle. This was no twenty-first century youth.

Still, vintage picture frames were back in vogue. That face might belong to the mysterious Someone's father or grandfather as a young boy. And surely some people held on to old tree lights and Swedish angel chimes long after they became outmoded.

Whether the objects belonged to the past or future or some shadowy in-between world, nothing in my view had arrived in a natural way.

Where was that unseen person who had transformed the parlor into a wondrous Christmas room? Watching me from the shadows in the hall? I felt that I was alone, and yet there was something here. A presence waiting just beyond my perception. Rather, a Presence.

I walked past the tree, close to the burning lights, feeling only cold, and looked out the window. By my watch it was five-thirty, but the sky still held bravely on to the last of its light. Snow fell in large white flakes. At least an inch of accumulation lay over the uneven grounds and the pond.

That at least was normal. So the strangeness was contained in the house. More accurately in the parlor.

You always suspected that. Now, observe. Find the answers.

My gaze fell on a wall clock, as silent as the fireplace flames and angel chimes. I didn't remember seeing it here before, but...pinpricks of fear traced a path up my body as I recognized the decorative spray painted on its gleaming mahogany surface. Delicate blue flowers and sprigs of heart-shaped leaves. This was the clock from the living room, the one whose chimes I'd grown accustomed to hearing. I was certain of it. But how could it be in two places at once?

It couldn't. However, in the past it might have hung on a different wall at Snowhedge, and, of course, I was dealing with different times.

The clock's hour hand pointed to three. I listened for the chimes but heard nothing. Parlor time lagged behind real world time by almost three hours. Or three decades? Or more?

This phenomenon needed to be documented on film, but I suspected that by the time I found my camera, still packed away, the furnishings and decorations would disappear. The developed pictures might show an empty parlor with a red stain in the middle of the floor. But maybe they wouldn't.

I decided to stay for a while longer. When I left, I'd take an object out of the room as proof for myself of what I'd seen. One of the framed photographs or perhaps a present. And I'd unpack my sketching materials and transfer what I was looking at to paper.

A small gold package tied with lacy white ribbon caught my attention. I reached under the tree and shook it lightly. Nothing rattled. It didn't have a tag or sticker, only the fancy handmade ribbon with long trailing ends.

What about the other gifts? They might be able to tell me something.

I knelt in front of the tree and examined them, one by one. All had name tags written in green ink: Richard, Mother, Dad, Cathy, Richard again, Aunt May, Juliette.

The ghost family, I thought. *The shadow people who walked on the cabbage rose carpet and sat in front of the fireplace.*

Where were they now?

I sank into the plush sofa and gazed into the impossible flames. I had to accept the truth, however inexplicable it might be. The blue Victorian had given me a phantom room, with a promise of a warm and happy Christmas celebration.

Cookies and chocolates, colored lights on a dark day, surprises in brightly wrapped packages. Scents of balsam and cinnamon. Warmth, acceptance. Joy, hope, goodwill. All the things I told myself didn't matter to me any more were mine for the taking in this enchanted parlor.

No, they're not. They belong to the shadow family.

The hour hand on the silent clock continued to move slowly. Five minutes passed. Ten. My eyes strayed to the cookies on the coffee table. Little trees sprinkled with green sugar. Red stars and meringue wreaths. Tiny gingerbread men. I reached for a tree but my hand froze in mid-air.

Don't. They may be poison, and they're certainly old and stale. They just look like they came out of the oven this morning.

Five more minutes went by. I couldn't stay in the parlor forever. But all I had to do tonight was cook dinner and get ready for bed.

I twirled the ribbon on the package around my finger, admired the ornaments, tried to guess what was in each glossy box, and, suddenly remembering Romy, called her name. She didn't come. I ought to see what she was doing, but the second I walked out of the room, everything would vanish. So I'd wait a little longer.

Leaning back on the sofa, I let my thoughts roam at will until they made their way back to me wearing strange colors and fuzzy faces, making no sense at all.

The fireplace flames leaped higher, and the room grew colder. The clock's hands kept moving. The Swedish angel chimes continued their

64

perpetual revolutions. Their candles burned down quickly. I closed my eyes. The only sound in the room was my breathing and a soft whine.

Romy?

I felt a brush of warm velvet as she rested her head on my hand. It was going to be all right. My dog was with me.

I awoke on the floor in front of the dead, cold fireplace, my right hand clenched in a tight fist and hurting. Romy slept at my side, her paw draped over my arm.

Harsh bright light poured in through the frosted windows. Even in my jacket and long scarf, I was freezing.

Everything was gone. The sofa I'd been sitting on, the coffee table with the server of chocolates and cookies, the magnificent Christmas tree, even the little gold present I'd been holding when I fell asleep.

Why didn't I wake up when the sofa disappeared under me and I fell to the floor?

I rubbed my eyes and glanced out the window. The world beyond the frosted panes was white. A new day dressed in October snow and possibilities had arrived. What would happen next?

I forced myself to sit up, then stand. A new pain spread across my shoulders and down my back.

How could I ever explain to an early morning visitor why I had fallen asleep on the hard floor when I had a comfortable bed and an electric fireplace down the hall?

What early morning visitor? No one would ever know what had happened here unless I told them.

The parlor was as cold as an ice cave. All the happy shades of red and green, the gold and silver, had drained away, leaving me in a surround of white and lavender and beige. Colors of bereavement.

I want it all back, I thought. *I have to find it again.*

Days awash in sunshine and normal activities have a way of neutralizing out-of-this-world experiences. Several times during the week I opened the parlor door, hoping to see again the room fully furnished and wearing its Christmas finery. It didn't happen.

The haunting, if haunting this was, had its own timeline. So I moved the feather duster across the mantel, carefully avoiding the tiny green star, and made yet another futile attempt to erase the red mark on the floor.

Don't fuss about what you can't change, I told myself.

The snow melted, and the sun brought warmer weather. Virgil appeared to blow the leaves into a high mountain and set them afire. I shopped for groceries and fresh bouquets, ordered a new crate for the puppies, and told Tara that I'd come by to pick them up on Saturday morning. In the meantime I unpacked their food dishes and toys.

Each busy hour moved my experience in the phantom room farther back to the past until it acquired the gauzy texture of a dream. At the same time, I was conscious of an encroaching sense of loss and longing that had nothing to do with my burnt-out kennel, Blue Frost, or Preston Anderson.

It seemed as if something wonderful was happening beyond the parlor door while I was trapped in the other rooms with their cavernous spaces and shadows, feeling unwanted and deprived.

That frightened me.

"There. It isn't so hard if you know what you're doing."

With a jeweler's screwdriver and a few deft movements, Mike forced the lock open. The waiting was over.

"Let's see what we have," he said. "You're looking for a hidden room?"

"Probably the attic," I said. "If it's another space to take care of, I want to have access to it."

He frowned. "No one expects you to keep an attic clean. Do they?"

"Okay. I'm just curious. I don't like secret places."

He pulled the door open. Cold, dusty air rushed out from the small, dim space beyond. My eyes began to water.

"It's a staircase," Mike said. "Let's see where it takes us."

"Is there a light switch?" I asked.

His hand swept over the wall. "I don't see one."

"Then it's lucky I brought a flashlight."

Mike held the door open. "I'll go first."

Romy pushed past me and sniffed anxiously at the floor.

"You stay," I told her, cringing as the first step creaked under Mike's weight.

"It's all right," he said.

I followed gingerly. Ten stairs. Ten ominous creaks. The old wood held. Mike helped me up to a makeshift threshold consisting of three wide boards nailed together. "I was right. It's an attic."

Almost as cold as the parlor.

"And packed with junk," Mike said.

I let the flashlight beam pan over the vast shadowy area, over hulking furniture shapes covered in sheets. The light danced off the dim surface of a hall mirror with cracked glass, mismatched chairs, boxes stacked up to the rafters, and other strange items.

Directly ahead a ghostly dressmaker's dummy leaned against a slanted beam. She wore a bib of shiny turquoise material and dozens of pins. The Someone Else's unfinished sewing project? Could that be a stone birdbath and a pink flamingo with one leg?

Mike picked up a lamp that lay on its side. "This baby weighs a ton."

"But it's beautiful." I touched the ornate ivory and brass base. The shade was coated with dust, and the frame was bent, but it could be straightened. That was more than I could say for the mahogany chair with the broken back or the cuckoo clock lying on a table in a jumble of weights, chains, and broken pieces of wood.

"Watch your step, Susanna." Mike set the lamp down and walked a few feet into the attic's interior. "There's no real floor. Stay on the boards."

I spied an old phonograph, its case gritty with age and neglect. "Why didn't the last owner move all this stuff out?"

"Miss Rose died unexpectedly, but her heirs or the Realtor should have done it. Whoever buys this old place can have a bonfire."

"Or a yard sale," I said. "Some of this might be valuable."

"Have you seen enough?" Mike asked.

I let the flashlight beam travel once more over the attic. Whoever had brought the discards up here had left a path down the middle, scarcely wide enough for a person to walk. Sifting through the wealth of treasure and trash would be a formidable but exciting task.

"I wonder what's in here," I said, spying a tall box with a caved-in top.

"I'll see." Mike tugged at the loosely tied string. As it fell free, he peeled back the cardboard edges.

"It looks like books," he said.

I peered over his shoulder at a row of slender volumes and picked one up. *The Storm Girls on Adventure Island.* Printed on brittle, yellowing paper, with a smudged orange cover, it appeared to be an old book-in-a-series for girls. The copyright was 1927.

"These are antiques," I said.

"Some rainy day you can sift through them. Maybe catalog the books and decide what to do with them."

Some day when Mike and I didn't have a date. As much as I was looking forward to dinner and a movie, I had a strong desire to stay in the attic and explore. Even in my good black dress with the long pearl earrings that dangled to my shoulder. However...

"That's not my responsibility," I said. "I'm just the house sitter."

But that wouldn't stop me from searching through the boxes. What better place to find clues than in an old attic? Every girl detective knew that.

"Your mystery is solved." Mike moved back to the top of the staircase.

"Not all of it. I don't understand why the door was locked."

"Maybe it was unintentional."

I let the light play over the attic one last time. "Or there's something up here worth guarding."

"Or something that should stay locked up." Mike broke off with a chuckle and reached for my hand. "Hey, Susanna, I'm just kidding. Let's go back downstairs. I'm getting hungry."

"In a minute." I squinted into the darkness. "Do you see a rose colored sofa and a pair of gold chairs?"

He looked at me, for just an instant turning into an inquisitor-state trooper. "You're looking for something specific?"

I hesitated, wondering how I could have been so careless. "I saw them in a—picture of the parlor the way it used to be," I said. "They were grouped around the fireplace."

"The chairs could be covered up, but I don't see anything large enough to be a sofa."

"That's odd. It looks like the previous families stored everything they didn't want up here. So I wonder..."

"What?" he asked.

Unwilling to let even one part of my secret slip out, I fell back on repetition. "Why nobody cleaned out the attic before putting the house on the market."

What really puzzled me was the fate of the parlor furniture. What had happened to it?

Chapter 11

After dark, the Blue Lion Inn shed its stuffy daytime image. Elegance and romantic atmosphere took over. Candle centerpieces contributed to the ambience, and tiny clear lights winked at the diners from every corner. The entrées were more elaborate and pricier than their lunchtime counterparts. Mike and I had dined on prime rib—Mike's favorite—and were waiting for dessert.

Our first date was going well, even if, in some part of my mind, I was anxious to return to the attic and start searching for a clue to the parlor mystery. I felt certain that it would be there, perhaps hidden in one of the boxes. Why else had the door been locked?

Well I wasn't going to do it tonight.

So relax, I ordered myself. The opportunity to enjoy a meal out with a congenial companion didn't appear that often, and I couldn't remember the last time I'd gone with someone to see a movie.

Mike had outdone himself to be gallant and entertaining, talking about Davey's birthday party, the new puppy's reception, and Maple Creek's next social event, the Halloween Haunted House Tour.

I sat opposite him in a cozy alcove, sipped Merlot, and tried not to look at the candle in the middle of the table. Its light altered reality, giving the painted knights on the wall a menacing look and casting shadows on their ladies and hounds. This was real fire, I reminded myself, not the cold blaze of the fireplace and the angel chimes. It could ignite a napkin or the tablecloth. The flickering glow was only inches from my face.

As a dull pain settled in my right hand, I set the wine glass down.

Someday I'm going to be able to coexist peacefully with fire, I thought. *I won't be constantly afraid of getting burned. And someday I'm going to feel at ease with a date and not remember that the last man in my life betrayed me.*

Mike made me nervous—a little. He was too attentive, the desire in his eyes impossible to misinterpret. I didn't know how he expected this night would end, and I wanted to keep him as a friend for now.

I was out of practice, a novice at dating again. It had been better in the attic when we were simply having a mini adventure. There was no pressure for me to be bright and chatty.

I should say something. Mike had noticed my preoccupation with the centerpiece.

"Is anything wrong with the candle?" he asked.

"Not really." I looked away for a moment. Then, noticing his quizzical frown, I added, "I'm afraid of fire."

I picked up the wine goblet again, let its cold surface soothe my hand.

"I'll take care of it." He blew the candle out. Thin wisps of smoke hung on the air for a moment and dissipated. "Have you always been afraid of fire?" he asked.

"It's a recent fear," I said.

He waited for me to go on.

"I was in a fire earlier this year."

The frown deepened. "Were you hurt?"

"A little. Mostly emotionally."

"I see. Now, Susanna, I don't know anything about you except that you like collies. What did you do before you became a house sitter?"

"Oh..." I sorted quickly through my past aspirations and achievements and chose what I wanted to share. "I taught art at Hazeldon Middle School until they dropped it from the curriculum. My collie kennel was more a hobby than a profitable business. Over the years I've worked at all kinds of jobs. None of them were what I really wanted to do."

"And what's that?" he asked.

"To rebuild my kennel on a couple of acres. To make it spacious and airy and safe."

"What's stopping you?"

"Mostly money. I'm hoping to be able to save now that I don't have to pay rent."

"What happened to your old kennel?" he asked.

"An arsonist burned it to the ground." I marveled that I could say those words in a steady voice. "But I rescued my collies."

"Ah, the fire," he said.

"This happened in July. I hope I'll get over it one day."

"Where are your other dogs?" he asked.

"I've been boarding my three pups. They're coming home tomorrow. To Snowhedge, I mean."

"You'll have your hands full. That little Jack gets into non-stop mischief except when he's asleep."

"I'm used to puppy antics." I took another sip of wine, holding the glass with my left hand. "Now, it's your turn. What do you like to do?"

He smiled, and the lines about his eyes crinkled. "Work and take my boys hunting or fishing when I'm off duty. I'm right where I want to be. In this job and in this town."

"It's good to be satisfied with your life," I said.

The waitress set our dessert on the table and refilled our coffee cups. At the sight of the chocolate caramel cheesecake, my mood soared. Caramel and October were natural go-togethers, and chocolate was right for any season.

"Tell me more about the Halloween tour," I said. "Do you have corn mazes or scavenger hunts?

He laughed. "Nothing so elaborate. It's trick-or-treating with a plan. We have some mysterious places in Maple Creek. There's a bed-and-breakfast with a ghost bride and an old country homestead where an entire family disappeared one winter night. Then there's Angelynn Carver's cottage. They say she was a witch. A grisly murder happened there in the 1930's."

"And these houses are all haunted?

"Probably not. The present owners tell their stories, serve cider and doughnuts, and arrange make-believe apparitions."

"In other words, they serve up candy and fright."

"That's been their goal. The Historical Society wants to change the name to the Autumn Walk and showcase fall gardens and decorations, but if they did that, the young people would stay away."

"Real spirits can't be happy with living people tramping through their rooms," I said, amused at the thought of volunteering Snowhedge for the tour. First stop, the parlor which would materialize on command. Second stop, the attic.

I couldn't tell anyone their stories. My display would be genuine, though, inasmuch as a phantom room could be described in that way.

Mike said, "I never met a ghost, but I guess they guard their privacy."

A ghost…

I looked up from my dessert plate, puzzled by something I couldn't identify. A sudden draft? An inaudible warning bell, an imaginary light that flashed danger? Something alarming, something near…

There it was. There *he* was.

A young man in a dark blue suit sauntered down the aisle, alone and looking straight ahead. He was lean and dark with sharp features and a familiar swagger. His mocking smile yanked me back to last summer, to the day I'd first seen him. Before the fire.

Morning sunshine. Fresh air. Romy begging for a bite of my apricot Danish. Amy trying to master her new digital camera, coaxing the puppies into cute poses for an ad in Collie Vistas.

A rusty red truck trundling up from the road with a dark lean figure behind the wheel. He'd stepped off the running board into the camera range, but we didn't realize that until later. He said he was looking for odd jobs.

As the man passed our table, I turned to stare at him, but he'd already vanished into another section of the Inn.

Like a ghost.

Logic insisted that he couldn't be the arsonist, Tag Nolan. I'd just been telling Mike about the fire. For Tag to appear at this moment would be too much of a coincidence—the kind that lurks in books and movies but rarely in real life. Besides, Tag was in jail.

The man I'd seen so briefly had to be his double or one of his relatives. Another possibility was the Merlot. A half glass of wine had sent my imagination spinning out of control. I'd better leave the rest in the goblet.

"Do you see somebody you know?" Mike asked.

"I thought so, but no. It couldn't be," I said.

"An old boyfriend?"

"Hardly." I couldn't stop my hand from straying to my throat. Lowering my voice, I added, "The man who torched my kennel and almost killed my dogs. Tag Nolan. But it has to be somebody else."

"Why do you say that?" Mike asked.

"Because he can't be here. He's behind bars."

Still, all the rationalization in the world couldn't slow the beating of my heart or bring back the warmth created by the Merlot, the cheesecake, and Mike. I'd thought this rural village was so isolated and safe. But first Amy and Preston materialized at the Apple Fair and now Tag strolled into the Blue Lion as if it were his favorite Michigan haunt. If it was Tag.

"I'll get you Ms. Kentwood," he'd said after the trial. *"You're going to pay for this and pay good."*

I said, "I must be mistaken."

"Maybe not." Mike's eyes turned to blue steel. "Let's check out his table. You can get a long, close look at him."

I said, "We can wander back to the restrooms and act casual."

He scooped the last bit of cheesecake into his mouth. "Then you won't have to keep wondering."

The man I thought was Tag, or rather, might be Tag, wasn't in the back section of the Blue Lion. He wasn't at the bar. According to Mike, he wasn't in the men's room. He'd probably gone out through the back exit or he'd never been in the Inn at all.

I couldn't have imagined that nightmare face. Could I?

"I'm sorry, Mike," I said. "I saw someone who resembled him, and it startled me. I'm not usually so jittery."

He reached for my hand and held it as we walked back to our alcove.

"You're cold," he said. "Let's have some more coffee. You can finish your dessert and tell me all about it. Did this man do something else?"

"He threatened me."

I told him how my one-time partner and I had identified Tag Nolan as the man who had brought a gallon of gasoline to Greengrove Farm and set fire the kennel with the sleeping collies inside.

"Just for the fun of it," he'd said after the trial in a low voice, meant only for me. *"I like to see things burn up. I like to hear animals screaming."*

"He dropped his glove at the scene," I said. "They traced tire tracks in the driveway to his pickup, but mostly it was our evidence that convicted him. Amy had a picture of him on the property. Then the owners of the stables he'd burned came forward with their identifications, but he blamed me for ruining his life, more than Amy. She kept a low profile the whole time."

I remembered Nolan's cold dark eyes and his face twisted into an ugly red mask. Clenched fists, mouth spewing obscenities, vows of revenge. His wolfish snarl. The police leading him away in handcuffs. For a while I was safe.

In the beginning, those dark moments played over and over in my mind. Lately they had stayed in the background with my fear of the man, emerging only when something reminded me of Tag and what he'd done.

Yes, I was afraid of Tag Nolan.

Even though I had quietly relocated to a relatively obscure village up north, I lived alone, and a maniac was out to get me. How did I know he wouldn't try to get even with me by hurting my dog?

Anyone could tell him that was the best way to do it.

"I assumed that Tag Nolan was still locked up," I said.

"I'll look into it. You can't afford *not* to take any threat seriously, Susanna. This former partner of yours should be concerned too."

"Amy," I said, keeping my bitterness and anger at bay. My issue with Amy was my own affair. "We've lost contact with each other. I have no idea where she is today."

Not even a common danger could bring us together again.

Three live wire puppies can peel the mystery away from the spookiest house, layer by layer. With endless energy and enthusiasm, my little ones tore through Snowhedge, staking out favorite places for naps and play. They left their toys underfoot and infused the old house with happy new life.

I set up their crate in the kitchen under the windows, but they preferred the shelter of the table with its proximity to the stove and refrigerator. Here they waited for biscuits, fresh water, and meals to appear or followed Romy wherever she went, which wasn't usually very far.

My collie family was together again. The parlor remained a cold, vacant room at the front of the house, and the October sun brought us what must be the last warm days of the season. I was happier than I'd been for a long time.

Mike was going to stop by later in the week to visit them. I looked forward to seeing him again. Very much. He wanted friendship, too, and was content with a goodnight kiss, at least for now. That suited me, and I felt safe, knowing that he was patrolling the roads of Maple Creek, although, technically, I was as alone as I'd ever been.

Late that afternoon when there was still plenty of daylight left, I changed into jeans and a white shirt and ascended the ten creaking stairs to the attic. On the threshold, I surveyed the jumble of stored items, letting the flashlight beam move slowly from right to left and back again.

Dust motes swam through the cold air, and grittiness seemed to rise up from the uneven floor and force its way into my throat. None of the autumn warmth and only a little of the daylight could squeeze through the narrow ventilation slats.

Without Mike at my side, the attic seemed spookier, almost dangerous.

If something happened to me, if I tripped and sprained my ankle, for instance, no one would know about it. The dogs couldn't go for help through locked doors. I could stay up here for hours and days—until Mike stopped by. Even then, when I didn't come to the door, he'd go away.

That isn't going to happen. Just watch your step.

I made a thorough search for the parlor furnishings, looking under sheets for an old rose sofa and gold chairs, for the tables, the winter painting, even boxes marked 'Ornaments'. They weren't here, but a green Christmas tree stand lay on its side next to a brass trunk. I couldn't know for certain if it was the one I'd seen in the parlor. But it might be. If so, it was a connection to the mystery.

What could I do with it?

Hoping to have better luck with the books, I carried the box Mike had opened down to the large third-story room. I moved a chair over to the windows and set out to examine the cold, musty volumes that had been kept away from the light for so many years.

They were old children's series and classics, many of them with color illustrations on the cover: *Rebecca of Sunnybrook Farm, Emily of New Moon, Heidi, Rose in Bloom, Pollyanna, Alice in Wonderland.* Girls' adventures, gentle artifacts from a bygone age whose owner had outgrown them and packed them away. Or somebody did it for her.

One by one, I leafed through yellowing pages, looking for an old letter or a name or inscription on a flyleaf. Occasionally, I came across a handmade bookmark, but I didn't find anything remotely resembling a clue. Before long, I grew tired of the project and began to feel queasy from inhaling dust.

Back in the attic, I set the books to one side and let the flashlight beam play over the boxes once again. What now? There was too much of everything here. I felt overwhelmed. The meager light that had filtered into the attic was fading, and the air seemed to grow colder by the minute. Suddenly I wanted to be gone from this gloomy place, to continue my search another day—or not at all.

As I turned to leave, I glanced at the hall mirror.

Dear God.

Behind my reflection, a woman in a long white dress stared out at me from the cracked glass.

Chapter 12

The turquoise scarf around her throat glittered with starry sequins. Its color matched her blue-green eyes. They were as clear and luminous as sea jewels uncovered in a secret cove.

I stumbled away from the mirror. The flashlight fell out of my hand, and the board shifted under my weight. I grabbed at a post to steady myself. A great cold unlike any I'd ever felt closed in on me.

Get a grip, for heaven's sake.

I was staring at my own reflection—my tousled dark hair and smudged white blouse. What I'd mistaken for a person was the dressmaker's dummy with her turquoise bib and silver pins. It stood behind me, tall and graceful like a living thing, its image trapped in the glass.

But a dressmaker's dummy didn't look anything like a woman. It didn't have eyes.

So what had I seen for that fragment of a moment?

The attic is haunted, just like the parlor, I thought. *No wonder someone locked the door. To keep the ghost inside.*

Even as I made my way down the rickety stairs to the third floor, I told myself that was nonsense. I had become too impressionable to go poking around in dark, atmospheric places with only a weak flashlight beam.

And when did a slab of wood ever keep a spirit from moving from one part of a house to another? Down to the parlor, for instance?

It's a dummy, I told myself. *Only a seamstress' aid made of metal and cloth.*

I closed the door, wishing I could lock it, but Mike's tinkering had weakened the mechanism.

A tiny whimper and a sharp pat on my ankle drew my attention downward. With wagging tail and sparkling eyes, Cindy waited for me to acknowledge her presence. I scooped her up and pressed her wriggling body to my breast. She licked my cheek.

"Let's get out of here, baby," I said, carrying her down to the first story.

Romy, Cherie, and Frosty were in the kitchen, all of them whining for their dinner. I cut equal portions of left-over prime rib into their food dishes, remembering Mike's amusement when I'd saved part of my entrée for the dogs. As for myself, I wasn't hungry, which was fortunate. I didn't have anything to turn into a palatable meal.

It was just as well. I felt a little queasy, most likely a nervous reaction from my fright. Still, in spite of my resolve, my thoughts strayed back to the attic.

If only I dared go up there again on a morning when bright sunshine would melt the shadows. When it wouldn't be so cold. With one of those lantern flashlights to cast a stronger light. There were so many more boxes to open and books to leaf through. A possible answer to find. I could throw a sheet over the mirror.

No!

I filled the teakettle with water, trying to decide between peppermint tea and Orange Pekoe.

No matter what elusive clue lay waiting for discovery, nothing would induce me to return to the attic again. Let its secrets stay hidden.

A loud pounding on the front door set my heartbeat racing. Whining turned to feverish barking as Romy dashed out to the hall, with the puppies scrambling after her.

It must be Mike. I brushed a trail of cobweb from my jeans, but there was no quick remedy for the smudges on my blouse.

I shepherded the pups into the living room, told Romy to Sit and Stay, and opened the door.

A tall lanky man with a gray mustache and a chunky little woman in orange and blue plaid stood close together on the porch. I noticed that dark clouds filled the sky, and the winds had picked up. Inside Snowhedge, I'd been unaware of changing weather conditions.

"Good afternoon," the woman said. She had pale blue eyes and brown windblown hair lightly sprinkled with gray. "We're the Tabors. Are you the owner of this gorgeous house?"

"That's Valerie Lansing, but she's out of town. I'm her representative."

Romy growled and sprang to her feet. The fur on her back appeared to rise with her. From the living room came the indignant yipping of three puppies being kept out of the action.

"Hush." I laid a hand on Romy's head, grateful for her warning stance.

"We'd like to see the property." Mr. Tabor peered beyond me into the hall where the flowers on the table were drooping again.

"You have a fantastic view," Mrs. Tabor said. "The pond, the hill, that little stream...it's just like a picture in a magazine. And look at these pumpkins and flowers! Everything is so fresh and pretty."

"Can we have a quick look around inside?" Mr. Tabor asked.

"Well, no, I'm afraid not."

I'd hoped for a prospective buyer to come along, but I couldn't admit strangers to the house. It wasn't done that way. It wouldn't be safe.

"You'll have to make an appointment with the Three Pines Realtor," I said. "Her office is in Maple Creek. Ask for Karenell Miller."

Mrs. Tabor frowned. Her voice rose slightly, and a modicum of her exuberance evaporated. "Oh, but they went out of business. Didn't you know? That's why we came straight here."

Her words stunned me, but the message made sense. The long silence, unreturned messages, my note ignored. My suspicion was reality.

"I'm going to have to check with the owner then," I said. "If you'll leave me your number…"

"You want to sell the house, don't you?" An annoying note of condescension crept into Mr. Tabor's voice.

"Mrs. Lansing does," I said.

"We're prepared to match any offer she gets," he added.

Mr. Tabor moved closer to me. So did Romy. She was silent, her body as hard as stone.

"We really *really* want this house," Mrs. Tabor said. "George, do something."

I said, "Tell me how to reach you, and we'll set up an appointment."

Mr. Tabor nudged his wife's arm. "Do it, Eleanor."

Mrs. Tabor opened her purse and scribbled numbers on a scrap of paper. "This is my cell, but please don't wait too long. We have to be out of our old house by the end of the month. There are plenty of places we could buy, but this one has…" She broke off, letting her eyes wander to the pond and the balsams growing on the hill. "It has…"

"Charm," Mr. Tabor finished. "And space."

"Everything we're looking for. I'm sure we'll love living here, if you'll just let us see the inside," Mrs. Tabor added.

In the kitchen, the teakettle whistled, its high shrill adding to the tension in the air.

I repeated the number aloud. "I'll give you a call as soon as I know something. Mrs. Lansing and I appreciate your interest."

"Any time will be fine," Mr. Tabor said.

As I shut the door, I realized that my hand was shaking. I didn't like these pushy people. They weren't right for Snowhedge. The real issue, of course, was the status of the house. If Valerie's agent had gone out of business, where did that leave me?

Romy whimpered.

"It's all right," I told her.

But it wasn't.

As soon as the Tabors left, I placed a call to Valerie. It went, as always, to her voicemail. Frustrated with interminable delay, I sat at the kitchen table, sipping a cup of mint tea and assembling my thoughts.

What should I do now? Remove the 'For Sale' sign? Keep trying to make contact with Valerie? Pack the car and move on, as I'd once been tempted to do? I could be ready to leave in the morning, or even later this evening. After all, an absconding real estate agent was Valerie's problem, not mine.

But Mike was stopping by to see the puppies sometime this week. I couldn't vanish without letting him know where I was going. I didn't know how to contact him, didn't have a destination in mind, and most of all, didn't need this indecision. How could I think about entering dog shows and rebuilding my kennel when my future had settled into a quagmire of uncertainty?

Early the next day, I drove to the Three Pines cottage. No one had cleaned the smashed pumpkin mess from the front yard, and the shuttered windows reinforced the truth of Mrs. Tabor's announcement. Apparently Karenell Miller had abandoned her office and her properties.

Couldn't she have informed her clients and referred them to another Realtor?

You're best out of this situation, I told myself.

But it was complicated. Along with not wanting to drive away from my growing friendship with Mike, I had another dilemma. If I left Snowhedge, what would I do with Valerie's house keys? Mail them to her in Florida with my resignation letter?

That seemed cowardly and careless, not the way to end our brief association. More importantly, if I left, who would watch over Snowhedge?

Unable to decide on an immediate course of action, I fell back on the routine: Shopping for the week's groceries, buying bouquets for the house, and stopping at the post office. Here I found the dog show application forms I'd requested and an envelope from Valerie. It contained only a check, but it was for a generous amount, fifty dollars more than the salary we'd agreed on.

So I decided to stay a little longer in limbo. In the meantime, I'd take the 'For Sale' sign down—just until I had a chance to consult with Valerie. Then I wouldn't have to deal with people like the Tabors without any guidance. By the time I reached Balsam Lane, I'd convinced myself that this decision was the wisest one I could have made under the new circumstances. It didn't occur to me to consider the consequences.

The bouquet with its bright Gerber daisies and delicate blue delphiniums was perfect for the parlor. The pale lavender walls and beige curtains needed a dash of color and life.

Poor lost room, I thought as I opened the door, preparing for a blast of cold indoor air to slam into me.

It didn't happen. I stepped into a dazzle of color and light. The phantom furnishings and decorations were back. This afternoon, someone was there.

A woman in a bright red dress stood at the round table, rearranging candy dishes. I couldn't see her face, but she was tall and slender, and her glossy brown hair fell in a smooth pageboy to her shoulders. A bracelet jingled on her wrist as she moved a green glass basket away from the candlelight.

It's the ghost, I thought, although from where I stood in the doorway, she seemed substantial enough, if slightly fuzzy, like an image on a television screen, out of focus while the props on the set came through sharp and clear. I'd always assumed that a denizen of the spirit world would resemble fog or mist with a vaguely human form. Here was a woman who looked as if she were made of flesh and blood, a living and breathing person I could touch or hug.

And I should be afraid of her, but I'm not.

I stood still in the doorway, clutching the vase with both hands, afraid to move lest I cause a disturbance and send the ghost woman away.

But why wasn't I frightened or even startled, when only a few hours ago a momentary glimpse of a face in a mirror had sent me into a full-fledged panic?

Because I'd been expecting her?

Yes, that was it; I knew it now; and I'd yearned to see the Christmas room again.

I didn't know what to do with the vase, only knew that I wanted my hands free. Holiday decorations and novelties filled every available surface. But I could move one of the plates on the mantel, or a sprig of greenery. If I found a place for the flowers, would the ghost woman see this strange new addition to her decor? More to the point, did she see me?

She turned then and glanced toward the doorway, affording me a brief but clear view of her features. I couldn't be certain if this was the face I'd seen in the mirror, but her eyes were blue-green.

She looked right through me as thought I weren't there. As if I were the ghost. Then, with a frown, she turned back to the table.

As if I were the ghost.

The phrase echoed in my mind, and this idea frightened me as the sight of the woman had been unable to do.

Lose that thought, I ordered myself.

Instinctively I touched my own flesh, and felt the familiar pain stab at my right hand. I was real. My dogs and my life and my dreams were real. This woman in the red dress was a lost soul in a lost room.

She must be someone who had lived at Snowhedge in another time, but why had she shown herself to me? There had to be a reason. It couldn't be simply because I made my home here now.

Finally I set the vase on the floor in the corner and watched the woman step back as if to admire her table. Then she sat on the sofa and added cookies from a holiday tin to the server. When the trays overflowed with jewel-iced confections, she moved to the tree where she relocated a tiny pear ornament to a higher branch and fluffed the feathers of a golden swan.

The fuzzy quality I'd noticed earlier was gone now. She was as sharp and clear as any object in the room, as natural looking as Mrs. Tabor had been.

Back on the sofa, she took a thick blue book from the coffee table and leafed through it for a few minutes before closing it with a deep sigh. Still holding the volume, she walked to the window and stared out into the night. Her gait was slow and stiff, as if she hadn't moved in a long time.

She's anxious, I thought. *Restless. Waiting.*

Quietly I stood at her side, resisting an impulse to touch her dress or her arm, even though I knew that she was unaware of my presence.

She pressed her hand to the glass. "Where is he?" Her voice was soft with a melodious timbre and a hint of...rust? "Richard, where are you?"

Out there in the real world, it was snowing. Thick flakes slanted toward the window, obliterating the view of the pond and the hill. But we two were in this warm and Christmas-bright place, brought together by some inexplicable twist in time, untouched by the wintry weather.

Only she didn't know that she wasn't alone, and it seemed that I was wandering through an exceptionally vivid dream.

For the first time since entering the parlor, I realized that I wasn't cold. The fireplace flames sent their warmth out into the air. Real fire threw off real heat that was almost uncomfortable in this small space. I backed up to the round table and listened.

The parlor had come alive with sound. I could hear fire crackling and the clock ticking. Its hands pointed to three-thirty. As I checked the time on my own watch, a chime note rang out.

I had five-thirty, a two hour difference. The times didn't match.

The woman in red continued to move. She glided from the window to one of the gold chairs and back to the window. Then she turned to the tree and moved a tiny red ornament shaped like a horn to a higher branch. I heard the swish of her dress, the jingle of her bracelet, and the delicate ringing of the angel chimes. All happy sounds of life.

I don't want to leave, I thought. *Not now; not until I know who she is and why she's here and what any of this has to do with me.*

The hot breath of the candle flames fell on my hand. Alarmed, I stepped back from the table. This fire could burn.

Somewhere in the room, Christmas music began to play softly. It was an unfamiliar carol with a merry rhythm that created an image of sleigh bells and trotting hoofs on a frosty night.

The ghost woman walked slowly to a small corner table that held a phonograph—the one from the attic?—and turned up the volume. I hadn't noticed it before. Nor had I seen the other painting on the wall, a nostalgic turn-of-the-century print of children feeding a white pony in a spring-flowering meadow.

The parlor was completing itself, more real and enticing at this moment than any other room of Snowhedge. It felt like the one place in the world where I wanted to be. It felt like home.

80

Snowhedge

Now, I thought, *what's going to happen now?*

Chapter 13

I stationed myself at a safe distance from the angel chimes and waited. The ghost woman stood at the bay window, watching the snow fall and scraping at the condensation on the glass with her fingernail, an action that set the silver bells on her bracelet jingling. She didn't speak again.

The book lay on the sofa, apparently not engrossing enough to hold her interest. But it caught mine. It might reveal something about the reader, her taste in literature or perhaps her identity.

Check for a name, I told myself. *Quickly now before she turns around. Quietly, even if she can't see you.*

I leaned over the sofa and read the lettering on the cover. *Gone with the Wind by Margaret Mitchell.* The edition looked new and fresh with a crocheted bookmark tucked in the middle. Holding my breath, I turned to the flyleaf and read an inscription written in a neat, slanting hand:

Merry Christmas to our dear daughter, Evalina, with all our love. Mamma and Dad.

Evalina was her name then—if the owner of the book and the woman were the same person. I shouldn't make this assumption, but I did. It was my only clue.

No—wait! I had another one. Mike had mentioned a writer named Eve or Eva who once lived in Snowhedge. Evalina?

A cold draft passed through the room, causing the candle flames to flicker. I'd better get out of the parlor before some dire cosmic shift brought our two time periods together and allowed the spirit to see me as I saw her.

If that were possible.

I didn't think it was, but an inner voice urged me to hurry back to my own world, back through the door to the safety of the hall before something terrible happened.

The clock chimed four times. As the echoes faded, the phonograph music changed to a discordant arrangement of bells. Suddenly the room seemed to fill with their tinkling, pealing, clanging, and tolling. Their voices came together, magnified many times. They were too loud for human ears, almost painful to hear.

Sound in the parlor was out of control.

Get out! Before it's too late. Don't forget the book! Take it with you.

What would happen if I did? Tampering with an artifact from another time might prove dangerous, and the woman would wonder where it had gone. I imagined her turning around just in time to see her novel floating across the room.

Live dangerously, I told myself. *You're doing it anyway.*

I reached down. As the shadow of my arm fell across the cushion, the book dissolved. The sofa, along with everything around me, vanished completely and without warning as if an invisible hand had swept every piece of furniture, every burning candle and bright ornament, into another dimension, leaving me alone in an empty room.

Disorientated, I groped in mid-air for something to hold onto. An anchor.

Nothing was left in the parlor except the vase of flowers I'd set down in the corner. There wasn't a fragment of log or ash to indicate that a fire had burned in the fireplace only moments ago. The candle wax stain on the floor seemed darker and wider, and the air grew progressively colder. A strong scent of balsam spiced the air, the smell so potent and intrusive that it nauseated me.

I staggered over to the bay window where the ghost had kept her vigil. White condensation crawled up to the panes' halfway point. There wasn't a single scrape in it, no message etched in the frost, no silent cry for help.

Beyond the graceful scrolls, I could see the grounds littered with the last of the autumn leaves, silvered pond water, and dark fir trees clinging to their hill, all washed in a soft, fading light.

There was no snow, not even a lone patch of white on the dull grass.

I slammed the parlor door and rushed across the hall to the living room. Loud clear chimes rang out into the silence. The clock's hands pointed to six. By my watch, it was six o'clock. The Tabors had driven away from Snowhedge at approximately five forty-five.

In the parlor it was four o'clock on an unknown day. Four, according to the same clock hanging on another wall in another time.

Although it seemed much longer, I'd only been away for a short while, observing the woman in red as she fussed with her decorations, scratched at the window, and pondered the whereabouts of a man named Richard.

Questions bounced around in my mind. What man? Was he traveling to Snowhedge for a Christmas party? What had detained him? Had he ever arrived? Most important of all, if the parlor's contents hadn't disappeared, would I have seen a second ghost?

I had to understand what was going on in Snowhedge. I couldn't abandon the house without knowing the phantom woman's story and the reason the parlor kept slipping back in time.

My greatest concern was that in some way the apparition connected to me. That was truly frightening but unlikely. My presence here was random.

I would never have heard of Snowhedge if Larkspur Kennel hadn't burned down—if Valerie hadn't read about the fire in the paper and offered me the job of house sitter.

Every mystery can be solved with the right clues and perseverance, I thought. *And if there's a connection to me embedded in this ghostly happening, I'll find a way to deal with it.*

But all I had was an inscription in a novel that might belong to somebody else. Still, for now I'd assume that the ghost's name was Evalina and that she was the writer who had once lived at Snowhedge. It was a beginning.

A thorough exploration of the attic might yield more information. For instance, that phonograph looked like the one I'd seen stored with the household's castoffs. Perhaps some of the parlor's furniture was there as well, along with old Christmas records.

A song that captured the sound of sleigh bells and an edition of Gone With The Wind, grown old with yellowing pages and packed in a box.

Of course, I was loath to return to the attic. The hall mirror and the dressmaker's dummy were there. The boards were unstable, and the place was as inviting as a crematorium.

No matter. After my latest experience, I had to go back.

I could ask Mike to accompany me, but I'd need to give him a plausible reason.

Like a whimsical desire for a Halloween costume. I could say that I wanted to look for an old-fashioned dress to wear when passing out candy to the neighborhood children. Or I could tell him the truth, which would be better as I didn't like to lie, especially to a man I admired.

Don't you dare!

Evalina was my secret, at least until I knew enough about her to figure out why she haunted the Christmas room at Snowhedge. Besides, if I took Mike into my confidence, he'd most likely think I was unbalanced. On a day like today, I half believed it myself.

The dogs were napping in the kitchen, oblivious of untoward events in their home, which was unusual. Canines were supposed to be aware of supernatural happenings and beings. Mine had let me fend for myself in a haunted room.

I lifted the lid of the teapot. Pale amber liquid lay on a bed of loose leaves. There wasn't enough to bother warming up, but I needed something hot. I should have a sandwich or a bowl of soup. The nausea had begun to recede as soon as I left the parlor. If I felt a little weak now, it was because I hadn't eaten anything since breakfast.

My collie family was fed and resting. Why not slip out to a restaurant? A breath of fresh night air and a chance to mingle with living people would balance an hour with a ghost. Picturing a hearty meal at the Blue Lion and a possible chance encounter with Mike, I almost reached for my purse.

The mere thought of noise and crowds overwhelmed me. In the end, I made a fresh pot of tea and a tuna fish sandwich. I didn't want to go out to eat; I didn't want to go anywhere. If the room materialized and Evalina returned, I needed to be home.

Sitting quietly in the kitchen with my sleeping dogs gave me time to think. I had more than a name in a book. Even without a return visit to the attic, it should be possible to figure out when the parlor had been so elegantly furnished—at least the general time period.

I knew that *Gone with the Wind* had been published in the late 1930's, before World War II, and remained popular to this day. So, any time after that year, a woman might have purchased a copy as a Christmas gift for her daughter.

What about clothing? The hemline of the ghost woman's dress had fallen just below her knees. That eliminated the 1960's with their mini skirts. But when had people set out Swedish angel chimes as holiday decorations and played records? Also, the local paper's archives should have a record of Christmastime snowfall in Maple Creek.

What else?

Multi-colored tree lights larger than the familiar miniature candles and flower petals. Tinsel, so seldom seen today. The release date of the Christmas album, assuming it was in the parlor.

I wished I could have jotted down every telling detail instead of relying on memory.

Romy lay at my feet, her eyes fixed on an uneaten corner of my sandwich.

I poured another cup of tea and saw that the puppies were awake, poking their noses in their empty food dishes and seconds away from whining. Before long, I'd have to wash dishes, take the dogs outside, give them fresh water, and get ready for bed. In about ten minutes.

I was running out of ideas, but my imagination leaped happily into the lull. Where was Evalina now? Did she ever leave the parlor to roam the halls of Snowhedge, wondering why the rooms were so bare and bleak? Did she look out through the windows at a long-vanished snowfall and wish that she could come home to stay?

Stop, I told myself. *You have to sleep here tonight.*

Did she wish that she hadn't ended her life?

I set the cup down with a bang and tossed the sandwich leftovers to Romy and the pups.

Where did that idea come from? The house's previous owner, Lila Rose, was the one who had committed suicide. True, but how did I know that the spirit wasn't Lila Rose?

I didn't. Speculation was pointless. I needed more information about both women. My neighbor, Flora Brine, could provide it, if she would. I especially wanted to know how long Lila Rose had lived at Snowhedge and if she had blue-green eyes.

The next day, the sun hid in a heavy gray sky, and a constant drizzle chilled the air. I felt as if a cloud had settled over Snowhedge, darkening the silent rooms and shadowing my hours. I filled out dog show applications, made countless trips to the parlor, which remained empty, and worked at my laptop, garnering scattered facts from the Internet.

Swedish angel chimes first appeared in 1948. Although some people undoubtedly held on to their hi-fi's, by the 1980's, they could buy CD players. Tinsel still existed, but environments considered it unfriendly; and every year there had been at least a trace of snow in Maple Creek for Christmas.

So anywhere from 1948 to 1980. Select a year, select a decade. And did *When* matter as much as *Who?*

After breakfast, I paid a visit to Flora Brine who promised to come over for lunch on Friday, which was Halloween. Later in the afternoon, Mike appeared. His arrival brought laughter and energy into the quiet house. I realized how much I missed company, specifically the companionship of a handsome blue-eyed man who was comfortable with dogs.

"This place reminds me of a castle," he said, settling into one of the kitchen chairs with an ecstatic Frosty on his lap. "Do you ever get lost in it?"

Yes—in the parlor, I might have said. *I lose myself there.*

"We live here in the kitchen and one bedroom and pretty much ignore the upper stories except on cleaning day," I said.

I glanced at the bouquet in the center of the table. The flowers were orange carnations, white roses, and baby's breath. This room at least was cozy and pleasant, a suitable place to entertain a male friend.

He said, "I noticed the 'For Sale' sign is gone."

"It's in the basement. The Realtor went out of business." I told him about my difficulty in contacting Valerie. "I'm not sure how long I'll stay here."

"What will you do when you leave then?"

"Move on. Somewhere."

"That reminds me. Tag Nolan isn't behind bars like you thought. They released him early, and he dropped off the radar."

His words fell through the air like heavy sharp-edged stones, each one chipping away at my fragile sense of security.

"How could that happen?" I asked.

"Somebody made a mistake. A clerical error."

"Then he could have been at the Blue Lion the other night." I recalled my brief glimpse of the man, his arrogant smile, and his disappearing act. "They have to find him. He needs to serve his time."

I touched Romy's head, searching for comfort and assurance. She whined and licked my hand.

86

"I agree, but he's not on America's Most Wanted List," Mike said.

"Nolan swore he'd get even with me."

"Chances are he won't find out where you're living."

"Maybe he knows already."

"I doubt it, if you haven't seen him around." He glanced out the window where the trees and stream were rapidly vanishing in darkness. "You're too isolated here. Do you have a friend who could stay with you? A roommate?"

"That's not an option," I said. "But I can protect myself. After the trial, I bought a gun. I won't be afraid to use it."

And I kept it in my nightstand, locked in its case, which wouldn't help me if Nolan took me by surprise. Thanks to Mike's news, now the shadow of Tag Nolan hung over Snowhedge. Tag or a ghost? Choose one. Tag *and* a ghost. My life was full these days. It just wasn't giving me what I wanted.

"If you have to move, there's a farm for rent over on Bridge Road," he said. "The house is small, but there's a barn on the property. From the road, they look like they're in good condition, and there are a couple of houses nearby."

"Thanks," I said. "I might look at it."

"You need a lot of outdoor space for all these dogs."

"Especially when the pups grow up."

They were acting like excitable toddlers now, Cindy and Cherie tearing through the first floor rooms, Frosty squirming wildly in Mike's arms, eager to join them.

"Okay, puppy," he said. "Down you go."

He set her on the floor, and she dashed out the door after her sisters. Seizing her chance for one-on-one attention, Romy padded up to him and placed her paw on his leg. Mike smoothed the fur on her head.

"The little ones are usually better behaved," I said. "Company makes them wild."

"Jack's like that." He paused and gave Romy a rough pat. Then he turned to me. "Could I interest you in joining me for a burger and coffee?"

"I'd like that," I said.

"Good. Are you going to let the pups have the run of the house while we're gone?"

"Oh, no. Never. They're going to bed down in the crate. Now you can watch them play a game of *Catch-me-if-you-can*."

We walked out to the hall together. It was long and cool and filled with shadows. There was no sign of the puppies. I called their names and waited.

The parlor door was closed. Just for a moment, I thought I heard a faint tinkling coming from inside.

It couldn't be, I thought. *And I can't check.*

Why not? Then I'd have a witness to the...madness.

Quickly I opened the door. The room was empty.

"Nice fireplace," Mike said. "Do you ever build a fire?"

"No. There's nothing in here. No reason to stay."

From the back of the house, I heard a chorus of yips.

"They come when they're ready," I said, closing the door again. "Mike, after we eat, do you have to go back on duty?"

His quick smile matched the merry glints in his eyes. "Not until morning. Why?"

"Would you go up to the attic with me again?" Abandoning my planned subterfuge, I said, "I need help carrying the boxes down to the room below."

"Sure thing," he said. "I can see why it scares you."

"That's not it. I don't want to trip on one of those boards and fall when no one's around to help me."

"You're right. That's one of the many hazards of living on your own in a rambling old country place." He stood up and reached for my hand. "I wish you didn't have to be alone, Susanna."

Chapter 14

Mike handed me a medium-sized box with the picture of a cookie jar on the side. The jar was inside, a ceramic likeness of a brown bunny with a broken ear. It was useless, unless the missing piece could be found or the next owner didn't mind imperfection.

But somebody had saved it. How could I toss it in the trash?

"That's the last of the boxes," Mike said. "Do you want anything else moved out?"

"Not tonight, and I think I'll leave this one up here."

Setting the bunny box on a small side table, I surveyed the remaining items: Assorted chairs, a loveseat with tattered upholstery, ornate Tiffany lamps, small paintings and prints, a clock radio. The phonograph. It was larger than the one I'd glimpsed in the parlor, with a different shape, rectangular rather than boxy. A label on the glass top identified the model as a Fisher.

I trailed my finger through the thick dust coating the panel. "I wonder if this old relic still works."

"You'll need the right size record to test the sound," he said. "I'll plug it in downstairs. Don't forget the lantern."

I'd left it on the floor. The beam illuminated the lower half of the attic, leaving the rest of the space steeped in darkness. It was late, almost ten o'clock, time to bring the project to an end. Mike had tackled the job with good nature and enthusiasm. Working alone, it would have taken me three times as long, and my only mishap was a snagged fingernail.

As I picked up the lantern, I caught a glimpse of my reflection in the hall mirror. Mike's tall form towered over me, but no stranger's face stared back at us with blue-green eyes. Still I pushed the dressmaker's dummy to one side.

Even as I did so, I realized that there might be no need for this precaution. I didn't feel apprehensive, and it wasn't just because Mike was with me. There was no hint of a Presence in the attic, no sense of anybody watching in the blackness, nothing the least threatening except for the uneven floor boards. This was just a gathering place for old, unwanted furniture. For orphaned things.

That's because you and Mike moved her out. She's in the room below now, hiding among the boxes, exulting in her freedom. Biding her time.

What a gruesome thought! Innocuous though the attic might be, it still set my imagination afire. But that thought didn't make sense. If the spirit walked anywhere, it was in the parlor. She didn't need us to release her.

"What are you going to do with all this stuff?" Mike asked.

"Sort through it. Get rid of the junk. Set aside some for a yard sale. Valerie mentioned once that I could do that, if I wanted to."

"You're looking for something specific," he said. It was a statement, not a question.

"All right. I'm searching for attic treasure. Valerie won't mind, and there's no one else around to object. She never seemed interested in the house. I think she's sorry she bought it."

Mike came down behind me, carrying the phonograph. I closed the door. Now I'd never have to come up here again.

"We could move that furniture down to the other floors and set it up in the emptiest rooms," he said.

"Yes, but another day. Thanks so much for helping me, Mike."

"Sure thing."

"Let's go downstairs now, and I'll get us something cold to drink."

"That sounds good," he said. "Then you can tell me exactly what you're hoping to find."

Back in the kitchen, over beer and pretzels, Mike asked his question again. I couldn't fool an experienced police officer. Neither could I tell him the whole story.

"I want to know more about the people who used to live here," I said. "In particular, the writer. She might have left her papers or books behind."

There. That was true, and I didn't have to include tales of a Christmas ghost on Halloween Eve.

I frowned, remembering the sound of a bell in the parlor earlier this evening. The house seemed even quieter than usual now. All four dogs were asleep in the corner, the puppies snuggled up against Romy. Mike and I were at ease with each other. And I felt guilty. The omission, or, rather, the lie, had come too easily to me.

"That makes sense, if you're not too busy," Mike said.

"With this job I have nothing but time."

"Then you may want to spend some of it with me."

I took a deep breath. "What did you have in mind?"

"A movie. Dinner. Something simple."

"I'd like that," I said.

Apparently Mike intended for our friendship to continue. But deception could doom a relationship. In some cases, so could truth:

This house is haunted, Mike. Sometimes, when I open the parlor door, I step into another time. A ghost is there. She's waiting for someone...

Snowhedge

I said, "I'll be looking forward to it."

"Next Thursday around six then?"

"Perfect."

We sat quietly together. I couldn't think of anything relevant or even frivolous to add. Finally Mike set his empty bottle on the counter. The clock chimed eleven times.

"I'd better go home and get some sleep," he said.

"It's been a long day."

He drew me into his arms and kissed me once gently, then deeply and thoroughly. I tightened my arms around his shoulders, let his warmth and the scent of his woodsy aftershave envelop me. For the first time in months, for a fraction of a moment, I felt safe and—almost—cherished.

"I'll see you soon, Susanna," he said.

He *did* want more than a goodnight kiss. Of course. That was why he'd been so generous with his time and help. Where is the man who does mundane tasks for a woman with no thought of recompense?

But what did *I* want? At this point, I wasn't sure.

Once again I was entertaining company in the blue Victorian. This time my guest was Flora Brine, and my goal was clear. I hoped she'd tell me whatever she knew about the two previous ladies of Snowhedge. So far, we'd talked about her vegetable garden, the old phonograph from the attic, and my collies who lay in a cozy group, keeping the spread on the table under surveillance.

I'd taken a quick trip to the deli in town and assembled a lunch of rotisserie chicken and pasta salad. Those were Amy's favorite foods, I realized now. When we'd traveled to out-of-town shows, we always bought take-out and ate our dinner in Amy's van, tossing bits to the collies.

The warm cloverleaf rolls and lemon squares were my choices, together with the peppermint iced tea. Flora had brought a jar of her homemade corn relish as her contribution to the meal. There was no need to remember Amy Brackett today or any day.

Flora stirred a spoonful of sugar in her second glass of tea. "This is such a cheery kitchen, Susanna. I love yellow walls with white curtains."

Her long fringed shawl, a soft daffodil shade, complemented her silvery blonde hair and the décor. Light and cheer surrounded me, but the view through the window was dreary with an overcast sky threatening rain. Lovely, gloomy Halloween weather.

"Somebody else chose the colors," I said. "All I added were the flowers."

They were fading, the petals of the pink sweetheart roses limp, their stems bending forward. Last night, when I'd sat here with Mike, they'd been fresh. Bouquets had a short life span in this house, which was puzzling as they had an abundance of fresh water and a cool temperature.

91

Dorothy Bodoin

"I'm so glad the place is off the market," Flora said. "You'll stay longer then."

"Or I'll leave sooner than expected. It's all up to the owner, and she's on an extended vacation."

In some secret place, I thought. I couldn't believe that Valerie still hadn't gotten in touch with me. Didn't she want to protect her investment?

"It's going to be nice to have a neighbor close by, especially in the winter," Flora said. "With all the snow we get in these parts, I feel like I'm in a box."

I leaped into the opening she provided. "Weren't you friendly with the lady who used to live here?"

"Lila Rose. Ah, yes. She wasn't the most sociable person in the world. When she moved in, I came over to welcome her to the neighborhood. We had a pleasant visit, and for a while, I thought we were going to be friends. As the years passed, I seldom saw her. She lived indoors, even on the nicest summer days."

"Do you remember what she looked like? The color of her hair? Her eyes?"

Flora stared at me. "Why would you want to know something like that?"

"I saw an image of a woman in a white dress the other day. She had beautiful blue-green eyes. They reminded me of turquoise jewelry."

"An image. You mean a picture?"

"Yes."

I felt my face grow warm at the lie, felt that Flora knew what I'd really seen and the reason for my curiosity. But how could she? To cover the awkward pause, I passed her the dessert plate. "Have another lemon square."

"Thanks. I will." She transferred half a piece to her plate and picked up her fork. "Her hair was gray. She had brown eyes—like yours. It's funny you mentioned turquoise jewelry. Lila Rose used to wear a pendant with a large bluish green stone and matching earrings."

"Did she live at Snowhedge long?"

"Around ten years. She bought the place, planning to turn it into a bed-and-breakfast, but that never happened.

Then Lila Rose couldn't have been the spirit, come back to relive a Christmas holiday from a long-ago time. Unless she'd purchased her old family homestead. But that was grasping at the proverbial straw.

"Did you know the woman who lived at Snowhedge before her?" I asked. "The writer?"

"That would be Evalina Allencourt," she said. "I've heard of her, but she was before my time. She wrote children's books, as I recall."

Allencourt! Armed with a surname, I could research the Snowhedge author. Surely her work must still be available, in the nearby Foxglove Corners Public Library or even on E-bay.

I'll find you, I thought. *I'll find the answers too.*

92

"This house was built for a large family, but it attracts single women," Flora said. "Isn't that strange?"

"Maybe the new people will have children."

"A whole passel of youngsters. Yes. Why are you so interested in all this, Susanna?"

I had an answer prepared. "The past fascinates me. I like antiques and old documents. I'll probably never have a chance to live in an historic house again."

"Not many people do, but it must be lonely for you out here in the country."

"I have my dogs—and a boyfriend," I said. "He's a state trooper. We met when he gave me a ticket."

"How unusual—but nice."

"I agree." A memory of Mike's kisses flickered in my mind. Very, very nice indeed. "Besides, I can't live in town with four dogs."

"No, I guess you can't," Flora said. "These little cakes are delicious. Did you bake them?

"They're from the bakery on Main."

"Oh. I was going to ask for the recipe..."

She trailed off and grew still. Her head tilted to one side, she appeared to be listening to an errant sound.

I was the one who heard invisible bells ringing in the house. At present the only noise was the hum of the refrigerator fan. Flora's hand appeared to have frozen in mid-air, and the color had drained out of her face.

"Is anything wrong?" I asked.

She set the fork down and with swift, deft movements arranged the daffodil shawl more closely around her shoulders.

I added, "Should I turn up the heat?"

"No—no, it's fine. I hate to eat and run, but that's what I'm going to do."

She got up quickly, grabbing her purse that she'd left on the counter, fumbling inside, taking out a key. Romy raised her head, her gaze on the uneaten portion of lemon square on Flora's plate.

"Would you like something else for dessert? A Halloween cupcake?"

"I just remembered I have something to do." She didn't quite meet my eyes. "Thanks for lunch, Susanna. Next time it'll be my treat, and we can go to a restaurant. Have you been to the Blue Lion yet?"

"A few times," I said.

She was already in the hall, walking briskly to the door, neatly avoiding the puppies who had sprung awake and were trying to nip at her shoelaces. A second later, she was outside on the porch, moving as if she couldn't leave enough distance between herself and Snowhedge. The ends of her shawl flapped madly in the wind.

"Goodbye," I called after her. "Thanks for coming."

She didn't look back. I closed the door and stood in the hall for a moment, feeling as if I'd been caught up in a gale.

I'd never been an accomplished hostess, but usually I kept my company interested longer than this. Had my not-so-subtle interrogation chased Flora away or something else? Something wrong at Snowhedge that I hadn't discovered yet? A sound I hadn't heard?

Here's another mystery, I thought. *Just what I don't need.*

With Flora's departure, the dogs retreated to the kitchen, and the house sank back into its accustomed silent state. I walked across the hall and opened the parlor door, listening for the faint ringing of a bell or muted holiday music. I fully expected to see remembered furnishings and festive decorations. Myriads of candles burning, lights twinkling amidst fir branches, and flames leaping in the fireplace. Christmas joy and a spirit dressed in bright red for the holiday.

A blast of cold air rushed out at me, almost knocking me off balance.

Nothing was there. Only the garish wax stain, white-frosted windowpanes, and a scent of balsam dancing lightly on the air. The flowers I'd left on the mantel were in no better shape than the kitchen bouquet. But wait!

I stood on the threshold, shivering and listening. Was that a soft swish at the window? A sigh? Footsteps passing so close to me that the unseen walker might have been trespassing in my space?

Was she here?

"Evalina?" I whispered and waited.

I could hear the refrigerator fan's hum and the puppies growling in their play and the first splatterings of raindrops on the windows. In the empty, dead room, there wasn't a sound.

I was alone. The spirit would come back again in her own time, and eventually reveal her reason for haunting the parlor.

"Rest in peace." I said the words aloud.

As they faded, I heard a muffled sob.

Chapter 15

I stood in the doorway waiting for the furnishings and Christmas decorations to materialize. Nothing happened.

Outside, a rain-hail mix pelted the windowpanes. Inside the parlor, the silence was deep and definite, but I was almost certain I'd heard a sob, cut off abruptly, swallowed by the still, cold air. Was the spirit trying to break through to my world?

I could think of other explanations for the sound: Wind wailing through the rain or a bird trapped in the chimney. One of the puppies might have wandered back into the hall and uttered a faint whimper before scampering off in another direction. There was also my wild imagination.

But I wanted the cry to have come from Evalina's throat; I wanted to see her again. Sound without sight and dimension added up to a major step backwards.

There was nothing to hear now. I waited a few more minutes but then closed the door and walked back to the kitchen. Phantoms adhere to their timetable, and I had lunch dishes to wash.

As I mixed leftover chicken into the dogs' dinner bowls, my thoughts stayed with Evalina. It wasn't surprising that a displaced soul would grieve, finding herself adrift in a world to which she no longer belonged. But what drew her to the parlor? What specifically made her weep in a bright, festive room where even a spirit should be happy?

If I knew the answers to those questions, possibly I could help her. That was what she wanted of me; that was why she tempted me with enchanting visions of Christmas Past.

Susanna Kentwood, house sitter, collie exhibitor, ghost comforter.

Just for a moment, I imagined that the parlor and everything in it belonged to me. That glorious balsam fir was my own. Those delicate glass ornaments that sparkled at the tree lights' touch were my prized possessions.

Through the bay windows, through frosty scrolls, I watched for Mike to arrive. He was going to celebrate the holiday with me. We would open our presents and drink eggnog on the old rose sofa. We'd exchange a hundred kisses while the fireplace flames sent their wondrous warmth through the room, and I'd never let him go.

No, not Mike, I thought. *Someone else. The man from Evalina's time. She's the one waiting. Not me.*

After washing the dishes, I climbed up to the third story and began a slow, systematic search of the Snowhedge papers. Many of the boxes were labeled and identified as the property of Lila Rose.

Cards, Records of Household Expenses, Paperbacks, Recipes, Patterns, Sketches. I set out to sort through mounds of memorabilia, making snap decisions about another woman's belongings because no one else had done this for her.

Much of the material could be discarded. Receipts and calendars from every year of the past decade, for example. Recipes for desserts on stained index cards. Other items like an old-fashioned sewing basket crammed with spools of thread and used patterns could be sold at a yard sale or donated to a women's shelter.

It seemed strange that Lila Rose would store recipes and sewing supplies in the attic, unless she was anticipating the end of her life. I couldn't know. Quite possibly she had simply lost interest in baking and dressmaking.

A box marked 'Miscellaneous' contained a hodgepodge of broken items. A small heart shelf with a missing screw; a blue and white teapot without a lid; a wooden Christmas goose planter in five separate pieces that could easily be glued back together. Another held old issues of dog-eared gardening magazines and one of those popular Anything books used for journaling. Finally. Something interesting.

Its smudged cover was decorated with sprays of rainbow-colored daisies. As I turned the pages, my hopes for a significant discovery faded. Instead of reflections or revelations, I found descriptions of the flora and fauna native to Maple Creek and day-by-day ramblings of a woman living a quiet life in the country.

Still, I set the book aside for further examination on another day. My eyes were itching, and my hands felt rough from handling so much paper. I needed to check on the dogs. They'd been too quiet which meant they were sleeping or getting into mischief. At any rate, I'd have to take them outside soon.

With a backward glance at the unopened boxes, I left the room. I had only one slight accomplishment to show for almost two hours of work, but tomorrow when I resumed my search, I might find another older journal, this one kept by Evalina Allencourt.

As I reached the first floor, I heard a series of rippling notes coming from the bedroom. There was nothing ghostly about this sound. Someone was calling me on my cell phone, the first time anyone had done so since I'd moved to Snowhedge. Only a few people knew my number. It had to be Mike, or Valerie responding to my many messages.

I followed the sound to the dresser and answered before the recorded message started.

"Hi, Susanna."

Slow, burning anger spread through me as I recognized Amy's voice, the last one I expected to hear. For a second, I considered hitting the 'End' button and throwing the phone in a drawer. I didn't want to deal with Amy; we had nothing to say to each other. Still, I was moderately curious, and if I didn't talk to her now, she'd only call again. She could be persistent.

"Susanna? Are you there?"

"Yes," I said.

"How—how have you been?"

Loud music played in the background above the hum of talking. Amy was in a public place, most likely a restaurant. She never phoned anyone when she was at home.

"I'm good," I said. "Busy. How's Frost?"

"Beautiful as ever. He's making a name for himself in Agility and having loads of fun."

He had been our dog. I should know this.

I could see her tanned hand gripping the phone and the circlet of tiny diamonds she always wore. It was her grandmother's engagement ring, Amy's twenty-first birthday present. The diamonds had sparkled as she stroked Romy's black fur. They'd flashed like lightning when she struck my world a death blow.

"Why are you calling, Amy?" I didn't care how rude that sounded. I owed her nothing, not even a minute of my time. Certainly not courtesy, although my mother's views on ladylike behavior were never far away. Then she'd never had an Amy in her life.

"I need a favor," Amy said.

Bitter memories paraded through my mind. Preston snatched away from me when I wasn't looking. My exquisite Frost stolen. My reputation in ruins. How dare this lying viper approach me for anything?

"And you're asking *me*?"

"We were friends for a long time," she reminded me. "Best friends."

"That isn't true anymore."

"I know, but there's a problem. Could you meet me for a drink? I want to run something by you. It's important," she added.

"Tell me now."

"I don't want to. Not on the phone."

In the pause that followed, the music swelled, louder, more intrusive than before. Amy's voice took on the strident tone she resorted to when she was nervous.

"Susanna, are you still there?"

"Yes. I don't know what you need, but you've come to the wrong person."

"Please. Hear me out." She lowered her voice. "It's about Tag Nolan."

My heartbeat quickened. "What about him?"

"He means to harm us."

"That isn't news."

"I think he already has."

She had my attention now. With my thoughts and energies centered on the haunted parlor and past times, I'd relegated the Tag situation to the back of my mind, which could be a serious mistake.

"All right," I said. "I'll make time for one drink. One hour. No more. When?"

"How about tonight?"

It was still raining and almost six o'clock. I'd have to come home to Snowhedge after dark...drive on wet country roads...leave the dogs alone...possibly miss Evalina's next appearance.

Well, why postpone the encounter? What if Amy's information really was important? On the other hand, I didn't trust her. Should I take the chance?

Yes. I'd meet her and hear what she had to say. Then I'd be finished with her finally. Forever.

"I'll come pick you up," she said. "Where are you living now?"

I sidestepped her question. "Name the place and time, and I'll be there."

"Whatever you like. There's a tavern called the Cauldron on Spruce Road. Say around six."

Was there a more perfect place to meet a witch on a night when tricksters plied their trade? The idea that Amy had concocted some vile new plan took hold.

But she sounded sincere. Still, how could I tell on the phone?

You're forewarned. Just beware.

"It's in Foxglove Corners," she added.

"I'll find it, but don't you think a place called the Cauldron will be packed on Halloween?"

"I'm sure it will, and that's good."

I could hear the relief in her voice and something else that I couldn't identify, something that bothered me. But I'd just given my word. Unlike Amy, I didn't break promises.

"Thanks, Susanna," she said. "Now it's going to be all right."

The Cauldron was a spooky old tavern set so far back from the road that I could hardly see its sign. I found one of the last available parking places in the unpaved lot and walked quickly up to the door through wind and rain, wishing with every step that I was at Snowhedge sitting in front of the electric fireplace.

Pushing back my hood, I opened the door to find myself face to face with a tall wood-cut witch strategically placed in the entrance. She had thin, sharp features, straggly green hair, and a malevolent yellow-eyed glare. At her feet an enormous black cauldron filled to the top with a dark liquid bubbled madly away. Her bony fingers clenched a long metal spoon as if she meant to squeeze it into powder.

Welcome to the witch's house, I thought.

I took a few steps and stood at the bar, scanning the crowd. The lighting was dim, the country music annoying, and the crowd boisterous, which was exactly what I'd expect to find in this spooky dive. Now where was Amy?

We saw each other at the same moment. She sat alone at a small table toward the back. As I walked over to join her, I was struck by a subtle change in her appearance. She seemed thinner than she'd been at the Apple Fair, her hair was lighter, and her tan had gone with the summer sun. Amy seemed a pale copy of her former self.

Was she ill? If she was, would I care?

"Susanna, I'm so glad you made it," she said. "Sit down. What would you like to drink?"

"Sparkling water."

Amy still wore her heirloom diamond, and she was dressed in black, a color she'd never cared for. In honor of Halloween, I imagined. She held her beer in a death grip, reminding me of the wood-cut witch with her spoon.

I unbuttoned my coat but left it on; I wouldn't be here long.

"Did you have trouble finding the place?" she asked.

"I just kept driving north on Spruce Road. Now, what's wrong? You said Tag Nolan had done something."

She pushed the bottle aside and twirled a strand of her blonde hair around her finger, a nervous habit she had been trying to break for as long as I'd known her.

"Do you remember at the trial—when Nolan threatened to get even with us?"

"How could I ever forget that?"

His fury had landed squarely on me, or so I'd believed, while Amy had tried desperately to make herself invisible. He blamed both of us for his downfall, but I happened to be sitting closer to him.

"He's been stalking me," she said. "I see him everywhere I go. At the dog shows, the stores, my favorite restaurants, on the street...at least I think I have."

"You're not sure?"

"It's just that he comes and goes so quickly. How can I be?"

I caught her surreptitious glance at the crowd. Tonight's clientele was predominantly male, and a few men hid their features behind grotesque masks. Nolan could easily be sitting at one of the tables or lurking in the shadows.

"I'm so afraid all the time," she said.

"Did you report this to the police?" I asked.

"Yes, but nobody knows where he's staying. They can't do anything until he makes a move. He's going to do something terrible to me."

"I don't know what to tell you except to buy a gun. I have one."

"Oh, I couldn't. I'm too afraid of guns."

"Then that isn't a good idea," I said. "Unless you're prepared to pull the trigger."

"There's more. This came in the mail yesterday." She pulled a paper out of her purse and handed it to me. "I know Nolan sent it."

Follow the fire. The three words, written in pencil, covered the entire sheet.

"This doesn't make sense," I said. "Why would you follow a fire?"

"It's a warning."

"You could read it that way. It *is* creepy, but consider the source."

"Have you seen him since the trial?" she asked.

"Once. I thought I did. Then when I followed him, he wasn't there."

"That's it!" she cried. "It's what he does. He shows himself and vanishes. It's some kind of weird game. What are we going to do? Wait until he kills us?"

"This is a matter for the law," I said. "I assumed that Nolan was all talk, that he wasn't really out for revenge."

"Look how he burned down the kennel," she said. "He's capable of anything."

I stared at her. Had she forgotten her claim that I'd set the fire? I had been too stunned and hurt to confront her. Maybe it was time I did.

"How does that jibe with the rumor you started about *me* being the arsonist?" I asked.

She looked away and twirled another strand of hair. "I never said that."

"Someone did, and people believed it."

"I swear it wasn't me. I stood up for you. That's what friends do."

So she was going to deny it, and I didn't believe her. There was no point in further discussion. My grievance and her treachery didn't have anything to do with our present problem.

"Getting back to Nolan, can't Preston protect you?" I asked.

"He isn't with me all the time," she said. "Anyway, we're breaking up."

"Oh…" I knew I was being unkind but couldn't stop myself. "You have Frost."

"I'm afraid for Frost. Nolan might try to get to me through him."

Oh, no!

Romy and my puppies might be at risk, too, all of us targeted by a psychotic man with a sizeable grudge.

"Again, Amy, I don't know what to tell you," I said. "Just be aware of your surroundings at all times. Nolan's release was a mistake. I'm sure the police will catch him eventually."

But he was clever and elusive with an uncanny ability to melt into a crowd. If Amy had communicated her uncertainty about her stalker, she couldn't hope for official help. She was right to be terrified.

"I just wanted to warn you," she said. "In case he comes after you."

"Well thanks for that."

"How are Romy and the puppies?" she asked.

"We're all fine."

I shifted in my chair, my unease about my canine family growing. No one had appeared to take my order, but I realized that it didn't matter. I didn't want to stay in this place with the noise and blaring music and the threat that seemed to wait in its dark corners. Then, apparently Amy wanted to restore our friendship. I didn't.

She might have lost her hold on Preston, but she still had Frost. And, even if I wished to, how could I ever forgive her for ripping my reputation to shreds? In spite of what she said, she was guilty; I didn't doubt it.

"It's pouring out," Amy said. "I hate this miserable Michigan weather."

"You always did." I buttoned my coat, noticing the sheen of rainwater on my sleeves. I hadn't been inside long enough for the material to dry. "I'd better head home. Take care, Amy."

That was all I could offer her.

Chapter 16

Leaving the Cauldron wasn't so easy.

I fought my way through a nightmare explosion of laughter, tipsy shouting, and loud, eerie music. The short distance to the door seemed interminable. At every step I encountered a human obstacle holding a drink, carrying a tray, or simply standing in the aisle blocking my escape route.

While Amy and I had been talking, the crowd had doubled in size. Bodies in grotesque costumes, faces hiding behind masks—they overwhelmed me.

So many people crammed into this small space surely constituted a fire hazard. Smoke filled the air. From cigarettes or candles? In the dim lighting, I couldn't tell. Probably cigarettes. It didn't matter. Either one could be lethal.

Mixed scents of aftershave, perfume, sweat, and beer took on a life of their own. I felt as if I were being pushed backward, felt the first stirrings of panic and a familiar pain jab at my right hand.

"Don't fear the reaper," sang the voice in the juke box.

And don't overreact, I ordered myself. *It's Fright Night at the local tavern.*

How many more steps to the wood-cut witch? How many to the door? I had to get out of here!

As I passed the bar, a voluptuous Marie Antoinette wearing an elaborate white wig and black mask turned around suddenly. Her drink spilled out of her glass. Red liquid splashed down my raincoat, and a shower of chipped ice landed on my shoe.

"Oh, sorry," she said with a giggle. "It's just a little rum. Here..." She grabbed a napkin and waved it in my face.

Biting back an angry retort, I said, "It'll dry. Eventually."

I turned away, but she took my arm. "Let me pay for the cleaning. If you'll give me your name..."

"Don't worry about it."

"Please. Wait."

Ignoring her plea, I made my escape, past the wood-cut witch, out of the door and into the night.

Thank God.

I pulled my keys out of my shoulder bag, ready for the quickest getaway in the history of the Cauldron. Cold rain pounded me as I sprinted down the lot, praying that no one was following me. The wind pushed me across wet gravel, past a cruising minivan. The driver, a chunky man in a skeleton costume, called out, "You leavin', miss?" I kept moving.

Here was my car! At last!

Once inside, I locked the door, started the engine, and drove out to the road. The worst was over. I might be soaked with rum and rainwater, but I was safe.

My headlights cut through the darkness, chopped into the irrational terror that had gripped me. The windshield wipers swished back and forth in a soothing rhythm. The numbers on the speedometer climbed steadily. Every mile brought me closer to home.

No one was behind me; no one in front; and although Amy had stoked my apprehension about Tag Nolan's intentions toward us, he couldn't possibly know where I lived now.

I had cautioned Amy to be aware of her surroundings. I'd do the same. Amy would have been easy to track down. She hadn't moved from the tiny house she'd rented after the fire, and her frequent presence at dog shows made her a visible target for a stalker.

Stop thinking about Tag. He doesn't know where to find you.

What if he had followed Amy to the Cauldron? Even more frightening, what if she had arranged to meet me at that strange and sinister place, hoping that Tag would be there, that he'd transfer his attention to me? Amy could be devious. But Tag intended to get even with both of us.

Don't borrow trouble, I told myself.

Still, from time to time I glanced in the rearview mirror. A truck followed me now, too closely and coming closer. He wanted to pass on this treacherous stretch of wet, curving roadway. I slowed down and caught a glimpse of a woman behind the wheel as the vehicle sailed by.

In about forty-five minutes I should reach Snowhedge where the first floor lights would be on, my dogs were waiting to greet me, and the parlor—I hoped—was empty.

Only, is escape ever that easy? A macabre thought slipped into my mind, a nagging fear that I'd picked up a deadly germ in Amy's unwholesome tavern of choice. Perhaps something brewing in the witch's cauldron had attached itself to me and burrowed beneath my skin. Like all germs it would ferment deep inside and ultimately strike a fatal blow when I least expected an attack.

Nonsense nonsense nonsense.

This was one of my more bizarre fancies, tailor-made for a night of trickery and evil.

But I couldn't rid myself of it.

The next morning, I turned the calendar to a new page. The first of November, All Saints Day. We were in a brand new month, but rain still fell from a low, swollen sky, and a trace of the unease that had begun last night remained with me.

I wished I could live through my meeting with Amy again. I should have stayed at the Cauldron a little longer, ordered a drink, and quizzed her about my other grievances, the theft of Preston and Frost.

Preston she could explain away. His interest in me had died. It wasn't in her nature to deny a handsome, available man. Why should she? In her place, I'd do the same. Or so she'd say. But Amy had stolen my share of our valuable dog. She had usurped his love and loyalty and kept him from me. That betrayal would always separate us, an insurmountable barrier to reconciliation.

Yes I should have made her talk about Frost and why she had written only her name on his papers, knowing that I trusted her and would never think to check them.

Well, it was too late for regrets. I was back at Snowhedge eating breakfast with my collies who crunched their biscuits with vigor and hoped for handouts from my plate. Tag Nolan was nowhere in sight, bygones were bygones, and I had a ghost to find.

Lila Rose's journal lay on the table where I'd left it yesterday. I poured a second cup of coffee and opened it, intending to skim through the book before resuming my search of the boxes from the attic.

She had dated the entries and recorded the main events of her days, including weather trivia, dinner menus, and new purchases. Then I came to several blank pages. When the writing resumed, the dates disappeared, and the ink was black rather than blue. I was looking at a long narrative with letters clumsily formed, at times almost scribbled. It had a title: *What Happened at Snowhedge*.

Hoping that I was about to make a significant discovery, I took a long sip of coffee and read on.

Right from the start, I knew there was something funny about the parlor. It's a good fifteen degrees cooler than the other rooms on this floor, and the windows are always frosted over.

When I mentioned the problem to the Realtor, she had no explanation for it. She suggested that when I built a fire, the room would be all warm and cozy. She was wrong.

No fire could generate enough heat to make the parlor comfortable. Even after I added a space heater, it stayed cold. It had a mind of its own. I know how crazy that sounds, but it's true.

It was an unhappy, lonely room. With beautiful bay windows and a picture postcard view, it should have been the most desirable part of the house, but whenever I crossed the threshold, I had to force myself to go farther. Something didn't want me in there.

I began to wonder if this had been the scene of a tragic occurrence in the past. Often, when I stood quietly in the doorway, a feeling of depression settled over me. That was puzzling. I had no reason to be unhappy. I was living in my dream house, soon to be a thriving bed-and-breakfast. My life had never been happier. Why did I feel like crying?

Depression doesn't need a reason. Sometimes it just appears, but as it only came upon me in the parlor, I didn't think I had a chemical imbalance or some other disorder that could be treated. The problem was this room, and the obvious solution was to stay out of it, but first I set out to change the ambience.

I painted the walls a lovely shade of lavender. Then I added my favorite colors. Yellow and pink pillows on the love seat, a rose crocheted afghan, and a green Tiffany-style lamp. I lit candles and brought in flowers. It didn't work. Nothing felt right.

The room was rejecting my possessions along with me.

I wondered how the former owners had managed. Maybe they'd kept the parlor primarily as a showroom or didn't mind sitting in an ice box. But when I opened the house to my future guests, no one would want to spend time in here.

In the first months, I experimented with different furniture and arrangements, tried three separate window treatments, and finally gave up. The house had plenty of other rooms. Only this one disappointed me.

So I wouldn't use it. I swept the fireplace clean, unplugged the heater, and scraped the frost off the windowpanes one last time. I closed the door and put the cold, inhospitable parlor out of my mind.

Then the voices came.

I heard them late one afternoon, as I was waking up from a nap, a constant conversational buzz, interspersed with bursts of laughter. At first I assumed they were part of a dream, but I kept hearing them even after I was awake and out of bed. I thought they originated on the first floor, directly under my bedroom. That was the parlor.

Suspecting that a group of ne'er-do-wells had broken into my house, I stood at the head of the staircase and listened, trying to summon the courage to confront them. It seemed that several people were talking at once, the way they would at a small social gathering. I could hear tones but couldn't make out words. The sounds faded and rose, soft, seductive voices, calling me to join their company. But by the time I reached the parlor, nobody was there.

The room looked the same as always, stylish and attractive with the color scheme I'd chosen but uninviting. There wasn't a thing out of place and no invisible revelers in sight. I couldn't hear anything now except ordinary household hums and creaks.

In the end, I decided that the voices were in my mind. How my so-called friends would laugh if they knew that dull, self-effacing Lila Rose was so desperate for company she had to make up an entire party. No one could ever know about this.

As it turned out, it wasn't a one-time happening. I heard them again and again, countless times over the years, disembodied voices in an empty room, always muted; the words indistinct.

One time only I was able to make out what they were saying. To the best of my recollection, this was the gist of the conversation:

"They're such a lovely couple, don't you think?"

"Who? Eve and Richard?"

"No, Juliette and Richard. Juliette is the girl for him."

"My money's on Eve."

"So is hers."

"I hear there's a storm moving in. I want to be out of here before it hits."

"No, stay. We'll ride it out together. It'll be fun."

It was like eavesdropping on actors rehearsing their lines. Taken out of context, the exchange didn't make sense. I always hoped to hear more about the people, but all further dialogue was unintelligible.

These days I hardly notice the voices. They're as unobtrusive as the wind blowing through the leaves. It's a comforting sound that makes me feel a little less alone. They come and go and mean me no harm.

I've accepted the fact that a gathering of ghosts assembles in the parlor at random times of the day or night. I don't understand how or why. It isn't necessary that I do. I only know that I live in harmony with spirits and that my love for the house grows stronger every year. I'm glad I bought it, and I'm never going to leave.

I keep the door closed and rarely look inside. When I do, everything is the way I left it so long ago. Frost covers the windows in all seasons, and layers of dust lie on the furniture. The colors of my pillows and afghan, once so bright and new, have faded. I don't go in there anymore, not even to clean. It isn't that I'm afraid. I just respect the room's desire to be left alone.

I never found the people. After all these years, I don't think I will, but whenever I hear muffled talking and laughter coming from the front of the house, I always hurry to the parlor, in the hope that just once I'll get there in time to see them.

"Oh, no, don't stop now!"

My voice sounded unfamiliar in the silent room, high and demanding. Romy opened her eyes and promptly closed them again. I flipped through the rest of the book, searching for more writing, but the remaining pages were blank. Lila Rose had ended her story and added a new element to the strange occurrences at Snowhedge. The disembodied voices. In her words, the invisible revelers.

If only we had been able to compare notes.

She had noted the unnatural cold in the room and the frosty windows but not the scent of balsam. She didn't mention a red candle wax stain on the floor. I tried to visualize her furnishings, but I all I saw were an old rose sofa in front of the fireplace, the gold chairs, the round table, and the decorated balsam fir.

My Christmas room.

With a heavy sigh, I closed the journal and set it back on the counter. I had many more questions now. For instance, why had Lila Rose never followed through with her plan to turn Snowhedge into a bed-and-breakfast? Was it because of the ghost voices?

They would have been an added attraction.

Calling all ghost catchers and lovers of the unknown! Spend your vacation at Snowhedge. If you're lucky, you'll hear the phantom party in the parlor!

Or because she wanted to keep her supernatural experience to herself?

She had looked forward to hearing voices. To her, they were like the wind.

It was blowing now. The wind was a constant presence in this part of the state, sometimes so powerful you couldn't walk or drive safely in the wild gusts.

Maybe all Lila Rose had ever heard was the wind.

But then what of the dialogue she'd recorded? Had she created it out of whole cloth? The talk of romantic parings? Eve, who had to be Evalina, and Richard, the name Evalina had uttered the one time I'd heard her speak.

Not likely.

Lila Rose wanted to hear the voices. According to Flora, she wasn't very sociable. Snowhedge was isolated. A quiet, introverted person could get lost in the rooms of the blue Victorian.

And I? Was I in any danger of losing myself in this house?

I didn't think so. We were different women. I had a life—in shambles. My teaching career was stalled, my reputation in the collie Fancy in transition. I had Mike. Maybe. You can never be certain about a man. Maybe I should be lonely, but I wasn't. I'd never describe myself as dull and self-effacing. I had, above all, curiosity, a quality Lila Rose apparently lacked.

My fascination with the unusual happenings at Snowhedge was completely normal. As soon as I knew Evalina's story, I would be satisfied, and, in the near future I'd be leaving Snowhedge. I couldn't possibly come to harm.

The dogs were still staring at me. They could smell the leftover toast on my plate. Four pieces. I set one in each eager mouth, keeping my fingers out of the way of sharp little puppy teeth as my mind teemed with plans for the day.

I'd look through the boxes, just in case Lila Rose had written more about the haunting in a different journal, but there were other, more efficient ways to track down the previous inhabitants of Snowhedge and learn its history.

Evalina, I thought, *it's time I find you.*

Chapter 17

My second search of the boxes from the attic yielded more of Lila Rose's belongings but nothing significant. Her books were mostly paperback romances and historicals with copyrights dating back to the 1980's. There were no other journals or diaries, and I didn't find the edition of *Gone with the Wind* that I'd seen in the parlor the day the ghost woman had appeared.

Lila Rose's account of the voices might be all I'd ever have.

After sorting through every piece of memorabilia, I ventured up to the attic to make one last sweep of the furniture.

Weak light filtered in through the ventilation slats, giving birth to shadows that lay still on the uneven floor. The deep silence magnified my every breath and footfall, and dust particles stuck to my skin.

Casting off a vague feeling of apprehension, I examined each item thoroughly, even the framed prints and lamps. Among the discarded furniture, there were no secret compartments or drawers. The chairs and tables were simply tired, threadbare antiques, all fodder for an estate sale or bonfire.

Finally I turned to an old steamer trunk with a scarred blue surface, my last hope for a major find. Setting the lantern flashlight on the floor, I opened the lid. A pungent odor of mothballs drifted out into the stale air. Blankets, well-worn sheets, tablecloths, and scarves with delicate lace edges lay in neat stacks beneath an empty top tray.

At the bottom, folded in half and serving as a liner, I saw a crocheted throw in a pattern of raised pink roses. If this was the afghan Lila Rose had described, she must have taken the parlor apart before her death, or at least removed the accessories, contrary to what she'd written in her journal.

That was all. How strange that none of Evalina Allencourt's possessions remained at Snowhedge. On second thought, maybe not. When Evalina left the house, she would have taken them with her, or they'd been cleared out before the sale. Only her spirit stayed behind.

I set the afghan aside, intending to use it in the living room. The bedding could be washed and donated to a shelter, and lovers of fine linens would be certain to snap up the scarves. Even the trunk in its distressed state might have value to someone.

Now I was through with this unpleasant place. As I reached for the lantern, my gaze lingered on the hall mirror. Like everything else stored in the attic, it needed a thorough cleaning, but why bother? With that disfiguring mark across the surface, no one would be likely to buy it.

But when it was new and unmarred, it would have been a handsome piece, a place to check your appearance before going out—to make sure every hair was where it belonged and not an inch of slip showed.

Flawed or not, I could use that mirror downstairs.

In the split second before I turned away, a face appeared in the cloudy glass. Behind the scratch, I had a fleeing glimpse of blue-green eyes and a neck swathed in turquoise material. Just for an instant. Then it disappeared.

It's not a face. It's only...

My heart pounding, I checked the position of the dressmaker's dummy, still wearing its scarf and pins. It was where I'd left it. From there the mirror couldn't possibly reflect its image. I hadn't seen an inanimate contraption made of cloth and metal. Something else, rather, someone else, had materialized behind me in that brief moment.

Evalina?

Who else but the Snowhedge spirit reminding me not to forget her.

I touched the glass. It was ice-cold and gritty. I stared at the dust coating my fingertips and my own face, framed with tumbling dark hair, eyes glazed with fear. The scratch on the surface created the appearance of a gash across my throat.

There's nothing there now. She's gone. Where?

Not here. I was alone with the shadows.

I'd once sworn never to come up to the attic again. Why remember this only now? With no reason to stay, I scrambled down the staircase and slammed the door, leaning against it, letting my breathing slow to a normal rate. The terror that had closed around my heart slowly loosened its grip.

The next time, don't forget. This whole floor is off limits. Keep hanging out in shadowy places, and who knows what will happen?

Putting a little distance, only a dozen steps, between myself and the attic gave me a chance to reflect on my most recent scare. If Evalina's possessions were gone from this section of the house, why would her face appear in the mirror? Good question. It didn't make sense. Nothing about the strangeness at Snowhedge made sense.

But perhaps the mirror had been left behind in the house when ownership of Snowhedge had passed to Lila Rose. On the other hand, what difference would the presence of Evalina's belongings make? Did ghosts care about books and candles and jewelry? I didn't know, but I was going to examine the mirror again, thoroughly, some day when I felt brave enough.

You just said you weren't going up to the attic again.

But if I wanted answers, I might not have a choice.

In the first floor bathroom, I soaped my hands thoroughly and rinsed off the dust. Illogically, with the attic door closed, I felt safe, but I wasn't. Not in this house; not until I learned its secrets.

Perhaps not even then.

My next project was to search for a biography of Evalina Allencourt on the Internet. Before settling down with my laptop, I needed sunlight and fresh air, and the dogs had to be exercised. We spent the next hour outside, walking on the lane, where we chanced upon Flora Brine raking leaves out of her flowerbed.

She appeared anxious to avoid us and immune to the friendly overtures of the puppies. After a few minutes of weather conversation, she made an excuse to go back inside and tend to the pot of stew she'd left cooking on the stove.

Why, I wondered, when she had been so friendly on our previous visits?

I called to my collie family and moved back to the pond where Romy and two of the pups jumped in the water for a quick bath. Cindy stayed close to me, whining and wagging her tail.

I scooped her up. "Don't you want to get wet, baby?"

She spun around in my arms and licked my face.

The other canines had the right idea. We had Mother Nature's swimming pool in our own front yard. In the winter, we'd have a private skating rink at the foot of Balsam Hill.

In Valerie's yard, I amended. And we won't be here when the water freezes.

Every now and then I tended to forget, just for a moment, that Snowhedge wasn't my home. It was Valerie's property, forever languishing in limbo while I tried to locate her.

But in truth I hadn't done that recently. I'd let myself drift into limbo, too, so preoccupied with the mysteries of Snowhedge that for long blocks of time I didn't remember that soon I might have to pack and move. If Tag Nolan ever found me. Or if Valerie returned and decided that she no longer needed a house sitter.

I glanced at the road. No cars were passing at the moment. Traffic was light in this area, at times non-existent, and the lane was dark and quiet. The houses were built far apart from one another, discouraging casual visiting. The only neighbor I'd met was Flora.

From here, I could barely see through the line of trees that formed a natural barrier between the blue Victorian and Flora's farm. The desolation of my surroundings communicated danger. No one would be around to hear my scream as a vengeful assassin crept out of the dark woods.

I had Romy, of course. My precious puppies could make plenty of noise, but they were too young and small to mount an adequate defense. And Nolan might shoot them.

"Romy," I called, hearing the fear in my voice. "Cherie! Frosty!"

They came, shaking water from their coats into the air. Their fur was soaked and limp. Cindy wriggled frantically in my arms, anxious to join them on the ground.

"Time to go back," I said.

Finding Evalina Allencourt in cyberspace proved to be easy. I should have typed her name into the Google search engine as soon as I knew it. Quickly I scanned the brief biographical paragraph, jotting down salient details. In the end, the facts were skimpy, and the three other articles I discovered contained variations of the same material. None contained the author's picture.

Evalina Allencourt (1930-1995) Michigan author of several short stories and books for young girls. Best known for her prize-winning short story, "Across the Pond" written at the age of seventeen. Miss Allencourt's books were popular in the 1950's through the 1970's. Among her works are Northwoods Summer, Memory's Island, and the Jessie and Joss series. She died in a boating accident on Lake Huron in August, 1995.

Evalina was definitely dead, then. Not that I'd ever doubted it.

I copied the accompanying bibliography, then searched the Out of Print sections of online bookstores. In the end I found three used books and ordered them. Armed with a list of Evalina's books, I could also peruse local bookstores, and libraries, if they existed. I could even look for her grave, assuming she'd been buried in the Maple Creek cemetery.

Not today though. While chasing phantoms, I'd lost track of time and my own life. It was Thursday, and Mike and I had a date. I fed the dogs early and took a long time getting ready, first relaxing in a bubble bath, then curling my hair, finally standing in front of the closet, trying to decide what to wear. By the time I had fully assembled myself, I had only a half hour to wait for Mike.

As I checked my appearance in the small bathroom mirror, I wondered what I'd see if I peered into that other one—in the attic.

A slender brunette in a black dress whose crystal chandelier earrings glittered in the dim light. And behind her, a face with blue-green eyes and a turquoise scarf draped around her neck?

Why couldn't I stop thinking about Evalina, even now when I was practically on my way out the door en route to a good time?

How I wished I could tell Mike every strange thing that had happened to me in the blue Victorian.

I could—if I wanted to see him back away from me. And he'd surely do that. Most likely I would react the same way if he told me an improbable tale about furnishings that appeared and disappeared at will. About a stranger's face in the mirror and a ghost in the parlor.

If Mike and I were going to build a relationship, our mutual attraction wasn't enough. We had to know each other. So if I wanted that connection—and I thought I did—at some point, I'd have to tell him the truth. All of it.

Maybe I would some day.

Maybe not.

I traced a shimmer of gloss across my lips and pushed my hair back so that my earrings could sparkle freely.

The clock chimed six times.

At the knock on the door, all four dogs came to life in a frenzy of barking and graceful movement. My time for aimless pondering had run out.

Mike had made a reservation for us at the Heidelberg Inn, an upscale German restaurant several miles north of Maple Creek. He must intend to make this night memorable, or we'd be having the evening's special at the Blue Lion.

As we drove down a quiet country road under a luminous full moon, I considered the pros and cons of taking Mike into my confidence about the Snowhedge secrets. I'd choose my words with care and, of course, wouldn't reveal everything.

First I'd tell him about Lila Rose's narrative.

I was reading that old journal we found in the attic the other day. The woman who kept it wrote about hearing voices in the house off and on through the years. One time she was able to make out what they were saying.

This revelation would segue smoothly into a discussion about the other world. Mike might remember that Lila Rose had been a possible suicide. Were these the ramblings of an unbalanced woman, or could there be a sliver of truth in her story?

Tonight, at the evening's end, I'd invite him in for a drink, take him to the parlor, and ask him if he had any idea why this room was so much colder than the rest of the house.

I might call his attention to the scent of balsam and the mysterious red stain on the floor. If our spirit-themed conversation went well, I'd tell him about the strange mirror with a surface so scratched and cloudy that sometimes another face appeared in the glass behind my own reflection.

Or was that was going a bit too far?

I'd better save the haunted mirror for another discussion. The last thing I wanted was for Mike to think I was eccentric or, worse, delusional.

The Heidelberg Inn was a picturesque fairy-tale cottage that captured the charm of old Bavaria. With its soft cream color and peaked red roof, it reminded me of an illustration in a fairy tale book. From the car we could hear the haunting strains of *Die Lorelei* floating out into the crisp night air. Who could resist the siren lure of that melody?

Mike had chosen a perfect place for our date. He took my hand, and I felt the threats of Snowhedge slip away. Suddenly the future looked promising. As we stepped inside, brightness and color surrounded us. Could romance be far behind?

"It's like we landed in the middle of the Black Forest," I said.

"That's the effect the owners want."

While Mike checked on our reservation, I looked around, mesmerized by the fanciful décor. A wraparound ledge showcased a collection of beer steins, and dozens of cuckoo clocks hung on the walls. They all appeared to be different. On some, birds perched on flowering boughs with nests of eggs. Others were more elaborate, adorned with majestic stag heads, hares, and playful forest creatures.

"There are an even hundred of them," Mike said, as we settled into our table. "We'll never lose track of time here."

"They're so beautiful."

"And they last forever," he added. "Some day I'm going to buy myself one."

"Everything looks like it came right out of a storybook," I said.

Especially the centerpiece in the middle of the table.

It was a large mushroom candle with a red and white speckled cap. The flame flickered softly, creating warmth and ambience, doing no harm. Still, I looked away. A faint draft wrapped around my arms.

Mike blew the fire out. "You don't need any reminders," he told me.

"Thank you," I said. "I keep running into candles. Everybody decorates with them."

He nodded. "It's hard to get over a fear of fire once you've had a bad experience."

"I'm trying."

I covered my right hand with my left. At present, I felt fine, but the pain might appear at any minute. I didn't want to feel anything now except the emotions Mike had kindled. I stole a glance at him. He looked so handsome tonight, so powerful and right for me, that I abandoned my plan of opening the ghost talk with a reference to the journal.

"I seem to be afraid of so many things these days," I said.

"That Nolan creep?"

"And the house I'm living in. Sometimes. Every now and then, something happens to spook me. Other times, I think of it as home. I'm ambivalent."

"Backtrack," he said. "What happens to spook you?"

I took a deep breath and told him about the face in the mirror, all the time wishing that I hadn't started down this dangerous path. But, having begun, I couldn't stop myself.

"At first I thought it was the dressmaker's dummy. Now I know it's something else."

"I'd start to see faces in a mirror myself if I lived alone in that gloomy old house," he said.

I smiled. "I don't believe that, Mike."

"What else happened?"

"I learned something interesting in that journal we found."

He listened intently as I summarized Lila Rose's account of the Snowhedge voices. I searched his face for a hint of disbelief but found only concern. Could he possibly believe me?

"I haven't heard them," I said. "But the parlor is unnaturally cold. It's impossible to heat. One day a candle wax stain appeared on the floor. I can't get rid of it. Once a little green star made of foil fell out of nowhere. And..."

My voice froze in mid-babble.

"What else?" he demanded.

I couldn't tell him about furnishings and Christmas decorations that came and went or that I'd seen Evalina Allencourt in spirit form. I simply couldn't go that far. Even though he appeared to take me seriously. Even though he could be my ally and possibly so much more.

A dull pain slashed its way across my knuckles. It felt as if someone had whacked a ruler across them. Or like the mushroom candle flame had sprung to life again and singed my hand.

"Old houses are full of odd sounds," I said. "But house sitting is my job. I can't let a little Gothic atmosphere intimidate me."

He looked at me for what seemed like a long time. At last he said, "If that's all it is. I think you should get out of there, Susanna."

Chapter 18

Like a fall of heavy rocks, Mike's words reverberated in my consciousness, drowning out the dulcet strains of "Edelweiss." I should never have mentioned the face in the mirror.

"That's what I'm going to do—soon," I said.

"The sooner the better."

"What's the rush?"

"That house isn't healthy for you," he said. "There's something unwholesome about it. I wish I could be more specific, but it's just a gut feeling."

"Well, it is full of atmosphere and mostly empty…"

"And it was on the market for months before your relative bought it as an investment. No one wanted to live there."

"Or nobody could pay the high asking price."

"Whatever the reason, it's still strange."

Everything Mike said was true. Nothing would make me happier than to drive away from Snowhedge in the near future, but if I didn't solve the mystery of the parlor first, Evalina Allencourt would haunt me for the rest of my life. Wherever I went, I suspected her spirit would follow.

"I entered the dogs in a show on Thanksgiving weekend," I said. "Moving now would be a bother."

He fixed me with a steely official look. "Is that your only reason for procrastinating?"

How could I dodge his question? "I'll admit I'm curious. I'd like to know what's going on there. Remember, the owner is somewhere in Florida, and I haven't been able to contact her. I can't leave without letting her know."

"In the meantime, you're on your own in an isolated house with no way to defend yourself if this Nolan character tracks you down."

"I have a gun."

"You might not get a chance to use it."

That was the police officer talking. But he was right. Again.

"Tag Nolan *is* a legitimate threat," I said. "My former partner claims that he's stalking her. I haven't seen him yet, unless he was in the restaurant that night, but I'm not letting my guard down."

"You say *claims*?"

"I don't know if Amy is telling the truth." I fidgeted with my napkin. The status quo was easier to deal with than the unknown. If I could just hold out until after the dog show. That would give me time to solve the mystery. "I'm going to find another place to live," I added. "But my situation is complicated."

"It's funny that this woman dumped the house on you and took off," he said. "Then the Realtor went out of business. Something isn't right."

A fair Alpine maid in traditional Bavarian dress handed us our menus. With a smile as bright as her long blonde braids, she said, "Tonight's specials are Wiener schnitzel and Sauerbraten. Would you like something to drink now?"

"I'll have the house beer," Mike said. "Susanna?"

"Just coffee. Thanks."

I scanned the menu, quickly discovering my favorites: Strudel, apple cinnamon streusel, and Black Forest torte. I'd do well to order a simple, light entrée and a fabulous dessert. But where would I find light and simple in the Heidelberg Inn? Potato pancakes, warm potato salad, potato dumplings, sausage? Ah, here was something promising.

"I'm going to order the mixed grill," I said. "That'll be a little bit of everything and leftovers for the dogs."

"I'll have Weiner schnitzel. My grandma used to make it."

"What a coincidence! So did mine."

Mike closed his menu and gave me a long look. "I'm not telling you what to do, Susanna. That's for you to decide. I just don't want anything to happen to you."

"Nothing will, if I can help it."

Because a phantom face couldn't step out of a mirror, and a spirit couldn't do me physical harm. Balsam scent and bells and green stars were lovely, innocuous things. Even candle wax was harmless—for someone who had never been burned. What was I missing? Just Tag Nolan. Always Tag Nolan, the man responsible for the Larkspur fire.

"Don't forget, the last owner might have committed suicide," Mike said.

"So they say, but not because of the house."

"We don't know that. It might have had an adverse affect on her."

"When she bought the place, she planned to turn it into a bed and breakfast."

"But she never did."

"I guess it proved to be too great an undertaking for a woman alone. All those rooms and space and the voices."

"That's what I meant," Mike said. "The place is downright unwholesome."

I agreed with him, but in this enchanted German inn, Lila Rose's frame of mind and her choices seemed far away. I wanted to forget about Snowhedge and mysteries for just a few hours. We needed a change in subject.

Davey's new puppy, I thought. *The dog show. Beer steins. The gnomes on the ledge. Scary grotesque little creatures. Maybe not gnomes.*

I avoided looking at their wrinkled faces and wicked eyes, gazed at Mike instead, and wondered what he was thinking. I was fortunate to have found him when I moved to this backwater town in the heart of nowhere.

Actually, he had found me—speeding on a country road, rushing home to Romy, convinced that she was in danger. Only she wasn't. Not that day.

Reality whispered a quiet warning in my ear. At present, I was a long way from Snowhedge, and I'd left my dogs there alone. I couldn't afford to forget that, not even for a minute. And once and for all, Snowhedge wasn't home.

Keep it in the back of your mind then. Keep Mike in front. Hold on to tonight's enchantment. Tomorrow all of this will be a memory.

The Alpine maid brought our beverages. A hundred tiny cuckoos sang out the hour. As the last notes faded, a rousing selection from *The Student Prince* blended into a hundred music-box tunes. I could almost believe that outside the window the river Rhine shimmered under a full moon and *die Lorelei* waited on the rocks to cast their spell on us.

Mike reached across the table to take my hand, the left one that had never felt the fire. "If we come back here some weekend night, we can dance to a live band."

"I'd love that," I said, imagining myself in his arms, gliding across the floor to a romantic German air. "Thank you for finding this place and bringing me here."

"I aim to please, ma'am," he said with a sly wink. "And I think that's our dinner coming."

I let Snowhedge recede a little farther back in my mind. We would be turning off Balsam Lane soon enough, and the old blue Victorian would be waiting for me at the end of the driveway.

I closed the massive front door behind us and bestowed a reunion pat on each of the four excited canines dancing around us in the hall.

"You have an enthusiastic welcoming committee." Mike said.

Frosty tugged on his trouser leg. With a laugh, he hoisted her up and spun her around. "Little fluff ball." He set Frosty down, and Cherie nipped at her tail.

"They're just happy to see the doggy bag," I said.

I set it on the table, along with my evening purse, and turned out the overhead light. In the other rooms on this floor, lamps burned brightly. Still, the long hall had a dim, forbidding look, and the uppermost stairs disappeared in heavy blackness. As they always did.

"I'm running up Valerie's electric bill, but I can't stay here at night in the dark," I said.

"She wouldn't expect you to. As an extra precaution, you should leave the porch lamp on."

"I will. I do."

And a night light in my bedroom, I might have added, with the lantern flashlight in quick grabbing distance. No matter how bright the moonlight, I needed these added measures of security.

Mike tightened his arms around my waist, trapping me in the shadow of the hall table. He brought his mouth down on mine in a crushing, thorough kiss.

I'd been waiting for this moment, longing to be closer to Mike, but before I could fully respond, an alien feeling of wrongness came out of nowhere. It thickened in the air between us like a cold mist forming.

I felt as if someone were watching me, not quite approving of this wanton display of affection in her home. No, that wasn't quite right. The emotions were stronger, almost primitive. The unseen watcher was envious, wracked with regret and angry, about to push Mike out of my arms.

He belongs to me!

I didn't know who had formed the thought or where it came from. It was loud and startling, like a sudden thunderclap in a cloudless blue sky.

I kissed him again, let my hands rest on his chest and wander up to his neck, longing to be nearer still, to let this kiss be the first of many.

This is my life. My man. My time. Go away.

Those surely were my sentiments. The clock in the living room struck eleven. The echoes of its chimes died in the silence, and I felt the cold mist dissipating. Whatever strange thing had happened here was over.

Mike still held me close. Romy had her front paws on the table, nudging the bag with her long nose. The puppies whimpered, keeping sharp eagle eyes on their treasure. Life in the present, my time, went on.

Determined to engage the alien presence on my own terms, I said, "Will you step into my parlor, Mike?"

"The haunted room?"

"I didn't say that. It's just the scariest part of the house. The place where Lila Rose's voices originated."

I opened the door, as always wondering what waited on the other side. Waves of cold air rolled out, with a scent of balsam in their wake. The room was empty and dark except for stray beams from the porch lamp breaking through the frosty windows.

I turned on the overhead light. "What do you think?"

He surveyed the silent expanse as if it were a crime scene. "It's cold in here all right. Could this be an addition? I have one built onto my kitchen. It's always cooler than the rest of the house."

"Looking at the floor plan, I wouldn't think so. There's no problem with the heat in the living room. That's on the opposite side of the hall."

"There has to be a rational explanation."

"You'd think so, but I can't come up with one."

"Someone installed a fireplace to do what the furnace couldn't?"

I walked over to the mantel where the green star lay next to an empty vase.

"This fell out of the thin air," I said.

"Are you sure about that?"

He took the star from me, let it lie in his palm, and turned it over. It was a tiny bit of shining foil, nothing more. How could I convince him that it had simply materialized?

"I heard a sound, a ping, and saw it lying at my feet," I said.

"Without being there, I can't explain where it came from. The bell is easier. Could you have heard something outside? Like wind chimes?"

"Possibly. My neighbor has wind chimes on her porch, but that's a long way for a sound to carry. What about the wax stain? I'll swear it wasn't there when I first moved in. At first I thought someone had been walking in the house with a candle."

"Again, I don't know, and I don't like anything about this." He set the star back on the mantel. "Have you seen any other signs of an intruder?"

"None."

"It sounds like somebody's trying to scare you."

"Not Tag. That isn't his style. He'd just pounce. I think." I had one last question. "Do you smell anything?"

"Your perfume." He pulled me close and buried his face in my hair. "It smells like flowers."

"Something else. Over here."

I took his hand and led him to the windows. Rich balsam fragrance surrounded us, conjuring memories of Evalina's Christmas tree. How could he not be aware of it?

"I just smell flowers," Mike said. "Roses or lilies."

What more could I say? "My imagination tends to run amok in this room."

After a moment, he said, "Let's have a look at that mirror."

I thought about the shadows on the landing. Up two flights of stairs to the second scariest part of the house? Did I want to do that tonight?

"It's still in the attic," I said. "Could we wait for another day? It's getting late."

"Then how about us finding a warmer room? I'm ready for that nightcap you promised me."

I closed the door and stood at his side in the hall, grateful for the mild air outside the parlor, trying not to be disappointed that our investigation had fizzled.

The dogs followed us into the kitchen, Romy whining and the puppies doing their best to trip me. I focused on what I had on hand to serve Mike. More beer. Cider. Chips. Everyday hostess matters were so much simpler than ghostly concerns.

I'd hoped that Mike would sense something off in the parlor and have a fresh perspective, but the house wasn't going to cooperate. The room wouldn't deck itself with boughs of holly as long as Mike was on the premises. There would be no stars falling through the air, no bells ringing, no new stains appearing on the floor.

For some unfathomable reason, those phenomena were reserved for me. Lucky me.

It was late when Mike left, almost two o'clock. The dogs had long since gone to sleep. So had the house. It was quiet and dark and, in this room, reasonably warm. I lay in bed, turning from one side to another, too wired to relax, marveling at the difference Mike's presence had made. Nothing untoward was going to happen tonight.

He was a bastion of practicality, an admirable Devil's Advocate, even when he couldn't give me the answers I wanted so desperately. But then, I'd expected too much of him. He didn't have all the facts. I'd withheld the most important one of all.

In spite of our new intimacy, he'd never believe me if I told him that the cold, empty parlor had the power to transform itself into a Christmas room from another time. He'd be convinced that it was too late for precautions, that the house had stolen my sanity. Anyone would think that. Only I knew the truth, and after tonight, I knew something more.

Evalina was aware of my existence. Her feelings lived on with her, and she begrudged me my happiness with Mike.

What could I do with that knowledge?

Nothing tonight. Everything tomorrow.

I closed my eyes, letting my mind take me back to the Heidelberg Inn. I longed to hold on to every precious second and aspect of my night with Mike. If I concentrated, if I tried really hard, I could bring them back.

Eventually they came, all the music and romance and moonlight and kisses, blending with a Black Forest torte that danced in a nonsensical mix of images.

As I drifted off to sleep, I heard a muffled ringing.

Chapter 19

When I awoke the next morning, something in my immediate environment was different. An incredible brightness flooded the room.

Ghosts, I thought. *Death?*

Raising myself up on my elbow, I focused on the intense light streaming through the window across the room.

Last night I had forgotten to pull down the shades. While I slept, a surprise snowfall had draped the world in white magic. Snow-coated branches sparkled in the sunlight, and the sky was pale and clear. It was daytime. Ten-thirty by the alarm.

Everything changes. The weather, the seasons, my situation. Mike is in my life now.

I'd slept later than usual, which hardly mattered as I didn't have any place to be. Only Snowhedge, and I was here.

I lay back against the pillows, yielding to a rare moment of self-pity. Instead of living in a haunted mansion, I should have a proper job and a nondescript house. One story, average-sized rooms with comfortable new furniture, and no phantom hovering in the wings. A place where I could sleep for six or eight hours without nightmares.

Soon. I promised Mike. I meant it.

Moments ago, I'd been floating through a dream version of the Heidelberg Inn, looking for my Student Prince. He had left me stranded on the dance floor in the middle of *die Lorelei.* I couldn't dance alone, and I couldn't find him. Dark-robed strangers crowded around me, jabbering in a harsh foreign language and raising their beer steins high in the air.

Listen to the bells, whispered a voice. *Follow them. Follow the fire.*

That ghastly scenario had been generated by heavy German food and inspired by the fears that shadowed my waking hours. But a nightmare couldn't sustain itself on a glorious, shining morning like this.

Listen to the bells...

The house was quiet, except for incessant whining coming from the kitchen. Romy and the puppies. My four reasons to get up.

Shivering in the waiting chill, I swung my legs over the edge of the bed, found my slippers, and remembered.

Last night I'd heard a bell ringing in the house. Was it part of a dream or another aspect of the Snowhedge haunting? Or perhaps nothing more than the protests of Cindy's squeak toy as she dragged it from room to room? Not that the little yellow chick sounded like a bell, but I had been on the verge of falling asleep and could have been mistaken.

Always the Devil's Advocate. Ever the shadow of a doubt. All those clichés. But I *had* heard an unexplained ringing on a previous occasion, before I'd bought the toys for the puppies.

There was only one way to find out what lay beyond the parlor door. Although I'd rather lie under my warm comforter and relive last night's date with Mike, I had to know whether or not the Christmas room had returned.

Throwing on my robe, I wandered out to the hall where the dogs waited to go outside.

"One minute," I told them. "Just one minute", and I placed my hand on the parlor's door knob, steeling myself to turn it. One heartbeat passed; then I did.

The room was cold and empty. There was the red candle wax stain in the middle of the floor. The green star on the mantel beside the vase. A snowy landscape framed by frost-edged bay windows The balsam scent, lighter than it had been last night, but still there. The status quo.

"We're okay," I said.

Closing one door, I opened another and watched the dogs dash down the porch steps into the snow. They tore around in crazed circles, chasing one another. At my third call, they came bounding back, bringing in a wet mess on their paws and shaking madly.

Now I could fix breakfast and start the day in a normal way. Who knew how it would end?

In the kitchen sink, I found the glass that Mike had used and pressed it to my lips, a sentimental schoolgirl gesture that Susanna Kentwood had never made before. Not even as a teen. Smiling at my foolishness, I filled it with orange juice.

He'll be back. He'll touch another glass or plate.

Now, tea. Toast. Strawberry jam. Milk-Bone biscuits and fresh water for the dogs. I assembled our food mechanically and let my mind create a mental plan for the day. First go grocery shopping; then stop at the nearest library. Find out the location of the town cemetery. Maybe haul that mirror down from the attic and let the sunshine burn the spookiness out of it.

That should take two or three hours at the most.

As I opened the breadbox, I spied the blinking light of the answering machine on the counter.

When did I get a call? And why didn't I hear the phone ringing?

You did. Last night. Rather, early this morning. One mystery solved.

I pressed the "New" button and listened to a voice I hardly recognized, for I hadn't heard it in weeks.

Hi Susanna. It's Valerie Lansing. Sorry I missed you. Sorry I've been out of touch. Just sorry. You know how it is. You're doing a great job with the house.

Hold down the fort a little longer. I'm flying home, and we'll get together and figure out our next move. See you then.

I replayed Valerie's message. There had to be more. After all this time, couldn't she have provided details? But that was the only call ever recorded on my watch, a series of terse sentences followed by silence.

If Valerie was still in Florida, how could she know what kind of job I was doing at Snowhedge? When was she coming home? By 'our next move' did she mean hiring a new Realtor or asking me to stay on as house sitter? Or perhaps firing me? And why place a call in the middle of the night unless she hoped I wouldn't hear the phone ringing?

How odd. No, how like her.

Incidentally, how much, if anything, would I tell her about the spirit who haunted Snowhedge?

Nothing. I'd do the asking. Valerie owed me answers.

I filled the teakettle with cold water and dropped two pieces of bread in the toaster, conscious of the minutes racing by. Possibly I had less time than I thought to solve the Snowhedge mystery. Now housekeeping chores would interfere with my sleuthing.

I'd better swing through the rooms with mop and duster, buy fresh bouquets, and start simmering potpourri on the stove again. Visits to the library and cemetery could wait for another day.

Everything changes, I thought.

Whether Valerie's visit would be good or bad for me gave rise to another concern. In case I had to leave the house in a hurry, I should search the classified ads for a house to rent and, incidentally, a job. I'd better check out the farm Mike had mentioned.

Suddenly I remembered Valerie's grudging allowance of only one dog in her house and no puppies. That was one more problem to deal with.

But I wouldn't move my babies again. If they were banished from Snowhedge, we'd all go together. All the more reason to develop a hasty Plan B.

The morning which had begun in boredom was rapidly filling up with matters that required prompt action.

By noon the snow began to melt. The branches lost their white covering, and the sparkle vanished under an overcast sky. Then the temperatures fell, and the winds picked up. Change trembled in the air.

As I unloaded grocery bags, I surveyed the exterior of the house with distaste. My outside decorations had gone from splendid to seedy. Cornstalks had shed, and the chrysanthemum plants were dying. The pumpkins had fallen prey to a scavenging wild creature who devoured huge chunks of pulp and left orange innards and seeds strewn about underfoot. Only the harvest wreath held on to its freshness.

I'd leave it up until Thanksgiving. Everything else had to go.

Whipping the house into shape seemed like a gargantuan task, but soon I had the porch swept free of snow and the tired Halloween adornments carried out to the roadside for pick-up. With its soft blue color and traces of snow caught in the hedge, the old Victorian still presented a handsome face to the world. Valerie would be pleased.

I devoted the rest of the afternoon to shopping and cleaning the inside. By dinnertime, the rooms looked as appealing as they were going to. The entire first floor smelled of apple pies baking, and fresh bouquets formed brilliant touches of autumn color in the hallway, living room, dining room— and in the parlor.

The owner was on her way home, Snowhedge was ready for inspection, and I was eager to move on to another activity.

At six-thirty, I fed the dogs, made a turkey sandwich, and sat down at the kitchen table with the *Free Press* and the *Maple Creek Tribune*. As I separated the sections, looking for the classifieds, I skimmed over the headlines. One short article on the front page of the *Tribune* caught my attention:

Forced Off Road, Woman Dies in Crash

A Macomb Township woman died when her car slid into a ditch, rolled, smashed into a tree, and caught fire on Fox Road in Lapeer County early this morning. Amy Brackett, twenty-nine, died en route to the hospital. Witnesses claim that a dark blue Buick forced her off the road and sped away. Anyone with information is asked to contact the sheriff's department.

I stared at the name in disbelief. Was the dead woman *my* Amy Brackett or another twenty-nine year old female Macomb resident with the same name?

It had to be Amy. I felt it. The letters blurred, as my eyes filled with tears. I touched the print, willing it to go away.

Not Amy, please!

A dizzying array of emotions crashed together in my mind. Once again, I scoured a message, looking for more, finding nothing beyond the stark facts of another fatal hit-and-run accident, probably a case of road rage. Unfortunately, they were all too common, but this one was different.

The victim had been my good friend for years. My partner.

Be honest. Toward the end, you hated her.

Yes, after a stunning series of betrayals, Amy had become my enemy.

The last time you met, you were barely civil to her.

She had warned me about Tag Nolan. I'd doubted her sincerity and couldn't get away fast enough.

What if Tag is stalking Amy? Let her take care of herself. That's what I have to do. I'm safe enough at Snowhedge. He'll never find me there.

124

I couldn't deny those hateful, self-centered thoughts, or the red-hot anger that had lived in me all these months.

My feelings were justified. Anyone would have empathized with me. But Death made all the difference. It was sudden, unfeeling, and definite. Death didn't allow time for mending fences or reconciliation. It was quite simply an end.

'Never hold onto a grudge', my mother used to say. 'Some day it will be too late to make peace.'

But you never believe that day will come.

My tears fell on the paper, smearing the type.

One by one, images of Amy and our shared lives formed in my mind. Her diamond ring sparkling as she moved a brush through Frost's thick coat. Her grief when our first litter died. Her proud smile as she showed off Blue Frost's trophies. Her laughter as she followed the dogs around with one of her many cameras trying to take the perfect photograph.

Plans and dreams and adventures in far-off places when we traveled to the shows. Amy in a hundred different moods and poses, always with a collie at her side.

We had been best friends.

I cried for words unsaid and opportunities lost. I'd never been able to understand why Amy had turned on me. Now I never would.

Romy laid her head in my lap and whined softly.

"Amy's gone," I said.

If only I'd known that Halloween night at the Cauldron would be the last time I'd ever see her, I would have...

What? Stayed with her a little longer? Demanded to know why she had stolen Frost? Cleared the air? Offered to help her?

Probably not. My hurt had been too deep. Besides, no one can undo past actions. What were the saddest words in the English language? *It might have been?*

She was so afraid of Tag Nolan.

A heavy coldness settled over me. Tag had done this. What kind of car did he drive? The red truck he'd had when I'd first seen him or a blue Buick? I didn't know. But of course, the driver was Tag, catching up with his nemesis on a country road, trying to make his vengeance look like an accident.

One score settled. One more to go.

Where would I be when he found me?

My sense of safety at Snowhedge began to evaporate. I felt it slipping away and longed to gather my beloved canines around me and move the gun to the kitchen counter, next to the answering machine. Wherever I was at the moment.

Would that help?

Not if Tag forced me off the road some evening or broke through my bedroom window while I was sleeping.

I imagined each of the scenarios in lurid detail. Terror and blood and fire.

Amy's car had burst into flames after impact. She'd received a note that upset her. From Tag, she thought. *Follow the fire.* Had Tag intended her to die that way?

The pain was back in my right hand. I let it rest on Romy's head, drawing warmth and comfort from her. Somehow I had to get a handle on my fear.

Mike might know more about the crash investigation than the *Tribune* reporter. He'd planned to stop over tonight. We could talk then.

"Oh Romy," I whispered. "What are we going to do?"

I glanced at my sandwich, surprised to find it was still on the plate, not surprised that I was no longer hungry. Tearing it into pieces, I tossed it to the dogs. I had to eat something eventually. Just not this minute.

Instead, I searched through the papers, looking for the Obituaries. Amy's name wasn't there yet.

My need to talk to someone close to Amy overwhelmed me. Her parents were still living. She had an older sister, Beth. They knew about our estrangement and undoubtedly sided with her. Then there was Preston, although she'd claimed they were breaking up. I didn't want to talk to him.

Except...there was Frost. What would happen to him? Was there a chance I could have him back? I had to find out.

Everyone in the collie Fancy, our friends and acquaintances, must have heard about the tragedy by now. Marsha Vernon was kind and discrete. She'd know what arrangements Amy's family had made for her burial. Quite possibly she would also know about Frost. I fumbled in my purse for my address book.

Taking action helped. Forgiveness helped. I needed to forgive Amy, for how can you harbor ill feelings toward the dead? And I needed to forgive myself.

I intended to go to Amy's funeral, even if no one wanted me there.

"I'm so sorry, Amy," I said.

But there was no one to hear me except the dogs.

Chapter 20

Once I knew what my immediate future held, I longed for Amy's burial to be over and the familiar rhythm of life at Snowhedge to return. I wanted to give my full attention to Valerie's visit, my developing relationship with Mike, and getting the dogs ready for the coming show.

That might be disrespectful, but, like all of my feelings about Amy, it was sincere.

As much as I wanted to say a final goodbye to her and leave our acrimony in the past where it now belonged, I dreaded the inevitable ritual.

Mourners in black, the nauseating scent of too-sweet flowers, somber music, prayers for the dead. *The priest and the bell and the holy well.* All of it.

I didn't like going to funerals. Who did? Does anyone appreciate a reminder of his own mortality? *Rest in peace* was an admirable sentiment, but it shouldn't apply to a young, vibrant woman.

Automatically, I rubbed my right hand, wondering when it had stopped hurting.

Amy must have been horribly burned in the crash. There would be a closed casket blanketed with white roses and a framed photograph of her on an easel. When I left the cemetery, Amy would be on her way to becoming part of the earth, and I would be alive, nourished and blessed by the sun. For as long as Tag Nolan chose to let me live.

No! I couldn't let that be Tag Nolan's choice. Because I was forewarned and forearmed, there was still a chance for me.

If only that were true for Amy. I grieved anew that once I'd wished her ill.

But not dead. Never dead. I only wanted vindication and justice, my share of Blue Frost back, and Amy relocated to some far distant corner of Michigan where I'd never have to see her.

After I discovered the *Tribune* article, time seemed to slide to a stop. Like an automaton, I moved through the house, doing unnecessary chores. When I grew tired of drifting, I looked through my albums for pictures of Amy and tried to recall our happier times. To my astonishment, they came flooding back, although Amy's face had already begun to fade from my memory.

Even when I stared at her photographs, she looked like a stranger. Like someone who had asked for my help, while I walked away, leaving her alone in a gloomy witch's tavern, not wanting to extend myself for a person who no longer had any connection to my life.

I couldn't rid myself of the guilt I felt over not finding a better way to deal with her.

Finally I made my call to Marsha Vernon. She'd heard about the hit-and-run accident on television but didn't know anything beyond the basic facts. Amy's family hadn't finalized her funeral arrangements yet. It was too soon; they must still be in shock. As far as Marsha knew, Preston Anderson was now the sole owner of Blue Frost.

"Frost is absolutely breathtaking, Susanna," she said. "He truly has no equal."

"He should be mine."

As soon as I uttered the words, I wished I could take them back or phrase them in another way. But again, they were sincere and true.

In the pause that followed, I imagined Marsha searching for a diplomatic response, not wanting to offend me or cast aspersions on the dead.

"Frost is in a good place," she said. "He and Preston work well together. They're a team. They have chemistry."

"You may be right. Preston always was a gifted handler. That's why we hired him. I just wish—"

"That he was still yours," she said. "I understand."

"I wish that things could have been different, and I'm talking about Frost, not Preston."

"Of course. I'm sorry you girls couldn't have ironed out your differences before this happened."

"We did. In a way."

I told her about our last meeting at the Cauldron. "At least we were speaking. Amy said that Tag Nolan was stalking her. He sent her a sinister note about fire."

Marsha gasped. "That vile man! I thought he was rotting away in jail."

"He's out. Somebody made a clerical error. Now they can't find him. He's free to do whatever he wants."

"My Lord! You don't suppose he caused Amy's accident, do you?"

"He could have."

"Then you're in danger too. Oh, Susanna, I'm afraid for you. Be careful."

"I will."

"Nolan warned Amy to follow the fire, and she burned up in her car. He did it."

"He's certainly on *my* suspect list," I said.

"Where are you living now?" she asked.

I hesitated. In my early days at Snowhedge, I'd guarded my location zealously. Now there was no reason to keep it a secret from Marsha.

"Upstate in a little town called Maple Creek," I said. "I've been house sitting for a relative, and the puppies are with me. Don't tell anyone."

"I won't, I promise. But that means you're worried."

"I just want to keep a low profile. Call me as soon as you know where the funeral will be."

She promised to do that. "I'll see you there," she said. "Amy had so much to live for. How could it end like this?"

The hours dragged on. Outside, a heavy rain fell through the darkness, and the wind whipped long branches against the sides of the house. I sat in my bedroom by the electric fireplace with my dogs stretched out in the doorway and my gun on the nightstand.

An illusion of safety settled around me. I had the absurd notion that as long as I stayed inside Snowhedge, Tag Nolan couldn't find me. Evil preferred the cover of a stormy night and treacherous curves with deadly drops.

But illusions are made of fragile stuff. They can vanish in an instant.

Gradually I became aware of a barely discernible change in the atmosphere. A cessation of sound. An electrical charge in the air.

The wind gusts had died down, and I couldn't hear the raindrops splattering against the windows. The weather forecast had included a possibility of rain turning to snow after midnight, but it was only eight. I hadn't taken the dogs out for their last run before bed. Mike hadn't come by yet.

How could the house have grown quiet so quickly? All I could hear were the dogs breathing. There had to be more.

I listened for the ticking of the clock in the living room, the hum of an appliance, the whir of the furnace fan—any sound to indicate that Snowhedge was alive and well.

Nothing inside. Nothing outside. But somewhere, something was happening.

Get up. Investigate.

I made my way across the room, stepping carefully over furry legs and still tails. Only Cindy stirred, uncurled herself, and padded after me as I stepped out into the shadows of the cold, silent hall.

A thin ribbon of light seeped out from beneath the parlor door where no light should be.

Finally, I thought, walking up to the door, *and finally sound. My footsteps, slow and light, Cindy's nails clicking on the hard wood floor, and in the parlor a delicate elfin tinkling.*

I turned the knob and stepped into a kaleidoscope of dazzling color. Splashes of red, green, silver, and gold blinded me with their brilliance. I blinked, and pieces of the room came crashing together, assembling themselves into elements I recognized.

The rose sofa and gold chairs. The glistening snow scene above the mantel. Garlands of holly and crimson bows. Orange flames in the fireplace. Christmas candles throwing their soft light on the faces in the vintage picture frames. The magnificent balsam fir tree with its glittering ornaments.

The reflection in the bay windows created a duplicate parlor on the other side of the glass, only real for as long as the lights were on. I was in that room, holding on to the doorknob.

Only real as long as the light lasted?

The eerie thought slipped through my mind and faded. Waves of warmth washed over me, reeling me in. I moved away from the door and found myself treading on the rose-patterned rug. My footfalls and their echoes vanished in deep silence.

Startled by a brush of velvet at my ankle, I looked down and saw Cindy, her small black form pressed against my leg. She held her ears smooth against the sides of her head and her tail still and straight.

She was afraid. My poor little lamb. I should take her back to the hall and close the door. Leave her safe with her sisters and Romy in our own world.

Instead, I picked her up and held her close to my pounding heart, squeezing her so tightly that she squeaked.

"Who's there?" Evalina said.

Evalina stood in front of the fireplace in a space that had been unoccupied a fragment of a moment earlier. She wore a red dress with a low scooped neckline and the jingle bell bracelet. Her complexion had a rosy, very-much-alive glow in the room's bright light.

She wasn't alone. A husky blond man in a military uniform towered over her, his hands placed firmly on her waist.

She turned her head and looked through me. "The door's open. Somebody's out in the hall spying on us."

"No one's there. The doors in your house are all mixed up. They spring open by themselves. Now where were we?"

"Here, Richard. Right here."

The bells on her bracelet jingled as she moved her hand languidly across his chest. She wrapped her arms around his neck and kissed him with an intensity that crackled like the fireplace flames.

After a while he gathered her up in his arms and carried her around the coffee table to the sofa. "Dear Evalina," he said, settling himself beside her.

She leaned her head against his shoulder. "I'm so glad you decided to spend your leave with us. This is going to be the best Christmas ever."

"It already is," he said. "Drink your cocoa before it gets cold."

So saying, he poured Evalina a cup of steaming liquid from a silver pitcher. She held it with both hands but didn't drink. She was looking at her handsome companion. His attention was fixed on the colorful array of holiday cookies.

I studied his features, emboldened by the knowledge that he wouldn't be aware of my scrutiny. Fair hair lightly streaked with gray, a rugged face chiseled in attractive angles and lines. A military man sporting insignia and medals. Although I couldn't tell what branch of the service he belonged to or his rank, his masterful bearing suggested that he was an officer.

Evalina's happiness was infectious, the joy and Christmas cheer in the room palpable. If only I could capture the festive colors and the emotion that sparked between Evalina and her lover on canvas, I'd have a once-in-a-lifetime painting.

Again I heard music playing in the distant part of the house, perhaps on the second floor. I recognized the old English carol, *My Dancing Day*, which suggested that another room had slipped into Evalina's strange other world.

Everything changes. Even a supernatural experience.

No longer was Evalina a shadow-presence in an impossibly furnished parlor that should have been empty, and Richard was as substantial as Mike and even more attractive. Well, maybe every bit as attractive. They were as real as anyone I'd met in Maple Creek. How could I think of them as ghosts?

That was what they were. Spirits reliving a long-past Christmas.

Still...it was as if we'd all met on the threshold of time and changed places, as if I were the spirit intruder who had stumbled onto a stolen tryst. The invisible one who couldn't be seen or heard.

But was that accurate? Although Evalina had reacted to my puppy's sound, she hadn't seen us. I stroked Cindy's head and whispered, "Stay quiet, baby. Just in case."

The pair on the sofa gave no indication of having heard my voice. They were thoroughly absorbed in each other, lost in deep kisses and ardent caresses, oblivious of holiday confections and hot drinks and unaware that someone was indeed spying on them.

I should retreat back to the hall and give them the privacy they thought they had. But how could I leave? My answers might be here, and the window of opportunity could close at any time. I feared the parlor and its occupants would dissolve around me as easily as they had appeared, leaving me in an empty, deserted room with a restless collie pup in my arms.

Or maybe I'd be trapped here in Evalina's world, a forsaken wraith longing for her own man. Maybe I'd never find my way back.

I will, and with my little Cindy.

Back to Snowhedge in the present day and the rest of my canine family asleep by the electric fireplace. Back to Mike. Somehow I had acquired the power to move freely between two times. By the parlor's leave. On its own terms. If only I understood the rules.

For now, I'd accept my role of reluctant voyeur and stay as long as the room allowed me to.

But in spite of my resolve, I began to feel uncomfortable. Almost feverish. The heat of the firelight and candlelight fanned my face. I breathed in the heady scent of balsam that had grown more potent since I'd entered the parlor. The perfumed air was too warm, stifling in this room that had always been as cold as a walk-in freezer. At least in my experience.

Stepping a little closer to the door, I brushed my hair back from my face, longing for just one short blast of that remembered frigid air.

Something was happening. Yet again.

The rug shifted under my weight. I grabbed the edge of the round table. The candle flames flickered wildly as though a hot wind had swooped down on them. Red and green and silver and gold ran together in an opaque no-color blur. The Christmas room was dematerializing.

Hold on, I commanded myself.

With a low growl deep in her throat, Cindy twisted herself around, nose pointed downward. I held on to her, ignoring her first attempt at a defiant protest, while the floor steadied itself and the colors regained their brilliance and returned to their proper objects.

Everything was back in place again. The Victorian cabbage roses at my feet shivered into clarity, the cookies lay still on their plates, and the candle flames on the picture table burned high and straight once more. Not a single ornament had fallen from the tree.

On the sofa, Evalina and her lover were still locked in their lovers' embrace, apparently unaware that the floor had almost given way under them. Left to cool while the mistress of Snowhedge pursued a matter closer to her heart, the cup of cocoa hadn't lost a single ounce.

Cindy growled again.

Something was happening. Something else.

Behind me, in the doorway, sounds broke the stillness: Footsteps, breathing, a swish of material.

Someone was coming.

I turned.

A sylph-like young woman with a cap of golden curls and a sparkling, coy grin tiptoed up to the sofa. She carried a pine cone basket under her arm which she turned upside down over the lovers' heads, shaking it playfully back and forth.

A multitude of tiny green stars showered down on Evalina and Richard. Bits of green glittered in their hair, on Richard's immaculate uniform, and on Evalina's red dress.

Green on red, ordinary aluminum decorations, making magic.

"Merry Christmas, you lovebirds," the girl said in a soft, lilting voice. "Come join the party."

Chapter 21

"Juliette!" Evalina patted gently at her hair and dress. "Look at the mess you made!"

"Don't fuss, Cousin. It's a merry mess."

With a hearty laugh, Richard scooped a handful of green stars from the cushion and tossed them at Juliette. She giggled as they cascaded down the ruffled bodice of her white blouse.

"What party is this?" he asked.

"We're having sandwiches and fruit cake in the music room. Aunt Ellen sent me to find you."

Richard glanced at the half empty plate of gingerbread men. "That's a good idea. I'm famished."

"It's snowing!" With a skipping gait, Juliette crossed the room. She passed so close to me that I caught a whiff of her perfume, an airy floral scent that dissipated in the waves of balsam wafting from the tree. "It's like a billion white feathers falling from the sky."

"I guess you don't see much snow in Louisiana," Richard said.

"I never saw snow till I came up north. Will you show me how to build a snowman, Richard?"

"I could, but I'm no expert."

"Anyone can do it," Evalina said. "You roll three snowballs until they're large, stack them for a body, and add a carrot and coal for the face."

"Don't forget branch arms," Richard added.

"And a hat and scarf." Juliette's voice fairly sparkled, and her Southern accent deepened. "That sounds easy. Let's make one!"

"Tomorrow, then, if the packing is good. We'll show Richard how it's done."

Evalina touched Richard's shoulder lightly and walked over to the window to join her cousin. "We can borrow the Claytons' sleigh and go for a ride one night. Would you like that?"

"Yes! And can we go ice skating sometime?"

"I don't know. That could be dangerous. You've never been on skates."

"I'm not afraid of a little fall," Juliette said.

"All right, but we'll practice on the pond first. I want you to enjoy every minute of your visit."

"I will. I am! And I'm going to be able to stay on a little longer. Mamma said I could."

Evalina's smile arrived a trifle late, but it was warm and full. "That's wonderful. For how long?"

"Until after New Year's Day. Then I'll ride home alone on the train. What a magnificent adventure!"

"We'll do all the lovely winter things while you're here," Evalina said.

Richard stood and brushed away a stray star caught in his collar. "Let's find this party. Are you ladies ready?"

He surveyed the room, as if searching for something out of place and abruptly froze. His eyes turned sharp, with steel glints. He was looking directly at me.

Startled, I took a step backward, but of course he was looking *through* me at his two companions standing together at the window watching the snow fall.

"Whenever you are." Evalina turned around. "Is something wrong, Richard?"

"I thought I saw something in the middle of the room. It's gone now."

A great chill stole over my body. Had the time barrier dissolved for one instant? Could Richard have seen us? What if it happened again? I imagined his consternation at the sight of a strange woman and a puppy in the parlor. If he discovered me, what would I do?

Evalina smiled. "My goodness. You must be hungry."

"He's hallucinating," Juliette added.

The carol I'd heard before was still playing, louder now. I knew the words:

> *Tomorrow shall be my dancing day;*
> *I would my true love did so chance*
> *To see the legend of my play,*
> *To call my true love to my dance...*

"That's my very favorite Christmas song," Juliette said. "Hurry, y'all!"

Evalina moved to the table and switched off the Tiffany lamp. "I'll just leave the tree lights on, but candles can't be left unattended. We may be gone for a while."

"Race you to the music room!" Juliette said.

Evalina watched Juliette dash through the door and Richard exit more slowly with a wink and a parting wave. Then, with a sigh, she began to blow out the candles. Their tiny fires died instantly, leaving a hint of sulfur in the air. Only the tree lights remained, multi-colored jewels floating in darkness. They were exquisite, but I felt cold. Oddly, the fireplace flames weren't giving as much warmth as they had earlier.

"I wanted us to have this time alone together," Evalina murmured. "Just this week. I wanted..."

She extinguished the last red taper and walked slowly through the door.

With a start, I realized that I was going to be left behind. I followed, hoping to find that other room frozen in time, the one in which the phantom guests waited to dine on sandwiches and fruit cake, where a choral arrangement of "My Dancing Day" played on a phonograph.

In her journal, Lila Rose's ghost voice had described Richard and Juliette as an ideal couple. Didn't they know about Evalina's romantic involvement with Richard? Or was nothing settled yet?

Based on my brief observations of the trio, I couldn't agree that the husky blond military man who had kissed Evalina with such ardor and the golden girl from the South would make a good match. Juliette seemed too flighty for Richard, but she was also refreshing and pretty, and they *did* make an attractive pair.

Still I knew what Evalina had hoped for; I knew how her unfinished sentence would have ended.

No you don't, I told myself. *How can you even think you know these people?"*

Sharp little needle teeth dug into my hand. It was Cindy's last desperate attempt to attract my attention. She wanted to run free.

"In a minute, baby," I whispered. "We have to find the music room."

But it was too late. The long dark hall was empty. The flowers on the table were the black-eyed Susans I'd placed there yesterday, burnished autumnal blooms, now limp with dry stalks. I'd moved too slowly and lost the ghosts.

I felt bereft, thoroughly chilled, and a little hungry.

On an impulse, I looked back through the open parlor door. No jewel-toned tree lights glowed in the dark, no flames crackled in the fireplace. The music from the other room had stopped.

I stopped too, peering into the kitchen. Everything was as I'd left it, neat and ready for Mike's visit, except for the *Tribune.* Spread out on the table, it brought me back to my own time and concerns.

Amy was killed this morning. I was reading about it.

As soon as I set Cindy down on the floor, she bolted for the bedroom. Alone in the kitchen, I glanced out the window. Low, dark clouds filled the sky, but there was no snow falling. According to the stove clock, I'd only spent about ten minutes in the parlor. It seemed more like half an hour.

Time is one of life's greatest mysteries. It can be an enemy or a friend. You can have too much of it or, like Amy, not enough. Sometimes you take a wrong turn in the dark and end up in a whole other era. As I had done.

But how and why? And would I ever find the shadow people again?

I had to. Their snatches of conversation hinted at stories that intrigued me. Would Evalina's romance culminate in a proposal or a winter wedding? Was Juliette casting her golden cap for her cousin's man? What had happened here that long ago Christmas? Snowhedge couldn't possibly bring me to this point in their saga and leave me hanging. Could it?

Of course. Snowhedge was a house of secrets. It guarded them jealously and doled them out one by one.

I held on to a slender reality. A single object, a tiny green aluminum star, had crossed over the misty timeways, traveling forward. Cindy and I had gone in the opposite direction. No doubt we would make the trip again. But not tonight.

An unaccustomed restlessness folded around me. I couldn't seem to move my mind beyond the contemplation of time's mysteries and the people who had left their spirits at Snowhedge.

Where was the music room located? And would Mike ever come? I needed human contact tonight. I needed him.

This is my time to be happy, I thought. *I've waited long enough.*

I folded the *Tribune* neatly, laid it on the counter beside the answering machine, and wondered what to do now. What needed to be done?

Wait for Mike. Change clothes. Touch up my make-up. Check on my dogs. Nothing momentous.

The collies were all right. Cindy was asleep, snuggled between her yellow chick and Frosty, the night's adventure forgotten. The gun lay on my nightstand. I stared at it, suddenly remembering why I'd left it there.

Tag. Don't become so engrossed in someone else's past that you forget the danger in your own present.

Back in the kitchen, I thought about making a cup of peppermint tea but looked instead for the cocoa. Now if I only had gingerbread men or Christmas cookies...

While the water boiled, I reached for my sketchpad and felt instantly at home. With broad sweeping strokes I drew the fireplace with the furniture grouped around the hearth and the Christmas tree in the window. I added an illusion of falling snow framed by the bay windows and topped the presents with fanciful bows.

But Evalina, Juliette, Richard...their faces eluded me, and I had no handy pictures to refer to. But I could pinpoint impressions: The air of austerity that enhanced Richard's handsome features. Juliette, with her childlike delight in her surroundings, was the easiest to capture. Then Evalina. Serenity and graciousness? Or was that right for her?

I sensed that two Evalinas existed in the same body. They had two different personalities and agendas. The wild possessive Evalina had tried to snatch Mike out of my arms on the night of our date at the Heidelberg Inn. She didn't completely welcome Juliette into her Christmas holiday but would never let her know it.

Evalina was the enigma. The first spirit to show herself. From the beginning, the heart of the haunting.

In the end, I portrayed the phantom trio as featureless forms of light, giving one distinctive tag to each. For Richard, it was military insignia shining on his broad chest, for Juliette a mop of curls, and for Evalina a jingle bell bracelet.

My three phantom friends, I thought. *Where are you now, this minute?*

I brushed a speck of dust from the paper and stood it against the centerpiece. The parlor itself turned out well, as faithful a representation of what I had seen as a photograph with every remembered detail in place. After admiring my work, I signed the sketch and scrolled a title across the top: *The Haunted Parlor at Snowhedge. One November Evening.*

Mike arrived while the cocoa was bubbling and the dogs were emerging from their before-bedtime naps ready for play and petting. He brought an enormous energy with him and a dash of normalcy, which was what Snowhedge and I needed.

He dropped a medium sized shopping bag on the table and took me in his arms. I couldn't remember when I had been so glad to see anyone.

"Are you all right, Susanna?" he asked.

"Pretty much," I said.

"I heard about your friend's accident and was worried about you. I had a feeling you might be in trouble."

I made an attempt at a smile. "Do troopers have premonitions?"

"Some do. It's unusual for me. Today was different."

He scanned the kitchen and nodded. "This all looks peaceful enough."

"It's the only truly cozy place in the house," I said.

I stayed in his arms a little longer, listening to the chimes ringing in the living room and plaintive begging sounds from the puppies who had discovered Mike's package.

The spirits were no longer at Snowhedge, and Tag was somewhere out there. Not here. It might be possible for me to enjoy a normal, pleasant interlude, freed from the trouble that shadowed my every step.

"Have some cocoa with me," I said.

"I brought you some comfort food." He took a package wrapped in foil from the bag. "My sister-in-law, Marjorie, baked chocolate chip cookies for you."

"They're my favorite. Please thank her for me."

I tried to keep my thoughts from straying to the parlor. It was a coincidence that Richard and Mike both liked cookies. What man didn't?

"I've been feeling terrible about Amy," I said.

"I knew you would. That's a hard way to die."

"I keep thinking about that note Tag Nolan sent her. *Follow the fire.*"

"Nobody could have known the car would burn," he pointed out.

"You're right. Maybe it wasn't Nolan after all, but I have a premonition, too. A bad one." I swirled a spoon through the cocoa, remembering the last time I'd had a similar drink. With Amy at a country diner in Ohio after a show early last spring. When everything was all right between us.

Would everything remind me of Amy from now on?

"Our relationship was complicated," I said. "We weren't quite friends again. Not even on our way."

"What happened today makes a strong case for patching up quarrels while there's still time."

"You're right, but there's no going back," I said. "I think Tag Nolan drove the other car. He followed Amy, waited for his opportunity, and took it."

"It could have happened like that. They haven't found the Buick yet."

"Then Nolan gets away with murder."

"You're afraid he's coming for you next," Mike said.

"Yes."

"I won't let that happen."

Before I could ask how he could prevent it, he added, "I have something else for you. It's a picture Marjorie found at a garage sale the other day. I talked her into parting with it."

He handed me a small oil painting of a blue Victorian house set in the midst of a wild snowscape. The façade blazed with light, and a magnificent Christmas tree sparkled in a first floor bay window.

"There's no hedge," Mike said. "Otherwise, it looks like this house. I thought you'd like it."

Chapter 22

Mike was wrong. For some strange reason I felt an immediate aversion to the painting. My reaction puzzled me. The house *did* look like Snowhedge, and Snowhedge was my temporary home, my shelter. It didn't repulse me. Why should the small canvas burn in my hand like a piece of smoldering driftwood?

I studied the graceful gables and classic lines, looking for an answer. No hedge heavy with snow stood sentinel on the grounds. The porch didn't wrap around the structure, and the gingerbread trim had been installed with a light hand. Only the soft blue color and architectural style were reminiscent of Snowhedge.

The house in the painting was simply a picturesque Victorian in a snowy setting with a Christmas tree in a bay window.

Like the majestic balsam in the Snowhedge parlor with a scent that wouldn't die.

"It would make a pretty Christmas card," I said.

Without a word, Mike took the painting from my shaking hand. "All right, Susanna, what's the matter?" His voice had a gruff edge.

I couldn't tell him what I didn't understand myself. "I have an unpleasant visit scheduled for tomorrow," I said. "I guess it's affecting me."

"Anything I can help you with?"

"Not this time. I'm going to the funeral parlor to pay my last respects to Amy Brackett."

"That's never easy, but it's something we all have to do from time to time." He peered into the saucepan and turned up the heat under the cocoa. "Let's have a few more cookies; then I'll be off. You'll feel better when you say a final goodbye to Amy."

"She died with this bitterness between us unresolved. It haunts me."

"She'll know how you feel now," he said. "That's what's important. Where is this place?"

"In St. Clair Shores where Amy's parents live. I wrote the address down."

He frowned. "That's a long drive. Be careful. We're in for a week of wintry weather. A little taste of what's to come."

"I wanted to be gone from here before the season changed," I said.

But not before I solve the mystery of the haunted parlor, I amended silently.

"You can," Mike said. "That farmhouse on Bridge Road is still for rent. Would you like to drive over with me and have a look at it on Friday? After, we can have dinner."

"It's a date."

I checked the cocoa. Once again, small bubbles broke on its surface, but now Mike's visit was winding down. It had been too short.

I could sit here all night with this man, I thought. *Sit and talk, eat cookies and be safe. Where did the old Susanna go?*

"Do you have any plans for Thanksgiving Day?" Mike asked.

"Just to keep the home fires burning at Snowhedge. Then, on the day after Thanksgiving, I entered the collies in the Fairoaks show in Lakeville."

"Good. Marjorie asked me to invite you to dinner—around four. You can meet the new pup and see Danny and Davey again. Will you come?"

"I'd love to. What should I bring?"

"Just yourself. Marjorie has the menu covered right down to three desserts."

"Well, I want to take something..." *Flowers,* I thought. They were always appropriate. *A good wine?*

"Yourself," he repeated.

A Thanksgiving dinner with Mike's family was a giant step forward. As pleased as I was at this sign of progress, I wondered if we were moving too fast. Building a relationship required a sizeable time commitment. Before I could begin to think about giving Mike a more permanent place in my life, I had something to do.

No, Susanna, you don't. Forget the little drama playing out in this house. Forget the ghosts. Any day now you're taking the dogs and leaving Snowhedge. You're going to make a new home for yourself and for them. And Mike will be with you.

But couldn't I have a life with Mike and the answer to the Snowhedge mystery too? A little more sleuthing, aided by another materialization or two, and I'd know what had happened in the parlor so long ago and whether or not I should be concerned for my own safety. It shouldn't take long. A week or two. Then I could leave this icy blue house of secrets and never look back.

As I sat in the kitchen drinking cocoa with Mike, thinking ahead to a holiday dinner with his family, my plan seemed feasible.

Please don't let anything interfere with it, I prayed.

If Mike was wrong about my liking the snow painting, at least he was right about the weather. The next afternoon, I donned a black dress and coat and drove out of Lapeer County on rain-slicked roads. As I rehearsed the Map Quest directions and entered the first of the freeways I had to navigate en route to my destination, I hoped the temperature wouldn't drop too drastically and that I'd be home before dark.

A journey to a dreaded destination always takes longer. Still I had to say goodbye to Amy, wherever she was now.

With traffic moving steadily and a mere smattering of police cars along the way, I had a chance to summon Amy's pale face and cold green eyes. I imagined her sitting in the backseat with a fearful new pup, comforting him as only Amy could. As she had done so many times before. And as she stroked him and spoke to him, her eyes grew as warm as sun-kissed lake water.

"I'm doing this for you, Amy," I said. "Because we were friends— once. I'd rather be anywhere else tonight. But here I am. Out in the storm. For you."

I half expected her to answer, to fling one of her signature witticisms my way.

The wipers traced their never-ending path across the windshield. Back and forth. Forth and back. Their swish sounded too much like Amy's sigh when she didn't get her way, which hadn't happened often.

"We needed more time to settle our differences," I said. "I should have stayed longer that night at the Cauldron."

I glanced in the rear view mirror, slowing slightly as the car on my right sped up to pass me.

"'Should have's' don't count," Amy would have said.

That was true. Those were empty words.

"I have a new man in my life now," I said. "But I'd still like to know how you managed to take Preston from me. One day, we were close, the next we were like strangers. He never called me again. Then I saw a picture of you two with Frost. It's true what they say. A man's girlfriend is the last to know."

The rain turned quickly to snow, falling steadily, turning the lanes into wide curving ribbons of white. When a car in front of me spun out on a slippery stretch of pavement, I ended my one-sided dialogue abruptly. Watching the other drivers required all my concentration, and for a while I gave my full attention to the road.

But the way ahead looked clear now. I could relax a little. I switched on the classical music channel to an eerie melody that sounded like a dirge. Perfect for tonight's visit.

An hour later I entered the last freeway and began to read the signs more carefully. I knew where I was going. At least tonight I did. It was a comfort to know something.

"Blue Frost was our dog," I reminded her. "Yours and mine equally. How could prestige and money matter more to you than our friendship?"

The precipitation on the window thickened. Ironically, the traffic seemed to speed up. I didn't like driving in snow, was wary of drivers who exceeded the speed limit in hazardous conditions, and wanted desperately to go back to Snowhedge.

"Couldn't we just say goodbye now, Amy? I'll send a few prayers your way. You wouldn't mind, would you? It's more than you gave me."

Suddenly my exit loomed ahead. I drove carefully down the ramp and out onto a well-lit road. If Map Quest was correct, the funeral parlor should be about ten miles ahead, on the right.

I switched off the dirge music. This was a pretty, festive drive with young snow-coated trees lining the street. I had the absurd notion that I'd driven from November into winter.

It's always colder and snowier near a lake, I thought.

Back at Snowhedge, the ground might well be bare. If snow fell, it was ghostly snow, seen only through a bay window rimmed with condensation.

"One more thing," I said. "Some day I'll breed another dog as magnificent as Blue Frost. I'll do it alone and never let anybody take him from me."

Dim outdoor lighting illuminated the Campbell-Carmelli Funeral Home, a rambling unadorned edifice set far back from the road. I found a parking place near the entrance and took a deep breath, not wanting to go in, but having no other choice now that I was here.

Unfortunately, my imaginary conversation with Amy had left me in a resentful and angry mood. I needed to switch to proper funeral parlor demeanor and do it quickly.

Inside I moved slowly up to the closed casket. Amy was lying inside the shiny wooden box. Or somewhere. Could she hear me?

I knelt down and said my prayer: *Rest in peace, Amy. I'm sorry you had to die. Sorry. Hail Mary...*

The elaborate funeral arrangements that surrounded the coffin distracted me. Their scents were too potent, and the heat of the vigil candles froze my blood. "Sorry," I whispered, as I rose from the kneeler, aware of a pain in my right hand that hadn't been there before.

I had done what I'd come for. Now I'd view the pictorial display of Amy's life and achievements and sign the guestbook. Then I'd go home, my somber mission accomplished, my duty done.

Without saying anything to a family member? That wouldn't be right.

But I didn't see Amy's parents or her sister. No one had taken any notice of me.

"Susanna."

Marsha Vernon emerged from a small group of chattering women and stood uncertainly at my side. Her long jet earrings added a whimsical touch to her appearance. I noticed them because she kept fussing with their beads.

"I'm glad you made it, dear," Marsha said. "This is a sad, sad day."

"I had to be here."

"It's such a long drive from Maple Creek—and in this ghastly weather."

Instinctively I glanced around, but no one appeared to have heard her.

"Remember my location is a secret," I said. "Anyway I may be moving soon."

"Because of that Tag monster." Marsha swiped at her eyes, leaving a mascara smudge on her cheek. "I'm sorry you have to do that, but it's better to be safe." She took my arm. "Let's check out the pictures. I'll bet you're in some of them."

"In a funeral parlor? I hope not."

But of course I was. I followed Marsha to the wall-mounted display and scanned it through tears. Amy and I in a dozen casual poses. Blue Frost. Our collies. Amy at her high school graduation in her cap and gown. Amy at her prom. Amy as a precocious little girl on a tricycle. Then, years later, Amy and her partner, Susanna Kentwood, with their beautiful collies, certain that the future was going to be bright.

There wasn't a single photograph of Amy and Preston, but, in a way, that was understandable. These were old pictures. Amy and Preston were a new couple. And—I looked away from the picture board—I didn't see Preston here tonight.

Hadn't Amy said that they'd broken up? Wouldn't he make an appearance though? They were still dog show friends.

"Susanna! Marsha! Thank you for coming."

A slightly older, more sophisticated version of Amy embraced Marsha and favored me with a cool smile. I recognized Amy's sister, Beth. Her green eyes were like Amy's, but her hair was dark.

"I'm still in shock," Marsha said softly. "That beautiful, sweet girl."

"My little sister," Beth added. "I can't believe she's gone." She turned to me. "Susanna, I'm so glad you two girls patched up your little quarrel. You'd have felt so bad if you hadn't. Amy was always a forgiving soul. She didn't hold any grudges."

"Amy..." The words I would have said died in my throat. This wasn't the time to set the record straight. There was never going to be a time. After tonight, I'd never see Beth again. Amy's take on our falling out was irrelevant.

I pulled an envelope out of my shoulder bag and handed it to Beth. "It's a mass card for Amy," I said.

Beth murmured a muffled thank you and looked beyond me, smiling at an elderly couple. Now I was truly finished here.

"I sent that basket of flowers," Marsha said. "Maybe Beth will take it home."

"It's pretty. Well..."

The comments of the mourners broke through the awkward silence that enveloped us.

"How could God have let this happen?"

"I for one don't understand it. She had her whole life ahead of her."

"I'm afraid to get in a car anymore. When did this road rage business start anyway?"

"Will all her dogs go to new homes?"

"So many of them. I wonder…"

Beside me, Marsha shifted restlessly. "Would you like to go out to dinner, Susanna? We can get caught up."

"Another time I'd like that," I said. "I have a long drive ahead of me, and it was snowing earlier."

"It's supposed to snow all night. Well, get along, then. I'll see you at Fairoaks."

"I'm just going to sign the guestbook, then I'll be leaving," I said.

I left Marsha standing alone, but I felt compelled to move—to do whatever I could to end this ordeal quickly.

More candles burned in the room's small alcove, casting their eerie light on the yellow pages of the guestbook. Quickly I scrawled my name and my old address—Marsha's place—and chose a holy card, a sentimental depiction of an angel leading a golden-haired maiden in a white dress through a flower-filled garden. Amy in Paradise, I thought. A long way from Larkspur Kennels. A long way from home.

I would keep the card and say the prayer. I'd think of Amy for a while and then over time she'd fade from my memory. I hoped.

Slipping it in my shoulder bag, I looked for Marsha, intending to wave goodbye to her, but she'd vanished into the crowd. In the few minutes I'd lingered at the guest book, the mourners and the floral arrangements had multiplied.

I clenched my fists and cringed at the pain in my right hand, tried to ignore the onslaught of panic. Hadn't I gone through a similar experience before?

I felt as if I were back in the Cauldron, leaving Amy alone at a table while I tried to find the exit. Just past the papier-mache witch. Keep moving. Don't stop for anything.

How many steps to the door? I longed to breathe fresh air again and to drive away from this place of death even if I had to slide all the way. Even if I had to spin out on an expanse of black ice.

That's not going to happen.

"Come back!"

The croak in my mind resembled Amy's voice.

"Come back, Susanna. We have more to say to each other. I have to tell you how it was between Preston and me. I have to explain about Frost."

Don't listen to her.

Clearly I'd been hanging around ghosts too long. My imagination had run amok. Besides, whatever Amy wanted to tell, I had no desire to hear.

"Easy there, miss."

In my haste to reach the door, I'd collided with a portly gentleman in gray, slamming him with the edge of my shoulder bag.

"Oh, I said. "Sorry."

"Are you all right?" he asked.

I pressed the bag against my side, found the outer flap open and hastily secured it.

"I'm fine," I said. "Just in a hurry."

"Slow down," he said with a chuckle. "You'll live longer."

I walked faster. There was the exit at last. It led to a dimly-lit hall. I turned right, passed an empty sitting room, and opened the front door. Cold air blasted me, and a wave of icy snow brushed against my face.

It was all right.

And there was my car. Liberation. In a matter of minutes, I'd be heading home.

No, I thought. *You're going back to Snowhedge.*

Chapter 23

That night before going to bed, I searched through my shoulder bag for Amy's holy card. One prayer for Amy, one for myself, and a brief thank you to God for a safe trip home over slippery roads. That was all I could manage.

Ah, there it was. But the card felt different. Coarse and larger...it *was* different.

I pulled it out and stared in horror at the images on the jagged-edged piece of construction paper. Pencil flames colored with orange crayon. A stick figure with wings leading a dark-haired maiden through a burning door. Three words printed in black marker: *Follow the fire.*

Dark-haired. The doomed girl wasn't Amy.

Dear God, I was holding Tag Nolan's calling card. But where was the real card, the one with Amy's birth and death dates and the prayer? Again, I fumbled in my purse until I found it next to my wallet.

Tag had been at the funeral parlor tonight, close enough to drop his latest warning into my purse, and I'd never been aware of his presence, never felt the hot breath of evil on my arm.

I remembered...bumping into a man on my way out of the funeral parlor. The crowd that had rapidly doubled in size. The open flap on my purse. People too close to me as I made my way to the door.

Usually aware of my surroundings, I'd been focused on Amy and Marsha and Beth. At any time, Tag Nolan could have slipped the fire warning card into my purse without my realizing it. Even as I knelt at Amy's coffin, distracted by the odors of the funeral flowers.

He had been there, biding his time, not yet ready to strike, wanting me to know that my death was imminent. Knowing I'd be afraid.

I let the vile paper fall to the floor and sank back on the bed, unable to stop trembling.

I was next on Tag's list, and he was near. He'd suspected that I would attend Amy's wake. He could have been tailing me across freeways and country roads, following me all the way to Snowhedge. Tag Nolan knew where I lived.

I glanced at my sleeping puppies. "I'm alone. Absolutely alone, except for you. My dear ones."

I called Romy to my side and buried my head in her fur. She whimpered and licked my hand.

"We're in danger," I whispered. "All of us."

It was almost midnight, too late to call Mike. Even if I did alert him, what could he do?

He's a state trooper. I'm his girlfriend. Tag Nolan is an arsonist and a killer who threatened my life.

I reached for my cell phone, started to dial his number, and stopped.

This was my problem. My panic.

Deal with it then, Susanna. Meet it head on.

I couldn't go anywhere tonight. Tomorrow then. At daybreak. I couldn't wait until Friday to check out the farmhouse on Bridge Road. I'd do it in the morning and take the dogs with me. Unless it was a dilapidated shack, which wasn't likely, I'd contact the landlord, hurry home, and pack the car.

Stay one step ahead of Nolan. If you can. And make sure he doesn't follow you.

Hastily I slipped off my nightgown and put on my black dress again, intending to lie on top of the covers all night, my gun within reach, the puppies and Romy close to my side. I'd try not to fall asleep, even though my eyelids felt as if they had two-pound weights on them. And if I slept, the dogs would wake me. Please, dear God, in time.

Being proactive was the only way I knew to fight Tag Nolan. Tomorrow I'd finally take action.

Tomorrow.

> Tomorrow shall be my dancing day;
> I would my true love did so chance . . .

The familiar melody pulled me out of a fitful doze, then ended in mid-refrain, leaving the old blue house steeped in silence. The music had been directly above me, on the second floor. Not in the parlor.

"My Dancing Day" was Juliette's favorite Christmas carol. The ghosts must be in residence. But who had turned off the phonograph so abruptly? Or did the song continue in that other time?

I pushed myself up on my elbows and cleared my mind of irrelevant thoughts so that it could catch a possible psychic vibration as it passed by.

Nothing.

Wait!

There was something. A kind of energy bristled just beyond the half-opened bedroom door. A sense of something moving in the hall, toward the parlor.

I slipped into my shoes and crossed the room, catching a fleeting glimpse of a slender, black-clad figure in the dresser mirror. Myself on the trail of a ghost, looking like a wraith in funeral attire.

Wrap the mystery up tonight, I thought. *Leave Snowhedge in the morning.*

Quietly I closed the bedroom door, trapping the sleeping collies in their safe cocoon. I tiptoed down the shadowy hall to the parlor, walking into an unnatural wave of cold air. Shivering, I pulled the door open, knowing that soon I would be basking in the heat of a long-extinguished fire.

They were both inside, Evalina at the bay window gazing out at the snow, Juliette standing at the round table holding a red taper in a tall brass candleholder. She must have entered the room a few seconds before I did, as Evalina seemed to be unaware of her presence.

I stood for a moment with my hand on the doorknob, then slipped past Juliette and sat on the sofa.

The parlor looked different, still festive and comfortable but in need of a little neatening. Unwrapped presents lay strewn around the room, with empty boxes and mounds of wrapping paper stacked in a corner. The punch bowl held a shallow pool of pink liquid. Crumbs and colored sugar layered the delicate tiers of the crystal server, and a lone gingerbread man languished on an oversized plate.

The long-awaited Christmas party was over, and I'd missed it. All that remained was for the fir tree to be stripped of its finery and dragged out to the bonfire.

But that wouldn't happen. The Snowhedge tree had never left the room.

Juliette watched Evalina silently for a moment; then she said, "Oh, it's you, Cousin. Where's Richard?"

Evalina turned quickly, relaxing the frown that creased her brows. "He's outside shoveling snow with Dad and Uncle Al. They're clearing a path to the road."

"Poor thing. He'll be freezing when he comes in. Let's make cocoa and throw some of that pretty paper on the fire."

A few drops of wax dripped down from the candleholder and pooled on a section of floor, just beyond the edge of the carpet.

"Juliette!" Evalina said. "Be careful with that candle. Put it on the table."

"Sorry, Cousin." Juliette set the candle down and stooped to wipe at the red mess with her fingers. "Ouch. It's hot."

"Well, sure it is. I'll take care of it later. Come see all the snow. This is a Michigan white Christmas."

Juliette skipped over to the bay window and almost, but not quite, nudged Evalina aside.

"Look at it coming down! Do you think we'll get snowed in?"

"Maybe," Evalina said. "But don't worry. We have a team of strong men to shovel us out."

Juliette pressed her face against the glass. "Our poor snowman is a shapeless blob, and I can hardly see the pond."

"It's snowed over like everything else," Evalina said. She stepped away from the window and settled herself in one of the gold chairs. Juliette followed, perching on the arm of the sofa. Too close to me. I moved as far away from the golden-haired spirit as I could.

"Did you have a nice Christmas, Juliette?" Evalina asked.

"It was wonderful, but I could have done without falling on the ice," she said. "I felt so stupid. Then my ankles ached the rest of the day."

"You're not used to wearing ice skates," Evalina said.

"I'm glad Richard was there to hold me up. It was almost like I was skating alone."

"I saw you." Evalina smiled. "Richard is handy that way."

Juliette began crumpling discarded wrapping paper into medium sized balls. "He is indeed." She paused and touched her dainty earrings. "Thanks again for the lovely present, Cousin. I'll keep them always."

"The emeralds match your eyes. Mamma always says that every lady should have good jewelry."

"That necklace and bracelet set Richard gave you is beautiful too," Evalina said. "What kind of metal is it?"

"Brushed silver."

"It's very pretty."

"Thank you."

Juliette tossed a green and gold ball of paper onto the fire. "Would you mind if I ask you a personal question, Eva?"

"I guess not."

"Are you and Richard serious about each other? I mean *engagement ring* serious?"

Evalina lifted her chin. "We're good friends. Maybe more. Why do you ask?"

"Well, naturally I'm curious, staying here with y'all. I can't recall ever meeting such an outstanding gentleman. And he's so cute. Now if you don't have any expectations—you know the kind I mean—you wouldn't care if he and I got a little closer, would you?"

Evalina looked away, into the fire. "Richard is his own man. Is there anything more to say?"

With a little giggle, Juliette said, "I can't think of a thing." She wrapped a strand of golden hair around her finger.

That was one of Amy's gestures! Now that I thought about it, Juliette looked a little like Amy. Blonde hair. Green eyes. Pretty. She was like her too. Self-centered, thoughtless, and treacherous. Why hadn't I seen this before?

"If you'd truly mind, Cousin, I'll just back away. Honest I will."

"Richard is free to make his own choices," Evalina said.

She turned to the tree but not before I saw a glimmer of tears in her eyes. "Oh, these aren't right. They're in the wrong place."

"Christmas is almost over," Juliette said. "Quit fussing with the tree. Aunt Ellen said it's coming down before New Year's anyway."

"I just want to move this . . ." Evalina gently relocated a string of white lights to a lower branch. "Now they shine on the little crèche. No one could see it before."

"People look at the whole tree," Juliette said. "Not just one little decoration."

"Nevertheless. Darn..."

"What's wrong now?"

"This whole branch back here is dried out already. The tree needs a long drink of water."

"Do you want me to get it?"

"I will; then I'm going to bed," Evalina said. "You stay here, if you like. Make yourself comfortable."

"I think I'll sit up for a while and watch the tree lights shine in the dark. That's my favorite holiday thing to do."

"Don't be up too late," Evalina said. "We're going to the after-Christmas sales tomorrow."

"Unless we're snowed in."

"That is a distinct possibility," Evalina said as she went swiftly through the door.

What now?

I could follow Evalina to the kitchen—my kitchen—or stay in the parlor with Juliette. In a few minutes Evalina would be back with water for the tree.

I'd learned that when I removed myself from a Snowhedge manifestation, it disappeared. If I tried to follow a spirit, it escaped into its own dimension.

You can't outrun a ghost or hold on to the impossible, but you can go back to bed. *Wait for the morning*, I thought. *It's going to be busy.*

Whatever I did, I was going to lose the parlor on Christmas night unless I curled up in one of the gold chairs and watched the tree lights in the dark with Juliette. Even then I might wake up to find myself on the bare floor, stretched out near the eerie red stain.

I knew now that it was a simple wax spill. Nothing ominous, except that it had endured through the decades and resisted countless attempts to obliterate it.

And wasn't that ominous?

"I'll take care of it," Evalina had said to her cousin. But she hadn't. Curious.

I glanced at Juliette. She had placed one of the plump sofa cushions under her head and closed her eyes. Her fair hair had a soft glow in the half-dark, and she'd set her lips in a small smug smile.

Of course. From her viewpoint, she'd received Evalina's permission to enchant Richard.

Maybe Richard didn't want to be enchanted.

When he came in with the other men from shoveling, would he repair to the dining room for a shot of bourbon to ease the winter night's chill? That seemed likely. He'd shed his winter jacket, maybe grab a snack in the kitchen, and go to bed in whatever room Evalina had assigned to him.

Or would he seek out Juliette in the parlor? Or Evalina, wherever she'd gone?

One aspect of the Snowhedge haunting continued to puzzle me. Apparently the house was filled with Evalina's friends and relatives, gathered to reconnect and celebrate the Christmas holiday. Uncle Al, Aunt Ellen, Cathy, Richard...I tried to remember the names on the gift tags.

Where were the other people now? Elsewhere in the blue Victorian, I imagined, trapped on another plain, their voices coming through clearly for Lila Rose, but not me.

I finally decided that the story—what happened at Snowhedge on that long-past Christmas night—revolved around three people only: Evalina, Juliette, and Richard. Everyone else was part of the background. For some reason that eluded me, I was the observer.

Stop speculating, I scolded myself. *Decide what you're going to do. Do it!*

By now Evalina would have melted away into that other plain. But Juliette was still here...

I'd waited too long to make my move. An ice-cold draft enfolded itself around me. Shivering violently, I turned around. Every single thing that had been in the parlor swam in a thick white mist. It was going. Going. Then it was gone.

Chapter 24

That night, as I tried to fall asleep, somewhere in the house, in that other dimension, the music continued. The chorus seemed to go on forever:

Sing, oh! my love, oh! my love, my love, my love,
This have I done for my true love.

So did the stanzas, but finally the carol ended. I wondered if Juliette knew that "My Dancing Day" wasn't actually a love song.

I lay still on the sleigh bed, wondering what was going on in the parlor. For the second time I got up to see if Juliette was still asleep by the tree or if Evalina had returned with the water, but the spirits had once again retreated. The room was a cold and empty space, thick with the rich scent of balsam.

Startled by the sound of a curious little whine at my feet, I looked down. Cindy had followed me out of the bedroom. She stood looking up at me, dark eyes filled with wonder at the prospect of a new adventure.

"Not tonight, little pooch," I said. "We're not going in there."

I picked her up, and, with a few spins and whimpers, she settled herself happily in my arms. The wondrous sensation of holding a velvet soft puppy brought me back to blessed normalcy. Cindy was the most affectionate of the babies, requiring three times as much attention as her litter sisters. She needed me the most. The thought disturbed me. As I carried her back to the bedroom, I realized that I had no idea why.

A new day's sun shining through a bedroom window makes the most appalling of nightmares dissolve into gray powder. During my few hours of sleep, just before dawn, Tag's face had haunted my dreams. I saw him everywhere: Staring out at me from the attic mirror, grinning at me through the bay window, spray painting *Follow the fire* on the glass.

"I'll get you, Ms. Kentwood. You're going to pay for this and pay good," he had said.

I woke up trembling and very cold.

He's here. Somewhere out there. Only I can't see him.

Then rationality took over. I'd been dreaming. Tag wasn't here—not yet.

Tag is gray powder on the floor, I told myself. *Like dust.*

The house was quiet, the morning bright. I'd slept until eight o'clock, and we were all still alive. Thank God. But I'd meant to wake up earlier. To rent the house on Bridge Road, to hurry back to Snowhedge, to start packing, to feel free again.

While I'd been sleeping, Cindy had leaped up onto the bed. She lay with her body under the comforter and her head on the pillow. My pretty babe. I stroked her gently. She stirred and yawned.

We couldn't afford a leisurely awakening today.

Without wasting a minute, I yanked off my black funeral dress and slipped into blue jeans and a warm green sweater. I brushed my hair but didn't take the time to apply makeup. We could all have breakfast later.

Trying to make a ride in the car sound as enticing as a walk, I led the dogs out to the Taurus where I settled three excited puppies in the back seat and allowed Romy to sit in front with me. Then I pulled my map of the county out of the glove compartment. We were ready.

The sunlight coaxed diamond sparkles from the thin layer of snow that lay on the ground. Although I tried to focus on the project at hand, I couldn't keep my mind from wandering back to the latest manifestation in the parlor. What had happened after the holiday ended and Juliette boarded her homeward- bound train? Had Richard placed an engagement ring on Evalina's finger? Or had Juliette stolen her cousin's lover?

Evalina had been too nice to Juliette. She should have revealed her true feelings about Richard and fought for him. Also, she might have reminded Juliette that you don't betray a relative's hospitality and threaten her happiness.

How could I find out what happened afterwards?

These people had lived. There must be a way to trace them. In a sense, I'd already found Evalina. Richard and Juliette might still be alive. Unfortunately, not knowing their last names could stop me.

Please, Susanna, enough, I scolded myself.

What did a love triangle from the past have to do with me or my collies and our survival? This wasn't a morning to wallow in idle curiosity, and once we'd moved out of Snowhedge, I wouldn't be able to spy on the ghostly goings-on in the haunted parlor.

I slammed the car door.

So be it. We couldn't stay here. I might never know the story's end, and that had to be all right.

No one was in sight as I drove out to Balsam Lane. That didn't mean that we were home free. The woods across from Snowhedge offered a safe hiding place for a watcher on foot. But I kept my eye on the rear view mirror. Nobody came creeping out of the underbrush, and no other car appeared behind me.

The route to Bridge Road was straightforward and quiet, and the farmhouse was easy to find. It was smaller than I'd imagined, but I felt immediately drawn to its sunny yellow color and simple, clean lines. It looked like a happy house with no dark secrets which was exactly what I needed, and the barn was spacious and looked as if it had been freshly painted.

I remembered my first sight of Snowhedge. Cold, blue, massive, mysterious, and unwelcoming behind its overgrown hedge. It had invoked a host of negative feelings in me. Now I knew why.

This time—this move—would be different. Taking only Romy with me and ignoring the protest yipping from the back seat, I walked down a snow-covered walk to a neat, compact porch and peered into the front window. The room inside was furnished in a cozy Colonial style as comforting for the mind as the body.

"This is perfect for us, Romy," I said.

Quickly I jotted down the telephone number on the 'For Rent' sign and headed back to my car to contact the owner. I never doubted that this small yellow house would be ours for the asking and that we could move in later today.

But is escape ever that easy?

Apparently.

The owner, Arthur Bramble, a jovial white-haired man who owned the local pharmacy, met me at the farmhouse a few hours later. He was delighted to have a tenant for his property at last. As he took my check, he assured me that he had no objections to four dogs living in the house and that I could move in anytime. The sooner the better.

"I always knew the right person would come along," he said with a broad smile. "And I could give you an option to buy..."

I dropped the receipt and keys into my shoulder bag. "Maybe in the future. Right now my plans are indefinite."

"When you're young, they always are," he said. "Oh, to be young! Everything should be in tip-top shape." He scraped the porch stairs clear of snow with his boot. "You let me know right away if it isn't."

He tipped his cap, got into his Jeep, and drove away.

As Romy jumped down from the porch and coaxed the pups into a game of Chase the Squirrel in the front yard, I thought *This is way too perfect. Something is going to jinx it.*

As soon as I'd formed the thought, I remembered Valerie. I had to deal with her, through her voicemail, which was the only way we had ever communicated, aside from our initial meeting and that one message on the answering machine. And how long ago that seemed!

All the way back to Snowhedge, I rehearsed what I was going to tell her, but nothing sounded right. In the end, I settled on an unembellished version of my decision.

Snowhedge

Hi, Valerie. This is Susanna. For personal reasons I have to terminate our agreement. You'll find the house clean and in good condition. There are fresh flowers in the vases and a jar of Autumn Memories potpourri on the ledge above the stove. The keys are in the post office box you rented for me.

I added, *"Thank you for giving me the opportunity to stay here and good luck finding a buyer. That's all."*

Yes, sometimes escape is easy.

I devoted the rest of the afternoon to throwing clothes in my suitcase and taking apart my bedding and the pups' crate. I made several trips out to the Taurus, each time looking in every direction to make sure that I was alone. Soon the trunk was full. I gave the dogs their last dinner at Snowhedge and packed their dishes, water pail, and food.

That was everything except for a few staples from the kitchen. I'd go shopping for groceries in the morning.

I hesitated over my Snowhedge File, the sketches I'd done of the shadow people, and my account of the manifestations. It had to go with me, of course. I couldn't leave it for Valerie or anyone else to see. On the other hand...

I studied my last drawing. *The Haunted Parlor at Snowhedge. One November Evening.* It was accurate and evocative, but, to my astonishment, my own work filled me with the same aversion I'd felt earlier when Mike had placed the painting of the blue Victorian in my hand.

I didn't want to take any of this with me.

Why not destroy them then?

Just as I remembered that I had to let Mike know what I was doing, my phone rang.

"I have an unexpected free evening," Mike said. "Are you up for a quick dinner at the Roadhouse? Say a burger and coffee? Apple pie with vanilla ice cream?"

"Sounds good. I forgot to eat today."

"Did you forget to feed your dogs too?"

"I'd never do that," I said. "Give me a few minutes to change."

"Come as you are. I'm in your driveway, calling on my cell."

Blue jeans, green sweater, no make-up. Suddenly appearances didn't matter. I only wanted to be with Mike.

"I'll be at the door in a second," I said and pushed the Snowhedge File to the back of the counter.

Mike looked up from his dinner and smiled. "You're leaving the house tonight? I'm glad. Surprised too."

"You've been telling me to get away from Snowhedge practically from the beginning."

"And you didn't do it. I thought..."

We were in the Roadhouse, feasting on thick bacon cheeseburgers, devouring mounds of cottage fries, and making brief passes at the garden

Dorothy Bodoin

salad. I couldn't remember when I'd been so hungry. And to think I'd been ready to drive away from Snowhedge without eating.

The waitress hovered over our table with a coffeepot, filling our cups to the top. With a sly smile for me and a wink for Mike, she moved on to her next customer.

"What did you think?" I asked.

"That you liked living in that fancy mansion."

"I'm a farmhouse kind of girl at heart," I said. "Snowhedge was only a job."

An obsession, I might have added. But that's over now.

"Again, I'm glad. I live a simple life, Susanna. There won't be any big houses in my future."

I dipped a cottage fry in the pool of ketchup at the corner of my plate. How could I answer that? With a smile. "Nor in mine. Snowhedge was my one and only mansion. Now that Tag got so close to me, I'm motivated to move on."

"I'll have that fire warning card you showed me back at the house tested for fingerprints," he said.

"Tag is too clever to leave that kind of clue."

"He's a bad artist. These pencil marks don't look anything like you."

"The dark hair is supposed to represent me," I said. "In Amy's card, the figure had light hair. He meant this warning for me."

"With luck he won't be able to find you for a while. That'll give us a fighting chance to catch up to him."

Those were his last words on the subject, but I suspected that he knew more about Tag than he was saying. That was all right. All I wanted was for Tag to be gone from my life.

Now he said, "That farmhouse seems to get smaller every time I drive by it. Do you really think you'll be happy living there?"

"I know I will."

"And will the dogs have enough room?"

"They'll probably hang out in the kitchen or bedroom. That's what they did at Snowhedge. They had three stories to roam through, but they stayed where I was."

"Isn't that what dogs do?"

"Usually. None of them liked the parlor."

"There were too many weird things in that house. Like the balsam scent, the stain, the green star, the face in the mirror..."

"You remembered? I'm astonished."

"Sort of." He pulled a small blue book out of his pocket and handed it to me.

Ghost Finder's Notebook: A Tour of Maple Creek. The cover was smudged, and the pages were yellow.

"With a little help," Mike said. "This is an account by Albert P. Lapham, who calls himself a ghost finder. He came to Maple Creek several

156

years back to record psychic phenomena. One of the houses he investigated was your Snowhedge."

I opened the book and leafed through it, sneezing as a drift of dust rose from the pages. Could this antique volume contain information about Evalina, Richard, and Juliette? "Where did you find it?"

"Marjorie bought it at one of her sales. The occult is her hobby. Ever since I told her that you were living at Snowhedge, she's been dying to meet you."

"I thought that was because we were seeing each other," I said.

"That too. She has a double interest in you."

"That's good. I guess."

"Marjorie reads everything she can about the supernatural," Mike said. "I just skimmed through the Snowhedge chapter. Apparently a lady in white haunts the parlor. She's been seen at the bay windows standing next to a Christmas tree."

That had to be Evalina, although I'd never seen her in a white dress.

But that half-finished garment in the attic draped around the dressmaker's dummy. The one with the turquoise scarf undoubtedly chosen to match the eyes of the spirit woman who looked back at me from the mirror.

How could Evalina wear a dress that hadn't been finished yet? Was it still in the attic where I'd moved it— a safe distance away from the haunted mirror? I could deal with transforming parlors and a trio of ghosts reenacting their special Christmas—somewhat—but I couldn't understand that.

Because it was impossible.

See if the dressmaker's dummy is still in the attic that troublesome inner voice whispered.

No!

"Did the author mention any other Snowhedge ghosts?" I asked.

"Only the one. He wrote about the extreme cold in the parlor, the red stain that appears and disappears, and a faint balsam fragrance. I thought of you right away. There's nothing about a green star or haunted mirror, though. He only stayed there for a few days," he added. "You've been living in that house for weeks."

"Months," I said. "Since October. I've been at Snowhedge too long."

"That's what I've been saying all along. You don't have to believe what this Lapham fellow writes, but it sure makes a good story."

I set my fork down. The time for honesty had finally arrived. The only downside to my full disclosure was the possibility that Mike would think I was unhinged. Still, his sister believed in the supernatural. He'd read the ghost finder's book. He'd introduced the subject into our conversation.

Go ahead. Talk.

"It's all true, and there's more," I said. "The problem is that the story doesn't have an end."

Chapter 25

I told him the entire Snowhedge story then, chapter by chapter, as the spirits had revealed it to me in the series of manifestations. It sounded fantastic, like a tale that had originated in an unbalanced mind.

Was that what Mike thought? Poor deluded Susanna. The kennel fire and the fire avenger have sent her tumbling over the edge.

Was that what *I* thought?

No. I knew what I'd seen.

Mike sat quietly, listening, occasionally frowning, not eating. His grim expression seemed to have darkened perceptibly in a very few minutes

I finished my account with my last glimpse of Juliette asleep in front of the Christmas tree.

"Evalina had gone to the kitchen to get water for the tree, and Richard was still outside shoveling snow with a couple of the other men."

"What happened then?" Mike asked.

"I don't know. I started to follow Evalina, but she was gone. Then, when I turned around, Juliette had vanished too. That's how it happens. I open the parlor door. They're there. Then they leave, and the furnishings disappear too."

"You talk about these ghosts as if they're real people," Mike said.

"That's what it's like. Imagine opening a door and seeing strangers in the house acting out a scene from a play. Only the play stops in the middle of the scene, and the people dematerialize."

"And you're left with an empty parlor."

"That's right."

I picked up the rest of my cheeseburger, took a bite, but promptly put it down again. True ghost stories and a good appetite don't go together.

"Why didn't you tell me this a long time ago? Say the first time it happened? I thought we were—close."

"We weren't close then," I said. "And it sounds so crazy."

"You told me some of it. The green star that fell out of nowhere and the face you saw looking back at you from the mirror."

"You don't believe me," I said.

"That isn't true." He reached for my hand and held it. The power of his grip and the intensity in his voice made me feel as if I had an ally for the first time since…since the fire.

"I'm afraid for you, Susanna. That house has a strong hold on you. It's unhealthy. Maybe deadly."

"I just wanted to know how it all came out."

He didn't answer.

"Now that Tag is in the picture, I'm moving tonight, so I'll never know."

"Let another ghost finder investigate," Mike said. "What time are you leaving?"

I looked at my watch. It was later than I'd thought. "Around nine. As soon as I take one last walk through the house to make sure it's in perfect condition and that I didn't forget anything."

"I'll be there at eight forty-five," Mike said. "I have a commitment I can't get out of, or I'd go home with you now."

"A police matter?"

He smiled. "Not tonight. I'm taking Davey and Jack to Obedience Class."

"You can't miss that," I said.

"Afterwards, I'll follow you to the new house and help you get settled."

"That'll be nice," I said. "Bring a cake. We'll celebrate."

"It so happens that I have access to one. Marjorie is famous for her cake baking. She has one with chocolate batter and coconut frosting on her kitchen cupboard right now."

I said, "So we'll skip dessert?"

"We'll have it in the new house," he said, with a smile that found its way straight to my heart. From now on, everything was going to be all right.

This is the last time I'll see Snowhedge like this, I thought, as I pulled into the drive. Icy blue and massive. Dusted with snow. Hiding behind its wild hedge. One light shining in the living room window.

I'd turned the lamp on, and no ghostly hand had turned it off. And—I couldn't resist a glance—the parlor was dark.

Mike was right. The old Victorian had an unwholesome hold on me, but I was breaking free of it at nine o'clock tonight. Never again would it tempt me with tales of love and longing and, quite possibly, loss.

Evalina, Juliette, Richard. I'm leaving you behind.

A great relief replaced my lingering curiosity about the shadow people.

The ghostly manifestations were like a soap opera. End with a cliffhanger. Tune in tomorrow. Tape the episode if you're going to be away from home.

Well, not exactly. I'd have to miss all further installments, but that didn't matter. I had my own life. Finally.

As I completed my customary survey of the hill and the woods, I noticed that the mailbox was open. That was odd. Mail never came to Snowhedge. I stopped and pulled out a package addressed to me. As I did, I remembered Evalina's out-of-print books that I'd ordered from Barnes and Noble. But I thought I'd asked for them to be sent to my post office box.

Odd. Everything about Snowhedge was odd, even the way the Allencourt books arrived.

Once I would have taken them inside, settled myself under a good light, and began reading. Now my interest had dwindled. Still, they were worth looking at some day, after I moved into the farmhouse.

I hurried on, walking in the path of light, up to the house. For the last time.

The dogs waited for me in the hall, Romy lying in her most regal pose, the puppies falling over themselves with joy at my return. Cherie, Cindy, Frosty. The silly little things. Their leashes were on the table next to the flowers—which should be fresh. I'd bought them yesterday.

I touched a lily petal. It felt limp and lifeless, and the ferns were dry.

No matter. By the time Valerie deigned to visit her property, the entire bouquet would be dead.

Now for the walk through. Start on the third floor.

"Come, Romy," I said. "You puppies, stay!"

See if the white dress is still on the dressmaker's dummy that persistent inner voice demanded.

"Not on your life," I said aloud. "No more exploring. No more curiosity. Never again." And I stated to climb the stairs.

If this were a ghost story instead of real life, something dire would happen now.

Holding her candle high, a girl ascends the staircase, coming closer to the Waiting Horror with each step.

I smiled at my foolishness. Only in fiction. Nothing like that was going to happen to me.

With Romy at my heels and a flashlight in my hand, I walked down the third floor hall, opening each door and quietly closing it again. In the large, airy room adjoining the attic, the boxes I'd intended to search lay on the floor like strange square-shaped ghosts. Valerie could do whatever she liked with them. Yard sale or bonfire. No one was left to care.

Second floor. Once again I opened and closed doors, shadowed by Romy. We came to the room with the rocking chair that had once seemed to move. It was still now. When I'd brought it up from the porch, I'd shoved it into a corner.

Leave everything in place. Nothing here is your responsibility. Not anymore.

The second floor landing. I'd never taken that imitation pine tree down to the living room, never bought green plants, never done so many things I'd planned. I'd only bought outside decorations, filled the vases with fresh flowers and every now and then simmered potpourri on the stove for buyers who never came. In other words, I'd done what Valerie had asked of me and allowed myself to be distracted by the ghosts who roamed through Snowhedge.

Ground floor. One last look at my bedroom. The closet was empty except for the hangers. I'd transferred all my belongings from the dresser and nightstand to my suitcases.

In the kitchen I found Valerie's pumpkin candle centerpiece at the back of the cupboard and set it in the middle of the table. As long as no one lit the wick, it was harmless. Why had I ever been afraid of it?

"Well, Romy, we're ready," I said. "Let's round up those pesky pups and be on our way."

The doorbell rang a harsh, grating sound. I realized that I'd never heard it before. My previous visitors had knocked. Flora Brine. Those aggressive house hunters, the Tabors, and Mike.

It was too early for Mike unless Obedience Class had been cancelled.

"Back, Romy," I said, as I opened the door, remembering too late that Tag might be in the neighborhood.

"Hello Susanna," Valerie said.

At my side, Romy growled softly.

"Your beautiful collie," she said. "You said she doesn't bite?"

"That's just a friendly warning." But I kept my hand on Romy's chain.

Valerie was as I remembered her. Tall, statuesque, wearing gold hoop earrings and wrapped in a fur coat with a fur headband in her chestnut hair.

"I got your message," she said with a backward glance at my car, obviously packed for a trip or a move. "I'm glad I caught you before you took off. May I come in?"

I stepped back and laid my hand on Romy's head. "Of course. This is your house."

She stepped inside, pausing to glower at the sight of the drooping bouquet on the hall table.

"I bought them yesterday," I said quickly. "They must have come from an old batch."

"At least they're colorful."

"I'm surprised to see you here," I said. "You only left me one message, and you didn't return my calls, not even when the Realtor went out of business."

"We'll find another one." She waved her hand lazily. "Let's sit in the kitchen, shall we? It's the most comfortable room in this old barn, and I could use a cup of tea. It's getting colder outside every minute."

"I hadn't noticed," I said. "But I'm in a hurry. I'm going to meet someone."

"Surely you can spare ten minutes."

Romy placed her body in front of mine as the puppies came tumbling out of my bedroom. With shrill little yips, they darted toward Valerie.

Valerie gasped. "Where did they come from?"

"They're mine. I had to bring them here," I said. "They haven't hurt anything."

She formed her lips into a thin line. "I hope I won't find any of this fine woodwork chewed or stains on the floors."

"Everything is exactly as it was when I first came here. We're all model tenants. Even the ones with sharp little teeth."

"I hope so." She attempted a feeble smile but held the edge of her coat away from the leaping pups. "What can I do to convince you to stay, Susanna? At least until Christmas?"

"Nothing, I'm afraid. I've made my plans."

"I could increase your salary," she said.

"It isn't a question of money. You've been generous."

She sighed. "But I need you. I have to fly back to Florida tomorrow. It's a matter of life and death. I can't leave the house unattended."

She sat down at the table. I stood over her, maintaining a slight advantage. Why did I feel I needed one?

"You've kept the kitchen clean and neat," Valerie said. "I see that old copper teakettle is still there on the stove. Do you have any tea?"

"No. I'm sorry."

I did, but it was packed in the car. The Snowhedge kitchen was closed. As far as I was concerned, forever.

"Every room is clean," I added. "Up on the third floor, I hauled some boxes down from the attic. You might want to go through them. I was going to do it, but..."

"Something else came up?"

"I ran out of time."

"It's a young man, I'll bet. He's the reason you don't want to stay." Her lip thinned again. "Did he make you a better offer?"

Romy growled again, and I bit back an angry retort.

"Are you sure that animal is friendly?" Valerie asked.

"Romy," I said softly, taking hold of her chain again. "My reasons are my own business, Valerie. Like your life and death matter in Florida. I have to leave now. You stay if you like. There might be a jar of instant coffee in the cupboard."

Her lips seemed to disappear. "As you say. But please take this." She drew an envelope out of her purse. "It's a little bonus. I came prepared, just in case I couldn't convince you to stay on for a while. I'm grateful for all you've done, but I have to tell you, I'm also a little disappointed. We are family, you'll remember."

"Thank you." I took the envelope and followed her to the door. She cast a disapproving look at the sad welcome bouquet.

"Thank *you*, my dear, for your time and effort."

I closed the door behind her, aware that my heart was pounding in a way that frightened me. Even though we were distantly related, I didn't like Valerie. Thank heavens I wouldn't have to see her again.

Now to follow her out of Snowhedge.

I stuck the envelope in my purse without opening it, grabbed my keys and called the pups.

They came, nails clicking on the hardwood floor. Two pretty blue merle collie babies bounced into the hall wagging their tails madly, ready for any activity I might suggest.

Two puppies?

I felt a pair of invisible hands yank me back into an old nightmare.

Where was Cindy?

Chapter 26

"Cindy! Here, Girl!"

I spoke loudly and firmly, wanting my pretty little tri to come bouncing into the hall, wanting to leave Snowhedge on schedule. Once and for all with no last-minute hitches.

There was no reason for panic. No reason for the tight band that began to close around my heart. Certainly no reason for tears. None yet.

Two puppies danced merrily around my feet. Frosty, Cherie, and Cindy were always together. Maybe not always. Cindy had an independent streak. She frequently left her sisters to their play and followed me. She must know that of the entire litter, she was my favorite, the one most like Romy.

So Cindy is the one I'm going to lose.

Not true. Cindy was just taking her time to answer my summons. For her, that wasn't unusual. She was probably in another part of the house, getting into some typical puppy mischief. Leaving teeth marks in Valerie's precious woodwork or fur on an antique chair.

"Cindy-Girl!"

The hall threw an echo back at me, taunting me.

She's gone. Gone. Gone.

No. That wasn't an echo. It was a cry coming from some deep, dark place inside myself. I had heard it before.

"Cindy!" I tried to give my voice a cheery note. It sounded hollow to me. Why would a dog believe it? "Hurry, little one. We're going for a ride in the car."

"Ride in the car," I repeated as Frosty and Cherie began to chase each other up and down the hall, turning into a gray-blue blur. Feeling dizzy, I grabbed the edge of the table and held on to it. A slight pain throbbed above my right knuckles.

Oh, no! The tears were close again. I wiped them away with my left hand.

Sensing my distress, Romy gave a little whimper and nudged me with her nose.

"Cindy!" I called again. "Come. Now! We're leaving."

She had to be here. A small puppy couldn't disappear inside a house. She had to be somewhere.

Answer. Please. Bark or whine. Cry. Let me know where you are, and I'll come get you.

The old Victorian had never been so silent.

Valerie did this!

The thought struck me with lightning bolt force. Valerie didn't like the puppies. They weren't welcome in her home. Furthermore, she wanted payback for my refusal to stay on at Snowhedge. She'd never tangle with Romy, but a small playful pup was easy to grab.

I'd go after her and demand that she give my puppy back.

Then I realized that Valerie couldn't have stolen Cindy. When I'd opened the front door, only Valerie had gone through it. Valerie Lansing wrapped in fur with no wriggling collie baby stashed in the folds of her coat.

But Valerie had brought bad vibrations into the house, and a bad thing had happened. Now I had to deal with the fall-out.

I couldn't do it standing in the middle of the hall calling Cindy's name while the band closed tighter and tighter around my heart.

"Frosty and Cherie, Stop that! Stay! Romy, find Cindy," I said.

But Romy didn't move. My normally obedient collie sat down, facing the door, as still as an exquisite dark statue, while the puppies ran around her, yipping frantically.

Why weren't they listening to me? Was there going to be a full moon tonight?

Once again, I started up the staircase, this time alone.

On the third floor, all was as quiet and innocent as it had been an hour ago. No mischievous puppy hid behind Lila Rose's memory boxes waiting to be discovered. The attic door remained shut.

But a clever little canine might have managed to open it and slip inside. Cindy might be in the attic now, in that dark, dangerous place where ghosts lived in mirrors.

No, she's not!

What if she is?

"Cindy!" I shouted. "Where are you?"

Silence.

Every room on the third and second floor was empty except for an odd table or chair placed there to create an illusion of occupancy. I opened and closed doors, moving quickly, followed by the echoes of my own tapping heels. Pausing on the landing I listened for a click of puppy nails on the floor or the jingle of a tag.

Nothing.

From here I could see the rest of my collie family in the hall. Romy still sat in front of the door, while Cindy and Cherie took turns nipping at her tail. Romy gave them a mild warning growl. They retreated in mock alarm. The clock in the living room chimed eight times, and my head began to ache.

One hour until departure time.

I looked in the bedroom. In the bathroom. In the kitchen. Nothing of mine remained in the house except for the Snowhedge File and the painting Mike had given me, both on the counter.

What could I do now?

Get along home, Cindy, Cindy,
Get along home...

I used to sing that song to her when I thought we were alone.

"Singing to a dog?" Amy would say with a sardonic lift of her eyebrows. "You're too strange, Susanna."

Mike was coming by in forty-five minutes to follow me to the farmhouse and our new life, but I wasn't leaving a family member behind.

Help me, I prayed. *Tell me what to do and where to look.*

My heartbeats were outracing my thoughts. I felt limp, like a poorly sewn rag doll whose stuffing is slowly dripping out of her body. I longed to sink into a comfortable chair and think. If only I could rest for a moment, maybe I could up with a plan.

There were no comfortable chairs in Snowhedge. Only solid, elegant contraptions with hard wood backs that required perfect posture. But the parlor had that marshmallow-soft sofa on which Juliette had curled up and fallen asleep with a smug smile on her face.

Look in the parlor! The haunted room that wants to keep you here forever.

Yes, the parlor. I hadn't looked there yet.

I opened the door, bracing myself for a blast of cold balsam-scented air or colored Christmas tree lights glowing in the darkness—whatever waited inside. Tightening my hand on the knob, I felt the pain intensify.

It was Arctic-ice cold inside, and the parlor was empty—except for Cindy's little yellow chick. It lay on its side like a dead thing that had been flung to the floor. Right next to the red stain.

I thought I'd packed it in the car. I *did* pack it in the car.

Of Cindy there was no sign.

I picked up the little chick and hugged it to my breast. In that moment I could think of only one scenario, and it terrified me. Cindy had found her way into the parlor, circa 1950, and the room had taken her. It couldn't have me, but an inquisitive little puppy was fair game.

Cindy was lost in time, and I had no way to follow her until the Christmas room transformed itself again and the spirits returned. Even then, there was no guarantee that I'd find Cindy waiting for me in that other dimension.

She's gone.

A single chime rang out in the living room. Eight-thirty. How could a half hour have passed already? Fifteen minutes until Mike arrived. He would help me. Mike would know what to do. For the first time in my life, I didn't.

"Oh, dear God," I whispered. "I don't know where to turn."

I heard the answer in my heart, spoken in a creaking voice that sounded as if it hadn't been used in decades.

"You're not going anywhere, Susanna."

Snowhedge wouldn't let me leave. It held on to me with cold blue hands the way the long branches at the sides of the house held on to the outer walls.

In a weird way, everything began to make sense. The ghost play wasn't over yet. I had to stay until the end. The parlor had snatched Cindy as bait to ensure that I remain in my seat, a rapt spectator at a spirits' reenactment.

All right, I thought, *I'll wait awhile. Just don't hurt Cindy. Don't let her be afraid or hungry. And when we're through, give her back to me.*

"Oh, no, no, no...how could you?"

The words were practically inaudible, lost in the music of the chimes, but I heard each one and recognized the pain in the speaker's voice.

Evalina stood in front of me, so close that we would have occupied the same space if we didn't exist in different time periods.

As the tenth chime faded, she backed up quickly. Drops of water spilled out of her pitcher. I felt them on my arm, dabbed at them, and watched Evalina run down the hall and disappear into the darkness.

I was back in the past. In the parlor, the cold had given way to a delicious warmth. The fireplace flames seemed to beckon to me, but I wasn't afraid of them.

Cindy might be here. A frightened puppy could hide in several places. Behind the tree, in the corner behind the phonograph...

I moved closer to the sofa, for the first time near enough to see what had sent Evalina fleeing into the darkness.

Richard and Juliette lay there entwined in an ardent embrace. A plaid throw covered their lower bodies. They resembled a pair of reclining statues washed in firelight, Juliette's blonde curls spilling over Richard's brawny arm like a golden waterfall.

The room was dark, lit only by the multi-colored lights on the tree and the dying blaze in the fireplace. The crystal servers on the coffee table had been replaced by a decanter of wine and two goblets, all empty. A 'Cookies for Santa' plate held a single slice of dark fruitcake and a layer of crumbs.

Remembering the ten chimes, I realized that it was later in Evalina's world than in mine, but the time between this materialization and the previous one puzzled me. When last I'd seen Evalina, she had left the parlor to get water for the tree, a short walk to the kitchen.

What had delayed her? Because the stolen tryst must have taken...I frowned. Ten minutes at least. Fifteen?

I could imagine how it had happened. Richard would have come in from shoveling snow outside, cold and ready for any kind of warming, perhaps craving a shot of bourbon. Instead, he found Juliette lying on the sofa and seduced her.

Ah, no. She had seduced him.

But in so short a time frame? In her cousin's parlor? With Evalina expected to come through the door to water the tree at any minute?

The shameless opportunistic slut!

You've come here for Cindy. I told myself. *Don't get distracted.*

Richard woke with a start and glanced toward the door. "Who's there?"

I stared back at him but knew he couldn't see me. Rather, I thought he couldn't see me. The blade-sharpness of his gaze frightened me. But it was all right.

He looked away and pulled Juliette closer. She awoke and stretched lazily, touched his cheek and laid her head on his chest. "I can't believe this happened."

Richard smiled down at her. "It did." He kissed her. "That was my Christmas present to you."

"It was—wonderful," she said.

He chuckled. "I'm glad you think so. This is only the beginning, dear Juliette. The first time."

She shivered.

"Are you cold?" He brought the plaid throw up higher so that it covered her breasts. "Let me throw some more paper on the fire."

"No; I'm warm enough. I was remembering my dream. It was scary."

"Were you cold in your dream?"

"Just the opposite. I was burning up. I had a fever, and I was trapped here in Snowhedge. I wanted to go home because I was so sick, but I couldn't. I'd much rather have dreamed about us—together."

"Our future is going to be better than any dream you could ever have," Richard said.

"Are we going to be together then?" Juliette asked.

"Sure we are. You and me. Forever. We'll travel all over the globe until I retire from the Air Force. Then we'll settle down in California. That's where I grew up."

With a sly little laugh, she let the throw fall to her waist. "In that case, I need more wine."

"Haven't you had enough for one night?"

"This is a holiday. A time for wine and fruitcake. For celebrations— and love." She sighed and pushed her golden hair back. "Maybe we shouldn't have done this. Not here anyway. We could have waited."

"Are you having a change of heart?" he demanded.

"About you? Never. I'm thinking of Evalina. She won't mind, will she?"

"We don't have to tell her."

"But she'll know something's different. She's a perceptive lady."

"Evalina likes to make people happy," Richard said. "Just look at this great Christmas party she organized. If we're happy, she will be, too. Besides, she has her writing. She's often told me that's her life."

"I don't know. She was supposed to come back to water the tree, but she never did." Juliette lowered her voice. "She couldn't have seen us together. Could she?"

"I closed the door." Once again he looked at me without seeing me. "But someone opened it. I don't know..." His voice took on a hearty tone. "It's late to be tending greenery. Evalina probably decided to do it in the morning."

Richard gave Juliette a long, deep kiss and reached for the last piece of cake. "I'll go see if I can find us another bottle of port."

"And more fruitcake. Aunt Ellen keeps them in tins above the counters. All of a sudden, I'm so hungry."

"You stay here, Juliette," he said. "Don't move. That's an order."

"Yes, sir."

Richard strode past me, as Evalina had, seeming to intrude on my space. Juliette scooped up a handful of crumbs from the Santa plate, ate them, and licked her fingers. Then she stretched like a contented little golden cat and closed her eyes again.

I stepped further inside the room and tiptoed past her, calling Cindy's name, knowing that Juliette wouldn't hear me.

At that moment something in the atmosphere changed. I tensed, bracing for some kind of psychic phenomenon: The furnishings around me dissolving, the fireplace throwing out cold flames, the floor turning into a quagmire, sucking me down to an underworld.

Something was about to happen. I took a deep breath and inhaled a strong, acrid odor. It drifted out from the tree and coiled around me like a furious demon.

I knew that demon. Its name was Smoke.

With an ominous crackle, the balsam fir tree burst into flames.

Chapter 27

"Juliette!" I cried. "Wake up. You have to get out of here!"

She lay motionless, trapped in sleep on the sofa, while waves of fire engulfed the parlor. She couldn't hear me, but it didn't matter. This disaster had already happened—decades ago. There was nothing I could do to prevent it.

The ghost fire was just another in the series of spirit reenactments. Its flames had no power over me. Still I felt the heat sear my exposed skin. As I breathed in ghost smoke and coughed, my old fear gurgled up to the surface. That was a real cough. What if this particular manifestation was different?

I had to get out of here! Cindy couldn't be in this room, or she'd have come running at the first scent of danger.

Still I called her name one last time before backing up to the door.

I couldn't see Juliette now. Or the sofa. Or the round table with its charming vintage photographs and festive candlesticks. In what seemed like moments, the inferno had devoured everything in its path, feeding on balsam needles, pretty trinkets, and human flesh. And it was gaining strength. Coming closer.

I might have been back at the Larkspur fire, except this one, however monstrous, would eventually disappear. It was only an imprint in time.

Could I be certain of that?

I coughed again and felt as if I were choking, as if my skin were melting.

Don't take a chance! Go!

I slammed the door shut and leaned heavily against it, let my heartbeat slow, allowed Romy's frantic barking to pull me back to my own world. Phantom fire couldn't spread through the rest of the house. But it had been so real. I still felt shaky and anxious.

Now I knew what had happened at Snowhedge all those years ago.

Juliette had perished in a fire started by Christmas lights, an unfortunate but common holiday tragedy. This one was subtly different.

While trying to illuminate the crèche, Evalina had noticed a dried-out branch and decided to pour more water in the stand. Then, on seeing Richard and Juliette together, she fled from the room without doing it.

Had that caused the fire? Would a pitcher of water have made any difference? If Evalina had left the lights where they were, would that have averted the blaze?

Maybe. Who could know? At any rate, fire moves rapidly. Juliette moved slowly, like a lazy golden kitten, but she couldn't have run fast enough to outrace the fire if she had been a jungle cat.

My thoughts came to a stop. Surely Evalina realized the danger of mixing dry evergreen branches with hot lights? In that moment of betrayal and grief, did she care?

I didn't want to venture down that dark road. Not tonight. But I had other questions.

How could Juliette have fallen asleep so quickly and slept so soundly? Why didn't the smell of smoke or the heat of the fire wake her?

The wine, I thought. *The bottle was empty. Richard said she'd had too much port for one night. It had dulled her reflexes.*

Inebriation was another common cause of holiday tragedies. But poor Juliette didn't deserve such a terrible fate. She had been young, self-centered, and passionate. She'd stolen her cousin's lover and celebrated on Christmas night with wine and fruitcake. Death by fire was a harsh punishment.

I recalled Juliette's dream of burning up with fever. She wanted to go home but couldn't leave Snowhedge. In a sense, it had foreshadowed her end. Shouldn't she be the tormented soul who haunted the old Victorian instead of Evalina?

That question must have an answer, but it eluded me. I didn't know the ways of spirits or why they had chosen me to witness their story. Or, for that matter, whether this was the last chapter. I hoped so.

No crackle or roar came from behind the parlor door now. There was no sound at all. The fire episode must be over, swept back into its proper niche in time as every other materialization had been.

Emboldened by the knowledge that I was safe from burning, I opened the door to a blast of cold air instead of hungry flames and killing heat. To frosty condensation formed on the bay windows; to my own grocery store bouquet fading on the mantel; to the red stain on the floor caused by Juliette's candle spill.

And how had that survived the blaze?

Cindy's yellow chick gave a tiny protest squeak. I still held it, obviously too tightly, but I didn't want to let it go. Would this be all I would ever have of my precious collie puppy?

I stood at the hall table, my hand hovering over Romy's leash, considering my options. Maybe I'd better drive the dogs over to the farmhouse before another one disappeared. On the other hand, I wanted to wait for Mike who should be arriving in five minutes. He was unfailingly prompt. What would he think if he found that I'd left Snowhedge without waiting for him?

I could explain. He would understand.

As I dropped Cindy's toy into my shoulder bag, I had the unsettling notion that someone had just pushed past me, almost knocking me off balance. It happened again. An invisible body brushed against my arm. Hot breath fanned over my face.

I sensed rather than saw people rushing through the hall toward the front door and out to the lawn. Unknown voices ricocheted around me, shouting, crying, screaming. For the first time since coming to Snowhedge, I heard the phantoms who until now had stayed in other rooms at Snowhedge.

Everybody out of the house! Here, Aunt, let me help you.

My jewelry! I can't leave my rings!

Don't be a fool! Ellen? Ted? Here you are! May! Cathy! Eva? Juliette? Where's Juliette?

In the parlor. That was Richard's voice. *Help me get her out!*

I could have told them that Juliette was already dead but had no way of communicating with spirits. Ah well, they'd know soon enough when she didn't join the others outside the house.

Quickly I grabbed my shoulder bag and all three leashes and raced out to the car, for once moving faster than my heartbeat. Away from the house and feeling safe, I stood outside in a light snowfall, shivering, sensing once again the phantoms of Snowhedge gathering around to witness the blaze.

Although invisible, they generated a cloud of emotion that was almost palpable in the cold night air.

I couldn't see anything burning. Snowhedge was intact, the parlor dark and silent. *Remember,* I told myself, *the fire is an imprint in time. Juliette died a long time ago and these survivors are shadows from yesteryear.*

I wanted nothing more than to be done with unnatural flames and spirit people.

Where was Mike?

High-pitched puppy screeches drew my attention to the small third-story balcony on the west side of the house. There at last was Cindy jumping frantically on the railing. The window behind her was closed. Unable to get back in the house or find her way to the ground, she did the only thing she could to attract my attention. She made noise.

How had she gotten out there?

That was irrelevant. One last Snowhedge mystery. I didn't need to solve it, I only needed to fetch Cindy.

I dragged and pushed the dogs into the car, threw my purse in the front seat, and went back through the heavy ornamental door into Snowhedge.

For the last time, I promised myself. For Cindy.

As soon as I stepped across the threshold, I became aware of a subtle difference in the house's atmosphere. Like the grief generated by the unseen mourners, it was all but tangible. I felt it creeping up from the floor like a noxious weed seeking a host for its slimy tentacles.

Too melodramatic, Susanna, and not possible. Stay with the facts.

Something was wrong, though. Something other than my puppy unaccountably trapped on a third-story balcony. A vague threat hung in the still air. Something...

But nothing from the other world. The spirits were gone.

And how did I know that?

The fire manifestation was over. They'd congregated on the front lawn to watch Snowhedge burn, then gone back to heaven or hell, or wherever they lived.

Still I had the feeling that I wasn't alone.

I shrugged it off and rushed down the hall. There could be many reasons for my growing unease: Losing track of Cindy, the ghost fire, moving to the farmhouse in a hurry, trying to keep one step ahead of Tag Nolan.

It could even be the deep quiet that had descended on Snowhedge, with the dogs and all my possessions in the car. We hadn't taken up much space in the house, but in the massive structure, every square inch counted. Every body, every breath, every voice, every shadow. Our absence would be noted.

I'd dealt with Snowhedge vagaries before. I could do it one last time.

Once again, I climbed up the stairs to the top floor. Cindy's cries filled the old Victorian, all three stories, quite possibly every secret corner. They grew louder as I passed the second floor, louder still when I reached the third.

"I'm here," I shouted.

Here...here...here, called the echoes.

Strangely, the feeling of unease, of not being alone, was stronger at this elevation.

You're not alone. This is the haunted house.

Okay. Spirits don't adhere to our timetables. Perhaps one or two restless souls on their way home to the other world had wandered back into Snowhedge to view the burnt-out parlor. I imagined Richard searching for his love, Juliette, hoping she'd somehow escaped the conflagration, or Evalina prowling through the first floor hall with a pitcher of water. Mine were ghosts worthy of any Halloween Fright Night Jamboree.

But I'm through with them, I reminded myself.

On the third floor, the air was cool and clammy. I walked swiftly past the closed door behind which Lila Rose's boxes waited for the yard sale or bonfire and didn't let my mind dwell on the sinister old attic. I kept moving toward the east side of the house, following Cindy's excited barking.

With each step, the feeling that I wasn't alone in the house intensified.

The balcony room didn't have any furniture in it, not even a stray chair or table, and it was dark, its view cut off by a low hanging branch. The door was ajar.

Seeing me, Cindy flung herself at the old glass and bounced back, out of my view. I rushed to the window and tried to open it, while she stood on the tiny balcony, wagging her tail, assured that deliverance was at hand.

The window refused to move. It wasn't locked. I turned the ancient lock in both directions and tried again, pushing up until I felt a sharp pain cut across my right hand.

I ignored it. "Just a minute, baby."

Countless coats of paint had sealed it shut. I'd have to find a way to break the glass and risk hurting Cindy or myself. But what else could I do? Wait for Mike? I peered through the window. I didn't see his car through the screen of tangled branches. Only mine.

I tapped on the glass, close to Cindy's nose. "How did you get out there, you silly thing?"

She gave three playful yips and ran around in happy circles.

I saw it then, a long strip of filthy wide gauze stuck to a toenail on her hind paw. A makeshift muzzle that she'd finally gotten off?

If that's what it was, no wonder she didn't respond to my earlier calls. Somebody would answer to me for forcibly silencing my spirited little puppy.

Possibly for the first time ever, my questions came late. Who would do this? Why?

I heard a footstep behind me. A sound of raspy breathing. A whiff of vile smoke. And a nightmare assumed a human form.

"Follow the fire," said a familiar voice.

I kept my grip on the windowsill, willing it to break apart and turn into a weapon.

"You," I said. "Nolan."

His vile form filled the entrance, creating an effective barrier between me and escape. One greasy hand rested on the doorframe; the other held a lit cigarette. Emblazoned on his threadbare red shirt was one word: *Firestarter*.

"In the flesh," he said with a sneer. "Weren't you expecting me?"

My thoughts went whirling through my mind. Wild, desperate, out of control.

Tag had found me. Come in through the front door. I'd left it open. Careless. Months of anticipating this confrontation, and still I wasn't prepared for it. The gun was in the car, packed for the move. Mike? Would he come in time?

Had Tag killed him? My dogs...

"You took Cindy," I said. "You muzzled her and put her out on the balcony."

"Guilty on all counts," he said. "I knew you'd come for her. You always come for the dogs. Wasn't I right?"

"What are you doing in my house?" I demanded.

"Your house. Ha! It belongs to me. You never figured that out, did you, Susabella?"

"Liar! It's Valerie Lansing's house. She's trying to sell it—"

"Where do you get your information? Valerie Lansing has been dead for seven years. Like you're going to be tonight. You and your four mangy mutts."

Let that pass. Think about Valerie later. If God lets you escape.

He will. He has to. But how?

"I said I'd make you pay for getting me convicted," Tag said. "You and that mealy-mouthed partner of yours. She already did. Now it's your turn."

My mind passed me a straw, and I grabbed it. "If this is your house, you must know it's haunted," I said.

"Crazy talk won't save you. Nothing will."

"Those ghosts have been pretty active tonight. I think I hear them now, moving around downstairs."

"What you hear is fire," he said. "Good old-fashioned, all-American fire. It's burning on the first floor. I guess the whole back of the house must be gone by now."

I smelled the smoke then, insinuating its way up the stairs, down the hall, past the bulk of Tag's body. Finding me at last. Smoke and fire. The death that had been stalking me all through the summer and the fall.

"No," I cried. "I won't let this happen. Evalina!"

175

Chapter 28

Tag bored into me with flat dark eyes.

"Who are you talking to?" he demanded

"Evalina. My friend."

"It's just you and me and the fire downstairs."

"Evalina was the previous mistress of Snowhedge," I said. "She's its resident ghost."

"Ghosts again, huh? You're going to need some heavenly help, lady. Pretty soon you're going to be frying in hell, like a French fry in a pan of hot grease."

He snickered at his comparison and tapped cigarette ash on the gleaming hardwood floor.

"Do you smell the smoke?" he asked. "Can you hear the roar? I wish you could see how beautiful the flames are. You will. Soon enough."

I didn't know why I'd called Evalina's name. No spirit could help me now. No one could. I had to save myself and my puppy from this pyromaniac, and I had no idea how to do it.

"The fire is hungry," he said. "I promised it two tasty meals."

If the blaze was spreading on the first floor. If Tag intended to lock me in the balcony room and leave me here to burn to death...

Did this door have a lock? Some of them didn't. But a long rusty key hung from a braided loop on his belt. It might belong to this room; it might be a decoration. I could only guess at Tag's method, but his intent was clear.

Snowhedge is burning. Again. Again.

That wasn't my voice, nor did it sound like Evalina; and it wasn't near. It appeared to originate downstairs.

Maybe not all of the spirits had left the house.

"If you started another fire, we have to get out of here!" I cried.

"Wrong. I'm the only one who's getting out of here. You're staying right where you are until the fire finds you." He sauntered over to me and swung the key in front of my face. "Dumb Amy Brackett never knew what hit her. For you, I planned something a little fancier because you stole my life. Because of you I had to rot in jail for weeks. You turned my girlfriend against me. I lost my job . . ."

"You did what you did, and I told the truth. I'd do it again."

"Even if it costs you those meat hounds you're so crazy about."

"Even then," I said, "but it won't."

"It already has."

On the balcony, Cindy started her panic yelping again. She scratched desperately at the old glass. I longed to hold her, to comfort her, even if it was only for a little while.

It'll be forever, I told myself. *Or as long as we live.*

"That's the only one you have left," Tag said, taking his stand in the doorway again. "That yappy little lump of tar."

"Liar!"

"Three bullets found their mark," he said with a smirk. "The targets were all in one place. Nice of you to set them up for me."

He was lying. My dogs were still alive. Beyond the great fire roar below us, I could hear Romy's furious barking and another sound in the distance. A siren, still far away but growing louder by the minute.

Someone must have noticed the smoke. Flora Brine, glancing out of her window across the stream, one of the infrequent drivers on Balsam Lane, Mike...Mike must be here by now. Unless Tag had ambushed him.

No, Mike was too smart to be taken by surprise. Tag didn't know about Mike coming to Snowhedge tonight.

"If you can make fire, you can control the world," Tag said.

Snowhedge is burning. Again. Again. Let it burn to the ground this time. Save yourself.

The unknown voice was louder now. Like the siren.

Fire moves quickly. It had spread too fast for Juliette to wake up from her wine-induced slumber and run from it. Too fast for Richard to drop the wine and fruitcake and race to her rescue.

But I had all of my wits, a reasonable amount of strength, and, most important of all, a desire to save myself and my collies. I could be a worthy opponent. If I acted now.

And did what?

Fight for your life and your dogs. Think!

The greatest problem was Tag blocking the doorway. He stood between me and freedom. I couldn't run past him unless he moved; that wouldn't happen unless something distracted him. Unless he decided to taunt me with that key again.

Evalina, I thought. *Any one of you spirits. Help me.*

"You and the mouthy little fluffmeister can go together," Tag said.

He crossed the room again, and, with a few upward tugs, lifted the window I couldn't budge. Cindy leaped inside, circling his ankles, nipping playfully at the cuffs of his pants. He kicked her into a corner where she lay crying and licking her side. The gauze muzzle still clung to her toenail.

"You creep!" I cried as I picked her up. "It's going to be okay, Cindy."

Slowly I worked the gauze off her nail and let it fall to the floor where it caught a spark from Tag's cigarette ash. He stamped it to powder with his shoe and returned to the doorway.

"Not yet," he said. "I want you to wait for the real fire. It's on its way. Eating up the stairs, I'll bet."

"You fool! You're going to be trapped up here too."

He laughed. "Not me. I know a secret way out."

Didn't the idiot hear the fire sirens? Or...was I imagining them? Wanting to be rescued so desperately that I was hearing things? Was Romy really barking or was she dead in the Taurus with my slaughtered puppies?

I hugged Cindy to my breast as I had cuddled her little toy. Maybe we had a shred of hope. Tag has just given me a possible way out of the room that didn't involve running past him. If I could move fast enough, I could make my escape through the half-opened window onto the balcony. And from there?

Jump down to the roof of the wraparound porch, which was still a great distance from the ground.

And from there?

Jump again. Hope that Tag was afraid of heights. Pray that the accumulation of snow would cushion my fall.

Choose, I thought. *Broken bones or the flames.*

"Amy Brackett was no fun," Tag said. "I never got to see her face. Never even heard her screams. That car burst into flames, and Poof! Poor little Amy was a goner. This is going to be much better."

I'll jump. Take Cindy with me. Take our chances.

Tag swung the key back and forth and reached for the doorknob. "I vowed I'd get you and get you good, Ms. Kentwood. Consider yourself got."

I barely heard his mad babbling. My mind presented me with a variety of possible outcomes. They went swirling by at a dizzying speed, but I managed to catch one.

Maybe it wouldn't come to that. Would the firemen be outside waiting for me? Would they have a net?

Susanna, listen!

The voice seemed to be in the room with me, but that was impossible.

When we were kids, we used to play on the roof. We'd climb out this very window and walk right across the front of the house to the east balcony. Down one side, up the other. It was steep, but we never lost our footing, not once. Sometimes we'd climb down the tree and go berry picking in the woods. It was forbidden, but we did it anyway. And do you know? We never got caught.

It was Evalina speaking, giving me my answer. But I wasn't a child to go walking on roofs, and I'd never been fond of climbing anything, even a sturdy ladder. Snowhedge rose up to the treetops. Up to the clouds. I could never do it.

Was there any other way?

You asked for Evalina's help. Take it.

"Nolan!" I screamed. "The fire! Look behind you!"

With a curse, he snapped his head around.

Holding Cindy so tightly that she squealed in protest, I eased myself over the sill and out onto the balcony. Straightening up, I slammed the window down.

We had only moments before Tag reacted, and I had an escape plan to figure out in that same timeframe.

I had two options. Jump or follow in Evalina's childhood footsteps. Down one section of gabled roof and up another, grab the closest tree branch, and climb down to the ground. All of this with a squirming puppy in my arms.

"Hold on, Cindy," I shouted as Tag raced to the window, his features twisted into a grotesque mask of rage.

Whatever happened next, it was better than being burned alive.

I stood on the balcony, holding fast to its slender post, calculating the distance to the roof. Snow mixed with smoke bathed the gables of Snowhedge in a thick ethereal mist, obscuring my perception. I thought I had three feet. Possibly four. A height beyond my reach.

But Evalina had done it as a child.

Stand on the balcony railing! Hope it holds your weight.

That was my thought, not Evalina's voice.

Take a deep breath. Say the most fervent, quickest prayer of your life.

Whispering *Dear Lord, help me,* I stepped up onto the railing's narrow top and groped wildly above my head, back and forth, until my right hand closed on the roof's edge. Snow blew white drifts in my face, and smoke forced its way into my throat. I fought the urge to cough.

There was only one way to do this. I set Cindy on the roof, shouting at her to stay. Then, using both hands and bracing my feet on the siding, I lifted myself up, clawing at the shingles, seeking a handhold, slowly inching my body forward until I was about five feet from the edge. Cindy, wildly excited, danced around me as I stood shakily on the slick surface. I scooped her up into my arms and surveyed the vast expanse of ice-glazed shingles.

I had nothing to hold onto, not even an outmoded television antenna. The chimney was on the other side of the house. The saving branches might as well be a mile away, and Cindy was so anxious to break free that I could scarcely maintain my grip on her.

But Tag hadn't followed me. I had a chance and no time to wonder why he'd given up the chase.

I looked down.

As Tag had said, the first floor of Snowhedge was on fire, sending its deadly light out over the landscape. Through the fog of blowing snow and smoke, the fire engines waited like red beasts eager to devour the flames, while men rushed out dragging their fire-fighting equipment and filled the air with light and noise.

I could see a vague outline of my car, but not my dogs. Mike's car, but not Mike. A police cruiser, strobe lights flashing through floating white shreds. People, miniature figures, huddled together along the hedge, as the phantoms had done earlier.

But there was no net.

Someone saw me and pointed. Mike? I didn't think so.

Don't look down, I ordered myself. Focus on the roof and the downward slope of gray shingles blanketed in snow. Forward, down, up.

As I started the descent, my foot slid on a slippery patch, taking me down to the roof's surface, almost stopping my heart. Cindy twisted and writhed in an attempt to save herself. Stunned, I caught my breath and tightened my grip on her.

Evalina's voice broke through the crackle of fire:

We never did it in the winter, but you can. You have to. Stand up straight. Walk slowly down. Keep going. Keep your eye on that long branch of the ash tree that leans on the gutter. It'll take you to safety.

I regained my footing and made my way down to the gable's base, took a deep breath, and started the upward ascent.

I'd forgotten about the smaller gabled room in the middle of the house with its small balcony. Here was something for me to hold onto in the wasteland of snow-covered shingles. I reached out for its post just as the light inside blinked on, trapping me in an eerie yellow glow.

Cindy uttered a low wolfish growl. The window opened, and a lean, hairy arm shot out into the night.

Chapter 29

"Still think you're smarter than me, Susabella?"

Long fingers stained with nicotine groped through the thin smoke pouring out of the balcony room. Tag's face filled the window. The hazy light of the overhead fixture gave him the appearance of a gloating demon. "Well you ain't," he said. "I got the element of surprise."

My leg was too close to that hideous hand. Within grabbing distance. I side-stepped away from it, slid on the icy shingles, miraculously righted myself and staggered away from him.

The drifts were high on this section of the roof. I held Cindy with my right hand, but with my left, I could throw snow at Nolan and blind him for a moment, giving me a momentary advantage over him. My own element of surprise.

I scooped up a handful of snow and glanced back as Tag slid his legs over the window sill and lurched toward me. My hastily assembled missile disintegrated at his feet.

"I'm quicker than you," Tag said. "They used to call me Tag-be-quick. You know: Tag be nimble, Tag be quick, Tag jump over the candlestick."

"You're crazy!"

"And you're dead. Just like I said. Hey, that rhymes."

Once again he reached for me, for my arm this time. He missed his target by barely an inch.

I kicked him and almost lost my footing, kicked again and closed my eyes as a shower of cold snow washed over my face. I swiped at it with my left hand and instantly felt it imprisoned by those long claw-like fingers.

Before I could raise my leg to kick again, Tag emitted an ungodly scream. My hand fell free as he went down, sliding a good safe distance from me. At least six feet. He lay writhing on the roof, screaming and pawing at his arm. His left leg lay under the right at an awkward angle, forming a strange dark cross in the snow.

I flinched as he started to rise and breathed more easily as he flopped down again, staring from his arm to his leg.

Could I possibly have demolished the formidable Tag Nolan with one well-aimed kick?

Then I saw his arm. It lay in a nest of shredded red material. Romy could have chewed Tag into mincemeat, but little Cindy had managed quite nicely, digging her teeth into his flesh and ripping a gash from his elbow to his wrist. And she'd done it so silently that I hadn't been aware of her attack.

Tag's arm was a mass of oozing red. Blood drizzled down on his filthy jeans and stained the pure snow. His curses fouled the air, none the less potent because they streamed from the mouth of a defeated man.

And he *was* defeated. I felt certain of it.

He tried to get up again, standing on his good leg, but slipped and rolled closer to the edge of the roof where it formed a deep V. "That little bitch!" he shrieked. "I'll kill her!"

"Over my dead body."

"Fine with me. You're both going back to the fire."

It was all meaningless bluster. Cindy and I were alive. Tag was courting death.

Still, I held Cindy back, but there was no need for protective maneuvers. With one more futile attempt to regain his footing, Tag fell back on the roof and rolled over and over on the shingles. Like a demented snowman forming itself, he added a new layer of snow with each revolution. At last he reached the edge and went over, disappearing in a fat column of smoke and snow, his last cries lost in the fire's roar.

I could hear voices below. Shouts. Screams. A howl that might have originated in the throat of a maddened wolf. Our would-be killer must have hit the ground. Could he still be alive?

"Follow the fire, Tag," I whispered. "Cindy, little girl, you saved the day. Brave, noble puppy."

Well, almost. We were still stranded on the roof, and the wind was stronger up here, threatening to blow me off my feet. Snowhedge was still burning, and the smoke was thickening. But Tag was gone.

I smeared my turtleneck with snow and pulled it high up over my mouth. That should help for a while. Through a smoky mist, I could see the chimney's dark bricks, which meant that the ash tree was near.

But how far was it? How many steps? I started a treacherous ascent again. "Let's guess. Fifty."

Evalina's voice floated in with the wail of the wind.

I love that old ash tree. It'll take you down to the ground, and it's far enough from the house so that the fire won't touch you.

I waited, wanting one more assurance.

I'll go with you, she said.

How strange to hear Evalina but not see her; how strange for her to be talking to me as if we were old acquaintances when she had never acknowledged my presence before.

"Where are you?" I asked.

I'll be there.

Fifty steps was an outrageous estimate. It was more like twenty, uphill all the way. Twenty giant slippery steps. Nineteen...eighteen...seventeen...I counted them, walking more quickly now, seeing a lifeline. The branches Valerie never bothered to have trimmed leaned heavily on the gutters like long arms extended in welcome. One looked promising. Thick and sturdy, a passage to the trunk. I touched it tentatively, hoping it wasn't rotten.

Yes. That one. We used to call it our wooden horse.

As I recalled, the ash tree had an impressive network of branches, hospitable places to sit and read or dream—if you were a child. Plenty of footholds and handholds if you were a desperate adult hoping to escape a conflagration. But I couldn't see them through the smoke and blinding snow. For the first time in my life I had to rely entirely on my sense of touch. The task ahead seemed impossible.

"I can't do this with only one hand," I said, "and I'm never going to let Cindy go."

I'll take her. Swing from the branch over to the trunk. You should be able to wrap your arms around the tree. Climb down slowly. Stop to rest if you find yourself tiring. You'll be on the ground before you know it. And don't worry about that devil, Tag Nolan. He's dead.

I climbed down the ash tree, using both hands, as Evalina had instructed me. Cold bark scraped my palms. Snow gusts slapped me in the face, and for one horrible moment, a jagged branch closed its mouth over my sleeve.

I yanked it loose and kept moving downward. I didn't think about how high I was and didn't dwell on the distance to the ground or what might happen with one small misstep. There was no time for thought. In any event, between the night, the blowing snow, and the smoke, I couldn't see clearly.

I could only trust that every step would bring me closer to the firefighters—and Mike. He was waiting for me, somewhere beyond the smoke and fire.

Or did he think I'd succumbed to the blaze?

Snowhedge was engulfed in flames, but the wind was blowing in the other direction. East, toward the stream. As Evalina had said, the fire hadn't reached the ash tree yet.

Tag had done his work well. Then, instead of running away as he had done at Larkspur Kennels, he'd stayed to make sure that I knew the name of my killer. I couldn't imagine where his secret way out was, assuming it existed. In the end, his revenge scheme had been more important to him than saving himself, and he'd been the one to die.

If he was dead. I half feared that he'd materialize above me, chanting one of his silly rhymes. But that didn't happen.

I took a few more steps down and almost stumbled when my foot touched solid ground.

Already?

I unwrapped my hands from the tree's trunk and leaned against it, letting the blessed cold of the ankle-deep snow ease the heat of the fire that radiated from the house's west wall.

You made it, Susanna!

"*We* made it," I said. "I couldn't have done it without you."

And suddenly my arms were no longer empty. A black collie puppy twisted her little body around and looked up at me. Her eyes held their usual dark sparkle and the merest hint of confusion.

Evalina had kept her promise.

The first person I recognized was Mike, still in his trooper's uniform. Thick snow layered his jacket, and glistened in his blond hair. He detached himself from the crowd of onlookers and ran to meet me as I stumbled and limped my way along the hedge.

"Susanna!"

I found myself locked in his arms, spent and bedraggled but safe, I and my wild, wriggling puppy. It was wonderful to be alive, and to be with Mike again.

I looked over his shoulder and saw my car, just as I'd left it, crammed with my belongings. But I didn't see the most precious ones of all.

"Where are my dogs? Romy and the puppies. Did Tag—"

"He never got near them. My buddy drove them over to my house when the fire broke out. I didn't know where you were. I thought...where did you come from?" he demanded.

"I climbed down that old ash tree."

His face darkened. "You were going to wait for me. What happened?"

"Cindy disappeared." I described my frantic search for her and her mysterious appearance on the third-floor balcony. "Nolan used her as bait. He knew I'd go after her."

"And you did. Into a burning house."

"I didn't know about the fire then, but I'd still have gone. Yes."

"And you fell into his trap." He hugged me so hard that Cindy yelped. "I saw you on the roof. Then you were gone."

"Tag was trying to pull me back into the house. He almost had me, but Cindy bit him, and he fell. I think he broke his leg. Anyway, he rolled right off the roof."

I smoothed the snow from Cindy's head. She flattened her ears and wagged her tail. "My little heroine," I said.

"Such a small thing to be so ferocious."

I hazarded a smile, my first in a long time. "Me or Cindy?"

"Both of you."

"Did Tag make it?" I asked.

"He died when he hit the ground. You don't want to look."

"No, I don't." But I did anyway, at the body of my enemy lying motionless in the snow.

It could so easily have been my body, with Tag looking on from the shadows, his revenge complete. If he'd been as quick as he thought. If Cindy had been as passive as her sisters. If...a dozen if's. I started shivering. Mike tightened his arm around me.

"It's over, honey."

"Then Evalina helped us," I said.

Mike walked us away from the firefighters and the crowd milling beyond the hedge. The only familiar face I saw was that of Flora Brine. I rubbed my eyes and looked more closely. The other watchers looked like the phantoms from the first Snowhedge fire. But that couldn't be. They were neighbors on Balsam Lane, all the people I'd never met, come out of their houses at the siren's wail to see a house burn.

"You saw the ghost again?" Mike said.

"Actually I heard her voice." I closed my eyes, recalling the burning Christmas tree, the wall of flames, and Juliette lying asleep on the sofa, unaware that her death was only moments away.

"Back at Snowhedge, before the fire, I saw Juliette die and couldn't do a thing to save her, but it didn't matter because it had already happened."

Another siren broke through the general chaos on the ground. I watched as the ambulance pulled up and two men rushed out on a mission that had lost the need for haste.

"That's for Tag," Mike said. "Or what's left of him."

Flora Brine came up to us. Her face was pale and drawn, the exact color of the scarf she'd wrapped around her head. "I'm so glad you got out in time, Susanna," she said. "I called 911 when I saw the smoke. Did you say someone died? A woman?"

"In another fire at Snowhedge. It was a long time ago."

Flora nodded to one of the onlookers, a tall, skinny woman shivering in a lightweight jacket. She looked vaguely familiar, like someone I'd seen in the grocery store.

"This is Bonnie Fairman," Flora said. "She lives down the lane. Bonnie, it's Susanna and...?

"Captain Mike Slater," I said.

Bonnie shook her head. "That was my favorite house in Maple Creek."

"It's evil," Flora said. "It should burn."

"Why do you say that?" I asked.

"I saw something through the bay window once." She moved closer to us and lowered her voice. "Something that just couldn't be."

"What was it?"

"A Christmas tree," she said. "All decorated and lit up, and the parlor was decked out like for a holiday party. Lila Rose never used that room. Never even stepped inside it. She said it was unlivable."

"Did you see this from the outside?" Bonnie asked.

"Yes. I went right up to the porch and looked through the window. The next day the tree was gone. It wasn't out in front or anywhere else to be picked up, and the parlor looked the same as always without a decoration in sight. This happened in the summer."

"There's nothing evil about a Christmas tree," I said.

"How about sleigh bells where there isn't any sleigh in sight? How about Christmas carols in April? I could tell you other stories..."

"I heard something similar," Bonnie said. "I thought it was just kids' talk. You may be right, Flora, but that's a fortune going up in smoke."

Mike said, "It looks like you're getting your wish, Mrs. Brine. Now, Susanna..." He took Cindy from my arms. "I'm taking you to the Emergency Room."

"But..."

"Don't argue. You've been breathing smoke all evening. Is that a scratch on your arm?"

"The ash tree did it," I said, noticing for the first time the missing part of my sleeve and the long red gash. "I left some of my sweater up there and some skin, too, I guess."

"If you check out okay, I'm driving you home. It's a good thing you packed your bags before the fire started."

"I have everything I care about," I said. "My parlor sketches with my story and the painting you gave me are inside. I wasn't going to take them with me."

"Then if they're burned to a crisp, it's no great loss."

"But I'm not going to Emergency," I said. "I've had enough trauma for one night."

Mike picked me up and carried both of us past the Taurus to his cruiser. "We'll see about that."

I felt as if I should object to Mike's sudden show of high handedness. I should demand that he put me down. But that would require too much effort. Besides, it felt good to be in his arms.

"Don't forget Cindy," I said. "Dogs can't go in a hospital."

"We'll figure something out about her," he said. "What are you looking at?"

"The parlor," I said. "There can't be much of it left."

"Just rubble in a burnt-out shell. Why do you care?"

"I think there's more to the Snowhedge story," I said. "I still have questions."

Chapter 30

I found the answer to one of my questions the next morning when I opened my purse. I'd forgotten about the envelope Valerie had handed me on her way out of Snowhedge. I opened it now, expecting to find a check or cash. Instead, the bonus was an orange index card with three words written on it: *Follow the fire.*

For one terrifying moment, it seemed as if Tag Nolan were back on my trail, as if I hadn't seen them take away his lifeless body. But just for a moment.

All this meant was that Valerie Lansing had been in league with Tag from the beginning. She knew what he planned. Furthermore, she wasn't related to me. She couldn't possibly be.

I should have known this at our first encounter when I had no memory of Valerie or her storybook doll gift. Why hadn't I been more curious? I could have asked a few pointed questions and tried to find an old greeting card with Valerie's signature on it or a photograph in a family album.

After the fire at Larkspur, I'd been too eager to get away and start a new life for suspicions and interrogations. Still I shouldn't have been so naïve.

"Valerie Lansing is dead," Tag had said.

Who was the woman who claimed to be my mother's cousin then? With Tag gone, I might never know.

But other pieces of the puzzle began to assemble themselves. The house sitting job and extended stay in Florida had been a set-up, a way to lure me to Snowhedge so that I would be in place when Tag was ready to initiate his revenge. He'd known where I was all along. I was never safe at Snowhedge, not a single day since my arrival.

"This is my house," he'd said.

About that one matter, could he have been telling the truth?

That would explain the invisible Realtor and my many voicemail messages to Valerie, never answered until I announced that I was leaving. My decision and refusal to stay on at Snowhedge caused Tag to change his timetable.

Dorothy Bodoin

I set the warning card aside, intending to give it to Mike. If the Valerie Lansing impersonator had aided Tag in his schemes, she must be guilty of some crime. Now with Tag's death, she would most likely try to disappear. That is, if she was aware of it.

She might well be. The *Maple Creek Tribune* had printed a front page article about the fire and Tag's fatal fall, along with a sidebar describing a previous fire from the 1950's in which a young woman had lost her life. That was Juliette Broussard, 20, of New Iberia, Louisiana, visiting her relatives for the Christmas holidays.

Could Tag and Valerie possibly have known about Snowhedge's reputation for being haunted? Judging from Tag's reaction when I'd mentioned ghosts, I didn't think so.

Evalina...

There was so much more I wanted to know. In truth, I wanted to see Evalina again.

Mike would never approve of what I was going to do. But then, I didn't have to tell him until it was done.

I glanced at the dogs. They were occupied and, most important of all, safe. I'd taken them out for a long outing on our new property and let them explore the barn. Now Romy was searching for a place to nap, and the puppies were playing with their chew toys. As for myself, I'd recovered fully from last night's ordeal and felt the pull of the parlor mystery again, even though the parlor as I knew it no longer existed.

Still marveling at how I'd been so easily duped, I finished unpacking the car and drove once more to Snowhedge—or what was left of it.

Last night's snowfall was melting away in an unseasonably warm morning. Temperatures were expected to rise to record highs for the Thanksgiving weekend. November sunshine and warmth were good omens for my new life. I felt happy and optimistic about the future. But again, I had to say goodbye to the past.

When I reached 7 Balsam Lane, I switched off the radio and turned into the driveway. The desolation that greeted me tore at my heart.

Most of the stately old Victorian was gone. Portions of the walls remained, stark blue skeletons stripped of their fancy ornamentation and standing uneasily in the embrace of the scorched ash trees. The fire had taken the antique furnishings, devoured them, and left dismal piles of charred bones behind.

The devastation reminded me of Larkspur Kennels. My first fire. *Never again*, I thought. *Please God. Let this be the last one.*

I walked across melting snow and debris to the west side of the house where the parlor had been. Vivid images of the Christmas room ran through my mind. The old rose sofa and gold chairs. The round table with its vintage photographs and candles. The holly garlands and crimson bows on the mantel. The angel chimes. Green and red, silver and gold. Sparkle and light. The magnificent balsam that had gone up in flames while its magical scent lived on through the decades.

Superimposed over those pictures were others. A cold empty space with a white brick fireplace, frosted windows, and a red stain in the middle of the floor. A shiny green star falling through time. The room that had called me back again and again until I became a willing spectator to the tragic events of the past.

A trace of acrid smoke lingered on the air, but not even a hint of balsam. Had the fire burned the ghostliness out of the parlor?

What a strange thought! Of course the Snowhedge spirits were still around, even though their haunt had been reduced to ashes. Stranger still, no sooner had I completed the thought than I saw a blur of white that slowly assumed a familiar form.

Evalina stood in the very spot where I'd first seen her gazing out at the snowfall and waiting for Richard. She wore a billowing white dress that seemed to be made of mist and a necklace of brushed silver around her neck with a matching bracelet on her arm. I thought she looked a little older than she'd been on that fateful Christmas night.

I knew that I was seeing the legendary lady in white and that she wasn't going to acknowledge my presence nor address any words to me. But she was talking to herself, and I could hear her clearly.

Maybe they're right and I did kill you, Juliette. They say I was jealous and wanted you out of the way. But it's possible that you started the fire yourself with that candle. You were always so careless. It could have happened that way. I'll never know. I just wish I hadn't moved those lights.

She turned slightly to the left and suddenly the Christmas tree shimmered into life, whole and brilliant as it had been during the materializations. Before the fire.

Evalina placed her hand on a string of white lights.

I saw that dried-out branch. I should have known what might happen. If I could undo that one act, it would have all turned out so differently—for Juliette, for Richard, and for me. If only I could have left the lights where they were, the tree wouldn't have caught fire. She clenched her fists. *I won't touch them. I will not.*

But she lifted the lights and draped them around a slender branch just above the crèche, as she had done on that long ago Christmas night. They cast their white glow on the Holy Family and the brittle yellow-brown needles that arced behind them. When she turned around again, I saw her tears.

"Evalina," I said.

She heard me. Her eyes filled with fright as she looked at me, or rather, through me. Ignoring a stab of disappointment at her failure to recognize me, I said, "Listen, Evalina. You didn't start the fire intentionally. You didn't mean for Juliette to die. And who knows? Juliette's candle might have tipped over and ignited the branch. You have to forgive yourself."

And you have to take your own advice, Susanna.

That wasn't Evalina talking. It was a voice deep inside myself.

You need to forgive yourself for not reconciling with Amy when there was still time to do it. For all the anger and resentment you still feel. For things you did in the past that can't be changed. That's the only way you'll find true happiness.

I'll try, I thought. To Evalina I said, "You have to leave this place now. Rest in peace."

And then, without another word, she was gone. And so was the Christmas tree.

"I saw Evalina again," I said the next day as Mike and I lingered over a carry-out lunch at the house on Bridge Road. My new home. I was moved in but not quite used to it yet.

Corned beef sandwiches with chips and dill pickles helped give it a homey feel, as did my four beautiful collies sitting in a row, waiting for a stray morsel to come their way.

It was the day before Thanksgiving, an afternoon of wondrous, unseasonable warmth. The sun was still shining, and my life was finally coming together. The dog show. Ribbons for my beloved pets. A holiday dinner with Mike's family. Every good thing life had to offer.

From across the small maple table, Mike cast me a sardonic look. "Did she follow you home?"

"I drove out to Snowhedge to view the damage and say goodbye. She was there."

"You have to stop seeing ghosts, honey," Mike said. "It isn't good for you."

"I think this is the last time Evalina will show herself to me. I wish I'd been able to ask my questions, but she wasn't communicating."

"You're still curious?"

"About some things, yes. For instance, I'd like to know what happened to Richard."

"He didn't marry Evalina, at least according to her biography."

"Then he really was in love with Juliette. Or he wasn't serious about either of them."

"Too bad you can't ask him," Mike said.

"Since he appeared with them in spirit form, I'm guessing that he's dead."

Mike smiled. "That's a safe assumption. He was in the military, wasn't he? He might have died in a war. Maybe Korea."

"Or of natural causes at another time. Without a last name, he'd be difficult to trace."

"Impossible, I'd say."

"There's one thing I *do* know," I said.

Evalina's three out-of-print books lay on the kitchen table. I'd skimmed them, but they failed to hold my interest, as the story lines were slanted toward the young girl reader, circa 1950: Dates and going steady; college and career plans.

I showed the dedications to Mike: *To the memory of Juliette Cecile Broussard, my cousin.*

"At times it seemed as if Evalina didn't like Juliette very much," I said. "But she blamed herself for the fire because she moved the lights too close to a dry branch. Apparently some people thought she did it deliberately. That she killed Juliette."

"That's a haphazard way to commit a murder."

"I guess Evalina didn't know about the part wine might have played in the tragedy. Darn..."

"What?"

"I should have told her yesterday. Now it may be too late."

Mike pinned me with a steely glance and passed me a packet of mustard. "Weren't you going to let the ghosts rest in peace?"

I nodded and opened our cokes. That was my intention. Starting tomorrow.

"Evalina kept coming back to Snowhedge to try to undo that one act, but she couldn't," I said.

"No. You can't change the past except in a science-fiction story."

"Still she kept trying. If someone builds a new house on the site, he may wake up one morning to find a ghost in white flitting through his dinette."

I shivered at the scenario I'd created. I wanted to think that, comforted by my words, Evalina had retired to some heavenly chamber. In any event, I didn't think I'd ever see her again, and I knew I'd never return to 7 Balsam Lane, no matter what stood on the site. Just as I'd never return to Greengrove Farm.

"I still can't figure out why she told her story to me," I said.

"I don't know about that, but I have one answer for you. Tag Nolan has an older sister, Beatrice. She might be the woman who posed as your relative."

"Can she be charged with anything?"

"I'm not sure. She hired you for a job and paid you well. Anyway, she appears to have left the state. The real Valerie Lansing died seven years ago."

"I've been thinking. This confederate of Tag's, whoever she is, might have been the red-haired woman who tried to buy the puppies when I was boarding them. She didn't really want them, but if I thought they were in danger, my anxiety level would rise. That's exactly what happened. And I brought them to Snowhedge, which is where he wanted them."

"Nolan expended a lot of energy on his revenge," Mike said. "Here's another piece of information I dug up for you. Nolan's mother, Anne, and Lila Rose were cousins. Anne inherited the house when Lila died, so in a way it did belong to Tag."

"That's a connection I never suspected," I said. "He probably knew ways to get in and out. I wonder what his sister felt about burning the house down."

Mike gestured toward the card. "We can assume she went along with his plan."

He closed his hand over mine and squeezed it. Rather intensely. Almost roughly. "I can't believe how close I came to losing you, Susanna."

Suddenly it was all back, invading the cozy sanctuary of my country kitchen: Tag Nolan reaching for me through the smoke, my flight across the slippery shingles, the fire's roar beneath me, the deadly smoke—all of it holding Cindy in my hand until Evalina took her from me. My right hand.

I stared at it now, at my long tapered fingers trapped in Mike's steely grip. My hand didn't hurt anymore. I couldn't remember the last time I'd felt the lightning stab of pain across my knuckles.

"I think it's gone," I said.

"What is?" he asked.

"The bad time." And I leaned across the table and kissed him.

After working as a secretary in Italy for Chrysler Missile Corporation, Dorothy Bodoin attended Oakland University in Rochester, Michigan, graduating with Bachelor's and Master's degrees in English. For several years, she taught secondary English and wrote during weekends in the summer. After leaving education, she devoted all her time to her first love, writing mysteries, Gothic romance, and novels of romantic suspense.

Dorothy's first published novel was *Darkness At Foxglove Corners*, the first installment of the seven-book Foxglove Corners mystery series. She has also written a Gothic romance, *Treasure At Trail's End*, and several novels of romantic suspense. Her work-in-progress is *Love, Love, Deadly Love*, set in the fictitious Maple Creek, Michigan, in which characters from *The Cameo Clue* make an appearance.

Dorothy is a member of Sisters in Crime. She lives in Royal Oak, Michigan, with her collie companion, Wolf Manor Kinder Brightstar, who inspired some of the puppy antics in *Snowhedge*.

Printed in the United States
126831LV00003B/176/P